PRAIS  

The Work of Art

"Matthews (*The Pug Who Bit Napoleon*; *A Victorian Lady's Guide to Fashion and Beauty*) weaves suspense and mystery within an absorbing love story. Readers will be hard put to set this one down before the end."

-*Library Journal*, starred review

"The author seamlessly combines a suspenseful tale and a soaring romance, the plot by turns sweetly moving and dramatically stirring."

-*Kirkus Reviews*

"If all Regency Romances were written as well as 'The Work of Art,' I would read them all...[Matthews] has a true gift for storytelling."

-*The Herald-Dispatch*

The Matrimonial Advertisement

"For this impressive Victorian romance, Matthews (*The Viscount and the Vicar's Daughter*) crafts a tale that sparkles with chemistry and impresses with strong character development... an excellent series launch..."

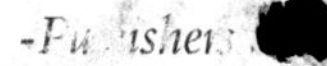

-*Publishers Weekly*

"Matthews (*The Viscount and the Vicar's Daughter*) has a knack for creating slow-building chemistry and an intriguing plot with a social history twist."

-*Library Journal*

"Matthews' (*The Pug Who Bit Napoleon*, 2018, etc.) series opener is a guilty pleasure, brimming with beautiful people, damsels in distress, and an abundance of testosterone…A well-written and engaging story that's more than just a romance."

-*Kirkus Reviews*

A Holiday By Gaslight

"Matthews (*The Matrimonial Advertisement*) pays homage to Elizabeth Gaskell's *North and South* with her admirable portrayal of the Victorian era's historic advancements…Readers will easily fall for Sophie and Ned in their gaslit surroundings."

-*Library Journal*, starred review

"Matthews' novella is full of comfort and joy—a sweet treat for romance readers that's just in time for Christmas."

-*Kirkus Reviews*

"A graceful love story...and an authentic presentation of the 1860s that reads with the simplicity and visual gusto of a period movie."

-*Readers' Favorite*, 2019 Gold Medal for Holiday Fiction

The Viscount and the Vicar's Daughter

"Matthews' tale hits all the high notes of a great romance novel...Cue the satisfied sighs of romance readers everywhere."

-Kirkus Reviews

"Matthews pens a heartfelt romance that culminates into a sweet ending that will leave readers happy. A wonderfully romantic read."

-RT Book Reviews

The Lost Letter

"The perfect quick read for fans of Regency romances as well as Victorian happily-ever-afters, with shades of Austen and the Brontës that create an entertaining blend of drama and romance."

-RT Book Reviews

"A fast and emotionally satisfying read, with two characters finding the happily-ever-after they had understandably given up on. A promising debut."

-Library Journal

USA Today Bestselling Author

MIMI MATTHEWS

PARISH ORPHANS *of* DEVON

THE WINTER COMPANION
Parish Orphans of Devon, Book 4

Edited by Deborah Nemeth
Cover Design by James T. Egan of Bookfly Design
Design and Formatting by Ampersand Book Interiors

E-Book: 978-1-7330569-4-6
Paperback: 978-1-7330569-5-3

www.PerfectlyProperPress.com

In memory of Ash
2006-2019

Chapter One

North Devon, England
December 1860

Neville Cross shut and latched the door of the loose box, giving Lady Helena's bay mare one last pat on her glossy neck. It was warm and snug in the Greyfriar's Abbey stable. Far warmer than the biting cold weather outside. The rain had stopped for the moment, but the sky remained dark with thunderclouds, the air pregnant with the damp fragrance of wet earth and churning sea.

Carriage wheels clattered in the distance, a faint but familiar sound. Like the Abbey itself, the stone stable block was set high atop the cliffs above the small coastal village of King's Abbot. The road up was precarious at the best of times. In wet weather it was positively dangerous. Nevertheless, over the past weeks the carriage had passed up and down, from the Abbey to the village and back again, with some regularity.

The coachman was delivering guests and supplies for the monthlong Christmas celebration. He never returned to the stable until his cargo had been unloaded. The carriage would simply roll by on its way to the Abbey. Neville had become as well acquainted with that passing clatter of wheels and clip-clop of horses' hooves as he was with the sound of the driving rain.

Until today.

The carriage didn't roll on in its usual manner. Instead it slowed to a halt. The door of the carriage opened. A swell of voices followed, unintelligible in the whistling wind. And then the door shut, and the carriage clattered on again.

"Good morning!" a soft feminine voice called out. "Is anyone here?"

Neville went still. His instincts told him to retreat. To withdraw to the feed room, or to the private rooms he kept above. It was a cowardly impulse, and one with which he regularly did battle. He had no good reason to avoid people. As long as he kept his speech to a minimum, he could manage very well in company.

But dashed if it wasn't awkward. Especially where ladies were concerned.

He wiped his hands on a cloth, dusted the straw and horsehair from his white linen shirt and dark trousers, and slowly walked out into the aisle.

A young lady stood inside the doorway. A shapeless woolen cloak billowed about her small frame, the hood shielding her face from view. As Neville approached, she pushed it back with one gloved hand.

He stopped where he stood, his mouth suddenly dry.

"I'm looking for Mr. Cross." Her chocolate brown eyes were large and luminous, with a peculiar sheen to them. "Neville Cross."

On a good day, the words Neville formed in his mind could be translated into short phrases with minimal difficulty. He'd learned over the years how to keep things from getting muddled. How to say what he intended with the least fuss, even if that meant he must occasionally sound like a child.

Today wasn't one of those days.

Not when the young lady standing before him had a face that made his heart beat faster.

It was a perfect oval, with a finely molded nose, a damask rosebud of a mouth, and wideset eyes framed by thick, gracefully arching brows that were several shades darker than the flaxen blond of her hair.

His thoughts, which were usually clear, proceeded to tangle themselves into a Gordian knot. With his brain in such a state, his speech didn't stand a chance.

"Are you Mr. Cross?" She stepped forward, a wash of pale pink tinting the sculpted curve of her cheekbones. "Mrs. Archer said I should speak with you about Bertie."

He stared down at her, fully aware that he must look as dumbfounded as he felt.

"Oh, I beg your pardon. I should have explained straightaway. This is Bertie." She opened the front of her cloak, throwing it back over her shoulders to reveal a black pug dog.

A very old pug dog, by the look of it. The little creature was cradled in her left arm, its face and body liberally peppered with gray.

Neville swallowed hard. His voice, when it emerged, was many steps behind the workings of his brain. "I'm Neville."

He could have groaned aloud in frustration. It wasn't what he'd meant to say. Not now.

But the young lady appeared unfazed by his inarticulateness. She extended her hand. "I'm Clara Hartwright, Mrs. Bainbridge's companion."

He hesitated an instant before shaking her hand, all the while conscious of how much smaller it was than his own. Every part of her was smaller. Good lord, her head scarcely reached his chest. He felt a veritable goliath looming over her. A clumsy giant who could crush her as easily as breathing. "Mrs. Hartwright."

"*Miss* Hartwright," she corrected. "Mrs. Archer said to speak to you about finding a place for Bertie in the stable. He must be kept warm, you see. And I haven't yet received permission to keep him in the house."

Neville reached out to brush his hand over the little dog's head. Bertie blinked up at him with rheumy eyes. A smile tugged at Neville's mouth. He was often shy around people, but he understood animals. He'd always had a way with them, long before his childhood accident on the cliffs and the head injury that, even now, affected his speech. It's why he preferred to work in the stables. Being around dogs and horses settled him. Helped to put his mind at ease. It helped his speech, as well.

"He belongs to Mrs. Bainbridge?"

Miss Hartwright's blush deepened. "Er, no. He belonged to the previous lady I worked for. She died last month, and poor Bertie isn't a favorite with her family. They were going to have him destroyed. I couldn't leave him behind. And I can't permit him to catch his death out here."

"It's warm enough."

"Yes, it's much warmer than being out of doors, but Bertie is accustomed to residing inside the house. He's spent much of his life on a velvet cushion in front of the fire, and I fear—"

"May I?" Neville reached for the little dog.

"Of course." Miss Hartwright helped to transfer Bertie into Neville's arms. "He's very sweet and gentle. Not spoiled at all. Not like some pugs. He won't be any trouble to you."

Neville scratched Bertie under the chin. Bertie didn't appear to notice. He was more than old. He was positively ancient, content to stare off into the distance and pant. Neville wondered if the little dog had all of his faculties.

Miss Hartwright moved closer. Close enough that he could smell the soft fragrance of orange blossoms that clung to her hair and cloak. "I understand you already have two dogs in residence. Mastiffs, Mrs. Archer said."

"Yes."

"Are they friendly?" She gazed up at him. "It's only that Bertie has no way to defend himself. If a bigger dog were to—"

"I won't let them hurt him."

"Yes, but—"

"He'll be safe here. I promise you." For once, the words came out strong and sure. They seemed important somehow.

"Oh." Her mouth trembled. "Oh, thank you. I've been so worried."

Neville's chest tightened. Were those tears glistening in her eyes? The very thought sent a jolt of alarm through him.

"I'm being ridiculous, I know," she said. "But might I see where you mean to put him? It would set my mind at ease."

He turned toward the feed room. Bertie's small body was a solid, warm weight in his arms. "This way."

She followed after him, the wide skirts of her gown rustling over the straw-covered floor. The stable boy hadn't swept this morning. He was busy up at the house with the rest of the staff.

Neville should be there, too. Lady Helena had asked him specifically. And he'd meant to go. But it was difficult.

More than difficult.

It was a month-long Christmas celebration. His three childhood friends would be in residence, along with their respective wives. The family of one of those wives—Mrs. Laura Archer—was joining them as well. Her invalid brother, and her widowed aunt, Mrs. Bainbridge.

And now Mrs. Bainbridge's companion.

Neville cast Miss Hartwright a sidelong glance. No one had warned him there would be an unmarried young lady in residence for the month. And they'd certainly said nothing about her being beautiful. Or about her having a dog.

She looked about the feed room. "Where will you put him?"

"Here." He carried Bertie to a stack of empty feed sacks in the corner. They were nothing like a velvet cushion, but when Neville lowered the pug down onto them, the little dog seemed content enough. He hobbled around in a half-hearted circle before plumping down with a grunt. "See? He likes it here."

"Do you think so?" Miss Hartwright sounded hopeful. She crouched down beside the feed sacks, her skirts and cloak pooling all about her. "You're all right now, Bertie." She stroked a hand over his back, her voice sinking to a whisper. "I'm not abandoning you. I'll return as soon as I'm able."

Neville clasped his hands at his back, uncertain what to say or do.

"Would you please give him a dish of water?" she asked. "And I shall try to beg some meat from the cook, but if—"

"I'll get meat for him."

She looked up at him, her eyes very bright. "Will you?"

He nodded.

Her face lit with gratitude. "Thank you, Mr. Cross. You're very kind." She rose and dusted off her skirts. "I must make my way up to the Abbey now."

He stopped himself from nodding again. It was easier than speaking. It also made him appear some manner of head-bobbing simpleton, or so he feared. But as he struggled over what to say to her, the silence stretched taut between them, on and on, until heat rose in his face. The words simply wouldn't come. Not the ones he wanted.

Outside, a clap of thunder rent the air. The rain began again, a light fall of it, pattering on the roof.

Miss Hartwright responded by fastening her cloak. "I can't linger. Mrs. Bainbridge expects me straightaway." She pulled her hood up over her hair. "Though I hope to be back soon, if all goes well."

Neville followed her to the doors of the stable. She glanced back at him once over her shoulder before ducking out into the rain.

"Goodbye," she said. "And thank you again, sir."

He made no reply. It was too difficult to muster one. He wasn't calm or clear-headed enough. And it was her fault, however unintended. She'd flustered him. Rattled him to his core. He could do nothing but watch her stride away through the mud and rain. A small cloaked figure on the cliffs.

Clara Hartwright.

Miss Clara Hartwright.

He heaved a sigh as he returned to his work. It was going to be a very long holiday.

Clara trudged up the winding road, her head half bent against the wind and the driving rain. The house loomed ahead at the top of the cliffs.

If one could call it a house.

From the outside, Greyfriar's Abbey looked positively medieval. It was composed entirely of weathered gray stone, with a steeply pitched roof, pointed arches, and a Gothic tower. The whistle of the wind, and the roar of the sea, sounded all about it. It seemed a sinister place. Nothing like the elegant home she'd been expecting.

She climbed the steps, raising her gloved hand to the heavy wooden door. A shiver of uncertainty made her hesitate before applying the iron knocker.

The owners of the Abbey were unknown to her. And her employer, Mrs. Bainbridge, was equally strange. Clara had only met the lady last month. As for Mrs. Bainbridge's relations—her niece, invalid nephew, and her niece's husband…

Well.

They had seemed kindly enough. Though how much could one tell about people during the course of a single railway journey and a cramped carriage drive?

It behooved her to remain on her guard, no matter how kind Mrs. Bainbridge and her relations might be. That was doubly true for the residents of Greyfriar's Abbey. Even that blond Sir Galahad of a groom in the stable. Yes, even him.

Especially him.

She wasn't about to have another position derailed by a handsome man.

Stiffening her spine, she once again raised her hand to the knocker. However, before she could apply it, the door swung open, revealing an elderly butler garbed in impeccable livery. He peered down at her from beneath a pair of bushy white brows.

"Miss Hartwright?"

Heat drifted out from inside the house, enveloping Clara in a warm embrace. She took an unconscious step toward it. "I am Miss Hartwright."

"Indeed, ma'am. Mrs. Bainbridge is expecting you." He drew back to admit her. "Welcome to Greyfriar's Abbey."

She stepped into the spacious hall. The interior of the Abbey appeared as luxurious as the outside was stark and grim. Daylight filtered in through the high, stone-framed windows, illuminating walls papered in softly shaded silk, and a floor covered in rich Aubusson carpet, spun with threads of crimson and gold.

There was no one waiting to issue a formal welcome, and no sign of Mrs. Bainbridge, or any of the others who Clara had traveled up with in the carriage.

"Allow me to take your wet things," the butler said.

She divested herself of her cloak and gloves, grateful to be rid of them. Her woolen dress underneath was nothing very special, but at least it was neat and dry. As she smoothed her hair and skirts, another servant appeared. An older woman in a plain black dress and starched cap. The housekeeper, Clara presumed.

"Miss Hartwright? You'll wish to freshen your appearance before tea is served. Permit me to show you to your room."

Clara followed after her up a single flight of oak stairs. The steps rose to a landing, after which they divided into two separate branches leading to opposite wings of the floors above.

"I've put you in a room next to Mrs. Bainbridge." The housekeeper stopped outside a wood-paneled door at the end of a narrow corridor, and opened it for Clara to enter. "She asks that you go to her after you've repaired your hair and dress."

"Yes, of course." Clara advanced into the room. It was as richly papered and carpeted as the hall had been, and equally as warm. At its center was a four-poster bed, curtained in dark green fabric. A wardrobe stood to the left of it, between two velvet-draped windows. At its right was a wooden washstand with a porcelain pitcher and bowl.

"There's hot water to wash with, and Robert has brought your cases in from the carriage."

Clara went to the foot of the bed, where her carpetbag and portmanteau had been neatly stacked atop a padded bench. "When will tea be served?"

"In a quarter of an hour." The housekeeper paused. She gave a delicate cough, her face a studied blank. "You received a parcel yesterday. I've put it on your dressing table."

Clara's gaze jerked to the dainty walnut table in the corner of the guest room. A large, overstuffed envelope was perched atop it, half propped against the looking glass.

Her pulse quickened.

"Will there be anything else, ma'am?" the housekeeper asked.

Clara willed herself not to apologize. After all, there was nothing irregular about giving out the direction of one's host. Not when one was staying longer than a fortnight. "No, thank you."

The housekeeper withdrew, leaving Clara to her thoughts—and to her parcel.

She flew to the dressing table and retrieved it. It was a solid, familiar weight in her hands. Her fingers itched to tear it open. To see if this time Simon had done what he'd promised to do.

But there was no time. Not now. Not with Mrs. Bainbridge waiting, and tea in a quarter of an hour.

She was already on thin ice with her employer.

Companions were meant to be next door to invisible. Rather like genteel ghosts, mutely shadowing the steps of their corporeal benefactors. Quiet and obliging, that was the companion's motto. Words, when spoken, were best kept to a murmured minimum. Yes, ma'am. No, ma'am. I'll fetch your shawl, ma'am.

That much Clara knew to a certainty. Her previous employers had known it as well. They'd been happy to overlook her very existence. During the course of the past four years, she'd been regularly trod upon, shouldered out of the way, or addressed by the wrong name.

But not today.

Today, she'd arrived to meet her new employer at the railway station in London with an unauthorized pug in tow. A sign of independence—nay, insubordination—that was unheard of for one in Clara's position.

That single act had shone a blazing light on her. Had drawn attention to her that was both unseemly, and unwanted.

Though she couldn't blame it all on Bertie.

The fact was, her disposition was not at all suited to her profession. She was too forthright, that was the problem. It was a formidable flaw. Companions were meant to be good listeners, not good talkers. And they certainly weren't permitted to speak their mind.

But paid positions didn't grow on trees. Not for women of her class. She would simply have to cut her dress to fit her cloth. To alter her disposition. To—in short—endeavor to become invisible.

Her parcel would have to wait.

She carried it to her carpetbag. The leather closure was equipped with a simple lock, its key suspended from a long, thin silver chain worn round her neck. She retrieved it from inside the bodice of her gown. The lock was tricky, but after some wiggling, the key turned it with a snick. The carpetbag opened and she dropped her parcel inside. It landed on top of a heap of near identical envelopes, each of them stuffed full to bursting.

She closed the carpetbag and locked it shut.

Soon.

Soon she'd be done with Mrs. Bainbridge. Done with being silent and subservient. With being a ghost. Soon she would shed the trappings of a lady's companion.

And then her real life could begin.

Chapter Two

Clara sat, as still as a statue, in her silk-upholstered chair in the drawing room, a teacup and saucer held motionless in her lap. She wasn't very imposing to begin with—only five feet three inches in her stocking feet—but she endeavored to make herself appear even smaller. She'd drawn enough attention to herself today. It wouldn't do to attract any more.

Far better to be still and quiet. To drink her tea, and enjoy the warmth from the blazing fire in the hearth. It crackled and sparked, taking away the chill she'd felt since first stepping down from the train at the railway station in Abbot's Holcombe.

Mrs. Bainbridge's nephew, Mr. Edward Hayes, appeared to have the same idea. He sat to the right of her in his wheeled chair, a tartan blanket draped over his legs. He was still a boy, really. Not more than twenty, by Clara's estimation.

During the journey from London, he'd been attended by a manservant. A brawny fellow who was kept far busier hauling about Mr. Hayes's art supplies than in hauling about Mr. Hayes himself.

As for Mrs. Bainbridge, she'd been too irritated with Clara to make any demands. "You never mentioned a dog, Miss Hartwright," she'd said in arctic tones. "Had I known..."

Clara had held Bertie all the tighter.

She wished she were still holding him now, truth be told, as much for her own comfort as for his.

Greyfriar's Abbey was an unsettling house, for all that it had a comfortable interior. The skies outside of it were too gray, the sea too thunderous. One felt as if one was sitting inside the eye of the storm.

"It often rains in Devon." Their host, Mr. Justin Thornhill, stood beside his wife's chair, a tall, imposing gentleman with raven black hair and a rather forbidding collection of burn scars on the bottom right side of his face. "One becomes used to it after a time."

"Do they indeed?" Mrs. Bainbridge drank her tea. She was a lady of magnificent size, clad in unrelieved black crepe, and as regal as Queen Victoria herself. "I must say, it's a relief after such a summer as we had in Surrey. We could scarcely move for the heat. I was quite undone by it."

"The climate in the South of France is said to be far more temperate." Lady Helena refilled her cup from a delicate painted porcelain teapot. A whisper of steam rose into the air. "I understand you'll be relocating there in the new year, to live with Mr. and Mrs. Archer."

"Nothing has been decided yet," Mrs. Bainbridge said. "My nephew wishes to go of course, but a woman of my age can't be too hasty. There is still much to be settled before I resign myself to leaving England."

Clara sent up a silent prayer that Mrs. Bainbridge would resolve to stay on this side of the Channel. It would save Clara from having to seek another position. She couldn't remove to France, not at present. And she had no wish to embark on another round of answering employment advertisements and submitting to intrusive interviews.

"Nevertheless, it all sounds very exciting." Lady Helena returned the teapot to the tea tray. She was garbed in a loose-fitting cashmere jacket and skirt, and had a soft glow to her gently rounded features. A result of her pregnancy, Clara guessed. The condition did nothing to detract from her ladyship's beauty. Though it was surely the impetus for Mr. Thornhill to hover at his wife's side, standing over her so protectively.

Clara felt a pang of envy for ladies who were fortunate enough to have a life and a home of their own. Perhaps that was why she'd been so stubborn about Bertie. It was a terrible thing to be alone in the world. To be dismissed and discarded. To never belong anywhere. What was a dog to do in his old age if no one wanted him?

More to the point, what was a *woman* to do?

"When do you plan on leaving for Grasse?" Mr. Thornhill asked.

"Early March, at the latest," Mr. Archer said from his place on the settee. He was a roguishly handsome gentleman. A newly married one, too.

His wife, Laura, was Mrs. Bainbridge's niece. She sat close at his side. So close that the hem of her voluminous skirts pooled over his booted feet. She was a lovely lady, though not in the doe-eyed, aristocratic manner of Lady Helena. Laura

Archer's beauty lay more in the confidence with which she carried herself. The intelligence in her slate-blue gaze and the compassion in her smile.

She seemed a level-headed lady with a genuine affection for her family. She was also plainly in love with her new husband, and he with her. One could see it in the way they looked at each other. The way they touched.

"We've found a house near to our perfumery." Mr. Archer took his wife's hand. "A grand old place atop a hill, with windows overlooking the lavender fields."

Mrs. Archer smiled. "We hope to be settled in before the first harvest."

"You must be looking forward to it," Lady Helena said. "And you, Mr. Hayes. I imagine that, for an artist, the French Riviera will provide a wealth of ready subjects."

"One hopes," Mr. Hayes replied. Like his sister, he was dark haired and blue eyed. But there was a wry humor to Mr. Hayes's expression that Mrs. Archer lacked—a sharpness which Clara suspected could cut as easily as it could amuse. "The new house is but ten miles from the sea."

"Do you prefer painting seascapes?" Mr. Thornhill asked.

"Of late I do."

Mr. Archer grinned. "I've challenged him to tackle the Devon coast."

"I intend to," Mr. Hayes said. "If the rain ever stops."

Mrs. Archer looked at Clara. "Which reminds me, Miss Hartwright, I must apologize to you."

Clara lowered her teacup to her lap. "Ma'am?"

"I expected Mr. Cross to accompany you back from the stable. I'd no intention of you walking up the road alone. Certainly not in this weather."

"It was no trouble," Clara replied. In truth, she was so used to being disregarded, it hadn't even occurred to her that Mr. Cross might escort her back to the house. She doubted whether it had occurred to him either.

He'd given her such a look before she'd stepped out into the rain, his face rife with impatience and barely veiled frustration. He'd plainly been anxious to see the back of her.

"Neville prefers being with the animals," Mr. Thornhill said. "He'll withdraw to the stables the whole of the holiday if we allow it."

Lady Helena took a delicate sip of her tea. "Quite. Which is precisely why we must keep him occupied here at the house."

Mrs. Bainbridge's gaze flicked to Clara. "I pray he won't be overburdened with looking after your dog."

Five additional sets of eyes immediately fixed on Clara. Heat flooded her cheeks. If a hole had opened in the ground, she'd have gladly leapt into it.

"You've brought a dog with you?" Lady Helena asked.

"Yes." Clara moistened her lips. "A very small one."

Mr. Thornhill gave her an interested look. "What kind of dog?"

"An antique pug," Mr. Archer replied with a laugh. "The oldest one I've ever seen."

"Too old to be any trouble," Mr. Hayes said.

"No, indeed." Mrs. Archer turned to Lady Helena. "But we didn't like to presume on your hospitality. Miss Hartwright has left him in the stable for the time being."

Lady Helena smiled. "You must bring him up to the house, Miss Hartwright. He can stay in your room with you if you like, or in the kitchens."

Clara couldn't hide her relief. "Thank you, ma'am."

"Not at all. We'll be so busy until Twelfth Night. You won't wish to be always walking down to the stables."

Mr. Thornhill rested his hand on Lady Helena's shoulder. "My wife intends to keep us well entertained this month."

"Do you have many festivities planned, my lady?" Mrs. Bainbridge asked.

"Oh yes." Lady Helena beamed. "We shall be trimming a tree, gilding walnuts and acorns, and hanging holly and mistletoe. The gentlemen have promised to find a yule log for us, and Cook is making a Christmas feast. I'm determined it will be the happiest Christmas in memory."

Mr. Thornhill gazed down at his wife. His harsh features softened. "And it will be."

Lady Helena covered his hand with hers, giving it a discreet squeeze. "I must delegate many of my duties of course, but with a little help—"

"You have mine," Mrs. Archer said. "I'm completely at your service."

Mrs. Bainbridge set her teacup down on the marble-topped table beside her chair. "If you're in need of an extra pair of hands, you must make free to utilize Miss Hartwright."

"Aunt Charlotte," Mrs. Archer objected under her breath.

"I won't need a companion with me every moment of the day," Mrs. Bainbridge went on. "Miss Hartwright will have plenty of time to spare. I see no reason she shouldn't help if she's able. And participate in the festivities, too. Young people must have their fun."

Lady Helena's gaze settled back on Clara's face.

Clara already had plans for her free time. An entire stack of them waiting in her carpetbag. All she could think about was getting back to her room, opening her latest parcel, and setting to work. She had no wish to spend any of her free time on trimming trees, or other holiday nonsense.

But this was Christmas. And her ladyship had kindly permitted Bertie to remove from the stable to the warmth and safety of the house.

Would it be so terrible to join in with the spirit of things? To, for once, endeavor to be something more than invisible?

It seemed a revolutionary idea. A dangerous one, too, based on past experience. But with all eyes in the room upon her, Clara could do nothing but acquiesce. "Thank you, ma'am. I would be glad to be of use."

Neville loomed over Bertie's sleeping form, regarding him with a troubled frown. The pug was still curled up tightly on his pile of empty feed sacks. He hadn't moved so much as an inch since Miss Hartwright had left the stables. And that was more than an hour ago. If not for the muted snuffle of his intermittent snores, Neville might have believed that the elderly canine had expired.

An unsettling thought.

The last thing Neville wanted was to have to tell Miss Hartwright that her pug had died while in his care.

"He looks contented." A deep voice sounded from the feed room door.

Neville's head jerked up to find Justin standing there. Neville exhaled, relieved it wasn't a stranger. With so many people coming and going from the Abbey, he never knew who he might encounter from one moment to the next.

But Justin was safe. He was a friend. Practically a brother. The two of them had grown up together in the orphanage, along with Tom Finchley and Alex Archer. Justin had been their fearless leader. He'd taken care of Neville. Protected him.

If not for Justin…

Well.

Neville didn't like to think of what might have become of him.

"He's sleeping."

Justin looked doubtful. "Are you certain he's not…?"

Neville shot another glance at Bertie's abdomen. It was still rising and falling, very slightly, with each softly snorting breath. "He isn't."

Justin turned to exit the feed room. "You haven't introduced him to Paul and Jonesy yet, have you?"

Neville followed after him. "Not yet."

The two mastiffs had been banished to the stables for the day. Last he'd looked, they were sleeping on a pile of straw in one of the loose boxes.

"The horses appear to be settled, each of them brushed to a high shine. And the saddles and bridles have all been cleaned and oiled, I see." Justin gave him an amused look. "You've been keeping busy out here."

Neville clamped his mouth shut. He wouldn't make excuses for himself. Not that Justin would have believed them anyway. He knew Neville far too well.

"Helena expected you at the Abbey this morning. And then again for tea when Laura's relations arrived." Justin stopped beside the loose box that housed his horse, Hiran. The chestnut stallion swung his head over the door to nip at Justin's sleeve. "You can't hide away here the whole of the holiday."

"I'm not hiding. Why should I?"

"No reason. Certainly not when it's just Tom and Alex and their wives in residence. But today, two new guests have arrived. Mrs. Bainbridge and Mr. Hayes. I suppose I can't blame you for feeling a bit reluctant."

"Not only them."

Justin's brows lifted.

"Miss Hartwright," Neville said.

"Miss Bainbridge's companion?" Justin gave Hiran an absent scratch on the neck. "Has she done something to make you uncomfortable? I wouldn't have thought her capable. She seems a harmless, mousy little thing."

Mousy?

Justin was usually so astute. So canny. But *mousy*? Had he lost his wits? Or, more to the point, his sense of sight?

"She's not mousy," Neville said. "She's…"

She was beautiful, is what she was. But he wasn't going to admit that. Not to Justin.

It wasn't that Neville didn't trust his friend, only that Justin was married now. He'd inevitably tell his wife, Lady Helena. And Lady Helena would tell her best friend, Jenny Finchley, who would then confide in Tom. And then, somehow, Alex and Laura would get wind of it. All resulting in Neville being made to look—quite unintentionally—like some variety of pathetic fool.

"She's what?" Justin prompted.

Neville's jaw tightened. "Nothing."

Understanding registered in Justin's gray eyes. "Ah."

Neville didn't care for that look. That knowing look that seemed to see—and understand—all of his private thoughts and feelings.

"Forgive me," Justin said. "Since I married, I find myself incapable of properly assessing the beauty of any lady, save my wife. But you're right. I misspoke. Miss Hartwright isn't mousy." He paused. "What is it? Are you worried she'll say something unfeeling about your condition? That she'll treat you poorly?"

"It doesn't matter."

"It clearly does. But there's a simple enough solution. Helena can have a word with her. Or, perhaps, Laura—"

"No!" Neville stifled a frustrated growl. "I wish..." The words were as thick as molasses. As slow as molasses, too. The more out of sorts he became, the harder it was for him to form them. "I w-wish I hadn't said anything about...about her."

Justin didn't comment on Neville's loss of temper. Not directly. "I've asked a lot of you this past year, haven't I? First, you were obliged to accustom yourself to the Abbey having a mistress. Then Tom married Jenny. And last week Alex returned to Devon, along with his new bride. It's been difficult for you, I fear."

"Not d-difficult. Just..."

"Traveling into Abbot's Holcombe wasn't difficult? You couldn't even manage to do so for my wedding last year. It can't have been easy for you."

It hadn't been.

Located thirteen miles up the coast from the Abbey, Abbot's Holcombe was now a fashionable resort town. But two decades ago, it had been a bleak and stormy place, more notable for its parish orphanage than for its pleasing prospects of the sea.

Neville had hoped to never see the place again.

He'd refused to attend Justin's wedding, it was true. A cowardly decision Neville had come to regret.

When Alex had arrived last week on the train, Neville had determined not to make the same mistake again. He couldn't refuse to meet his childhood friend at the station. The very friend who'd saved Neville's life on the day of his accident. Abbot's Holcombe was just a place, after all. It wasn't a person. And it certainly wasn't responsible for the ills that had befallen him.

Nevertheless…

As he'd climbed down from the carriage and onto the railway platform, his palms had grown damp, and his pulse had accelerated with alarming swiftness.

"Tom and Jenny will be returning for dinner this evening," Justin said. "I won't insist you join us. I'll only remind you that this is your home, and that you're among friends. Don't isolate yourself down here. It serves no purpose."

"I'm not. I—"

"I know you prefer it, even at the best of times, but this is Christmas. And we're all together at last. The eloquence of your speech will be the last thing on people's minds."

Neville shook his head. "You don't understand. You can't."

"Oh, can't I? Do you think I don't know what it's like to be looked at askance?"

"Yes, but…" Neville scarcely noticed Justin's burns anymore. And when he did, they didn't alarm him. They were merely a reminder of his friend's bravery and strength of character. "You're a hero."

Justin snorted. "Hardly."

"Lady Helena says—"

"Of course Helena says so. She's my wife." A smile edged Justin's mouth. Any mention of Lady Helena always served to boost his spirits. "How is your speech any more repellent than my burns? And what about Laura's brother? He's in a wheeled chair, for God's sake. A dashed nuisance, I expect, for a young lad like him. And yet he's here—among strangers, no less."

Neville's gaze dropped to the straw-covered floor of the stables. He knew what Justin was trying to do. He was attempting to make him feel better. But one's infirmities weren't any easier to tolerate simply because some other poor chap had it worse.

Besides, faulty speech was different from burn scars or a wheeled chair. Language went to the heart of a person's humanity. It was the dividing line between men and beasts. And for a man of his size to stammer, and stutter. To forget his words entirely, or to blurt them out like a disordered child… It was worse than embarrassing. It was shameful.

"You spend too much time alone of late," Justin said. "You're in danger of sinking into a melancholy."

"I'm not."

"Don't deny it. Not to me. I've had personal experience with the state. I recognize the signs when I see them." Justin clapped a hand on Neville's shoulder. "Come. Enough moping about. Gather your things—and that little dog—and return to the Abbey with me."

Neville looked up. "The pug can come up to the house?"

"Naturally. I'll rouse Paul and Jonesy. We can get all the introductions over with at once—God help us."

Neville grimaced. "God help the guests."

Justin appeared unperturbed by the possibility of canine havoc. "They seem a sturdy enough bunch. A pair of ravening mastiffs aren't likely to send them running back to the railway station." He paused, adding dryly, "One hopes."

Chapter Three

Back in her room at last, Clara lifted her carpetbag onto the dressing table, unlocked it, and opened it wide. Inside were her most prized possessions. Her most valuable, too. Six months' worth of them. She withdrew the topmost packet, feeling the familiar sensation of nervous butterflies in her stomach as she broke the seal.

It contained, as it always did, a thick stack of papers covered in lopsided script. A note was scrawled in the right-hand corner of the first page.

Dear Clara,

Apologies. Here's the latest.

Fond regards, Simon

It was the same note Simon had written on most of the sets of papers he'd sent to her this year. Apologies. Always apologies. As if nine hastily dashed-off words could make up for his carelessness. Heaven's sake, he used to enclose an entire letter!

"I ask only one thing of you," she'd said when he'd first left for Cambridge. "That you tell me everything. Describe it all so that I may experience it with you."

And he *had* done, initially. But as the years passed, Simon had become less inclined to share the rarified experience of his education with his older sister. No matter that her wages paid his tuition.

She sank down at the dressing table with a sigh.

It didn't signify. All she really wanted was his lessons, and those he continued to send—albeit belatedly.

She turned the first page. The words written across the top were oddly familiar.

Notes on Classification of Natural Objects and Phenomena

A soft knock sounded at the door. "Miss Hartwright?"

Clara's pulse jumped. She leapt up from her seat, shoving the stack of papers back into her valise and clicking it shut. "Yes?"

Mrs. Archer quietly entered the room, shutting the door behind her. Her ebony hair was drawn back into a delicate silk net, the same shade of blue as her eyes. "I thought you might have already gone to retrieve your dog."

A flicker of guilt stung at Clara's conscience. She'd hoped to fetch Bertie after tea, but her curiosity over her parcel had been too great to resist. After assisting Mrs. Bainbridge in settling in, Clara had returned to her own bedroom rather than departing for the stables. It was only for a moment, she'd promised herself. Just long enough to open her parcel. Bertie wouldn't mind a brief delay, surely. "I'll be going down shortly."

"I won't keep you," Mrs. Archer said. "I only wanted to make certain you were comfortable, and that you have everything you require."

"Oh yes." Clara stood beside the dressing table, hands clasped in front of her. "The housekeeper is looking after me."

"And my aunt? She's not too tired from the journey, I trust."

"Mrs. Bainbridge is having a lie-down. I offered her some of her tonic, but she refused it. I was unable to persuade her."

"Aunt Charlotte won't take her tonic unless it's strictly necessary. You needn't keep after her. She'll ask for it if her heart begins to pain her."

"Yes, ma'am." Clara hesitated. "She did seem a bit weak after the journey."

"She's only tired, I expect. Travel overtaxes her. And with the change in the weather..." Mrs. Archer's mouth curved into a pensive frown. "I wonder if I was selfish to encourage her to spend Christmas in such a climate? Dampness has always worsened her aches and pains."

"It's not damp inside the house," Clara pointed out. Rather the opposite. She was toasty warm. Warmer than she'd been in an age. Her last employer had guarded the coals for the fire as if each one was a precious jewel. As a result, Clara's former bedroom had been the approximate temperature of an icebox.

"No. It's really quite modern, isn't it? Despite the remote location. Mr. Thornhill has even had gaslight installed in some of the rooms." Mrs. Archer's features brightened. "I daresay my aunt will warm up soon enough, once she's recovered from her journey. And then we can all set our minds to having a merry Christmas."

"Yes, ma'am." Clara managed a smile, certain it looked as brittle as it felt.

She hadn't had a merry Christmas in a very long time. In truth, she couldn't remember ever having had one. And it wasn't only because they'd never had a bean to spare for gifts. Or because Mama found the fashion for Christmas trees frivolous—never mind that it was favored by the Queen.

It was hard to imagine Christmas here being any merrier.

There was an aura of gloom about the Abbey. No matter its warmth and modernizations. She supposed it was the age of the place.

"You mustn't feel as though you can't take part. You're not a servant here." Mrs. Archer paused, studying Clara's face. "Forgive me if I've got the wrong end of things, but I sense that your last position may not have been entirely agreeable."

Clara's cheeks warmed. "I was very grateful for it."

"Of course you were." Mrs. Archer moved to the door. "I'll say no more on the subject. You're sure to get an earful on the role of ladies' companions when you meet Mrs. Finchley. She was once Lady Helena's companion, you know."

Clara's brows shot up. She hadn't known. "And they remain on good terms?"

"Indeed. They're the best of friends." Mrs. Archer smiled back at Clara as she opened the door. "We're an eccentric bunch, Miss Hartwright, even at the best of times. Consider yourself warned."

With Mrs. Archer gone, Clara once again sank down into the chair in front of the dressing table. She didn't retrieve her papers from her valise. She didn't have to. The lesson on classification of natural objects was an old one, the notes drawn straight out of *Herschel's Preliminary Discourse on the Study of Natural Philosophy*. It was a lesson she'd read before.

Helpless frustration rose in her breast.

She didn't want to relearn the principles of classification. She was past the fundamentals of natural philosophy, and so was Simon. At least, he *should* be.

Her fingers drummed absently on the inlaid surface of the dressing table.

There was nothing for it. She would have to involve her mother.

The prospect was as grim as it was necessary. Mama wasn't fond of receiving personal letters, nor of writing them. Indeed, Clara hadn't heard from her since the summer, and only then in the briefest terms.

"Don't forget your brother's school fees," she'd admonished in the short missive.

As if Clara could.

She'd always considered them her own school fees, after a fashion. That is, until Simon had grown lazy in sending her copies of his lessons. And now, a duplicate lesson!

Is this all she had to show for four years of being a lady's companion? A thorough knowledge of dratted classification?

Oh, but it wasn't fair. It simply wasn't.

She stood, smoothing the skirts of her plain gray day dress as she crossed the room. She needed paper, pen, and ink. Surely Mr. Thornhill must have some in his study.

Another knock sounded at the door, harder and brisker than before.

Was it Mrs. Archer come back again? Or Mrs. Bainbridge? Schooling her features, Clara went to the door and opened it.

Neville Cross's large frame filled the doorway.

Her breath caught in her chest. She pressed one hand to the front of her corseted waist. In the stable, she hadn't properly appreciated how extraordinarily big he was. But here in the house…

Good gracious.

He appeared an absolute giant. He was taller, even, than Mr. Thornhill, with the sort of bronzed skin and lean, well-muscled build that spoke of hours spent out of doors engaged in some physical pursuit or other.

When she'd met him in the stable, Clara had thought him well favored. But now he struck her as something rather more than that.

His features were roughly hewn, with straight blond brows, lean cheeks, and a jaw so firm it could have been chiseled from granite. He might have been intimidating if not for the sun-streaked splendor of his fair hair and the slightly faraway look in his pale blue eyes.

She wondered, briefly, if he had a wife or a sweetheart.

A stupid thought. The sort of romantic schoolgirl fancy that was designed to get her in trouble again. And this time with a servant, of all people.

Mr. Cross *was* a servant, wasn't he? The head groom, or something like.

Yet his clothing was well made. And hadn't Mr. Thornhill and Lady Helena mentioned his taking part in the holiday festivities? As if he were a friend or a family member.

She waited for him to say something, but he only looked at her. Stared at her, really.

"It's not Bertie, is it?" she asked at last. "Something hasn't happened?"

Mr. Cross's throat contracted on a swallow. "No. I've brought him to you."

Her brows lifted. Mr. Cross's arms were empty, hanging loose at his sides. She gave them a pointed look, and saw—for the first time—that one of his hands was clenched into a fist. Odd that. And slightly unsettling. Her eyes met his. "Where is he?"

"In the kitchen. Eating with Paul and Jonesy. I came to tell you—"

"I'm sorry, who? Paul and—" She broke off in dawning horror. "Not the two mastiffs?"

Mr. Cross nodded.

She pushed past him into the hall. "Which way is the kitchen?"

He caught her by the upper arm. "Miss Hartwright—"

She stopped short, her skirts swinging about her legs. "I *beg* your pardon. Will you please unhand me, sir?"

He abruptly released her, taking a step back, as if he'd been scalded. "I didn't—" His face was stricken. "Did I hurt you?"

She straightened her sleeve. "Not at all. But I don't care to be manhandled. And I won't tolerate anyone taking liberties with Bertie. You should have told me you intended for him to meet the other dogs. I'd have been there to help. You can't just—"

"He's fine. He's...happy."

Clara stared up at Mr. Cross. A creeping feeling of confusion dulled her outrage.

Was something wrong with him?

She hadn't noticed it in the stable. She'd been too focused on Bertie. But now that she thought of it, she realized Mr. Cross had faltered over his words there as well, his sentences short and riddled with uncomfortably long pauses.

Was it a speech impediment of some sort? A newly banished stutter? Or was it something more insidious?

Mr. Cross turned a dull red about the collar. "He's fine," he said again, his voice gone gruff. "That's...that's all."

Guilt twisted in Clara's bosom. Good lord, she'd hurt his feelings. Embarrassed him. And he didn't deserve it. Not from her. She was a guest here. A stranger.

As he turned to go, she laid a hand on his sleeve. He stopped immediately, as if her touch had turned him to stone. "Forgive me. I didn't mean to scold you."

Mr. Cross's eyes met hers.

"You must understand," she said. "Bertie is my first dog. All I have, really. And I'm terribly afraid that I won't be able to care for him properly. To protect him. I'm in no position to—"

"It's all right."

"It isn't. You've been nothing but kind since I stormed into the stable this morning and interrupted your work. A demanding lady with a pampered pug. It exceeds caricature."

"You weren't..." His jaw tightened. "You're not."

"That's very kind of you to say, but I know I can be demanding at times. The trouble is, I never realize it until afterward. An unfortunate failing, to be sure." She dropped her hand from his arm. "Is Bertie truly all right? The other dogs didn't bully him, did they?"

A shadow of a smile edged Mr. Cross's mouth. So faint, she might have imagined it. "Come," he said. "I'll show you."

Miss Hartwright followed Neville into the hall, shutting her bedroom door behind her.

He slowed to accommodate her pace. "Paul and Jonesy liked him. They didn't bite or growl."

"Well, that's something." She folded her arms at her waist. "And what did Bertie think of them?"

"He didn't notice them."

She huffed a short laugh. "I can well believe that. He doesn't seem to notice much of anything these days."

He guided her not to the main staircase, but down a narrow corridor in the opposite direction. It opened onto a set of curving stone steps.

The servants' stairs.

Miss Hartwright gave him a questioning look.

He shrugged. "It's easier."

Easier for him, anyway. It saved him from running into anyone. From having to talk. The servants he passed along the way rarely engaged him. Unlike the Abbey's guests, they hadn't any time for conversation.

Miss Hartwright didn't seem to be interested in conversation either.

At least she was no longer upset about her dog.

It hadn't occurred to him that he was being high-handed by introducing Paul and Jonesy to Bertie. He'd been trying to be helpful. To do her a service. The idea that he'd put any animal in danger was so far from the truth as to be laughable. But how was Miss Hartwright to know that? She was a newly arrived stranger. A lady who didn't know him at all.

He went down the narrow steps ahead of her with an ease born of familiarity. When she didn't follow, he looked back, brows raised in question.

She was poised at the top of the stairs, her skirts clutched in her left hand, revealing a glimpse of sturdy leather half boots—and a rather trim pair of ankles. "If you wouldn't mind?" She extended her right hand to him.

He hesitated for what seemed an interminable length of time. And then he took her hand, engulfing it carefully in his.

He was grateful the staircase wasn't properly lit. Had it been, she'd have no doubt marked the heat that rose in his neck and face. He felt it everywhere, that peculiar warmth, as if he were a furnace that had been stoked with a sudden shovelful of glowing coals.

It was unsettlingly intimate. Bare skin to bare skin. But Miss Hartwright didn't appear to notice it at all.

"I don't know how a lady is meant to navigate such stairs in the present fashion," she said. "My skirts are as wide as the steps."

An image of the Abbey's housemaids in their smart dark dresses and white aprons formed in Neville's mind. Miss Hartwright was equally smart and starched. Neat as a pin, in fact, in a long-sleeved gray dress with a form-fitting bodice and a set of delicate buttons that marched from her impossibly small waist all the way to her collar.

But unlike the dresses worn by the maidservants, Miss Hartwright's skirts were full, standing wide over layers of petticoats and crinoline.

"The housemaids don't..." Neville faltered. "They..." He tried and failed to get the words out. It was impossible when his thoughts kept drifting to the sensation of Miss Hartwright's slim hand clasped so snugly in his.

"Their skirts aren't quite like mine? I daresay they aren't. It wouldn't be very practical."

"N-no."

She stepped down after him, clutching tight to his hand.

It was two flights before they reached the kitchen. A line of evenly spaced gas wall sconces lit the way into a cavernous room with a stone floor and a long wooden table and chairs. A footman was seated there, absorbed in polishing the Abbey's collection of silver. Nearby, Cook stood in front of a steaming pot on the stove, talking loudly to one of the kitchen maids.

At the opposite end of the room, a fire roared in the hearth. Bertie was asleep in front of it, along with Paul and Jonesy.

Miss Hartwright dropped Neville's hand as she crossed the floor to her dog. Her steps were brisk and purposeful. Though small, she wasn't weak or timid, he didn't think. Not in the normal course of things. And if she required assistance—as she had on the stairs—she seemed to have no qualms about asking for it.

Neville flexed his fingers. He could still feel the delicate curve of her hand cradled in his. The sweet, uneasy warmth of it. As if she'd branded herself on his skin, leaving an indelible mark.

Jonesy chose that moment to lift his head and growl.

Miss Hartwright stopped short.

Neville strode to her side. "No," he said to Jonesy.

The mastiff obeyed, though he continued to watch Miss Hartwright with a hostile eye.

"That's Jonesy," Neville said. The older mastiff was crochety at the best of times, downright aggressive at the worst. "And that's Paul. Paul is… He's younger."

Paul lifted his head at the sound of his name, his tail thumping.

"He doesn't look half so fearsome." Miss Hartwright reached out to pet him. "May I?"

Neville nodded.

She stroked Paul's head before crouching down in a pool of skirts to give a pet to Bertie. The pug continued to snore. "He's sound asleep."

"He's old."

"Should I leave him here? I'd intended to bring him to my rooms, but…" She frowned. "I wonder if he's happier to be with the other dogs?"

"It's the fire," Neville said. "He wants to be warm."

"There's a fire in my bedroom. Perhaps I'd better take him there. He'll have a soft carpet to sleep on. And no servants coming and going to trouble him." She scooped the little pug up in her arms.

Bertie woke, blinking his bulging eyes up at her. His tongue lolled.

"There you are, Bertie," she whispered. "Good boy." She moved to rise.

Neville stepped forward and offered her his hand. She took it gratefully, permitting him to help her to her feet.

"Thank you." Her cheeks flushed pink. She glanced back down the corridor. "Would you mind walking back with me up the stairs? I wouldn't care to slip and fall. Especially not while carrying Bertie."

"Of course."

She walked ahead of him, the pug cradled close to her chest. "And I don't suppose you have any idea where I can procure ink and paper? I'm desperate to write a letter."

A letter to whom? He didn't dare ask. It was none of his business. *She* was none of his business.

But that didn't mean he should be rude, or careless of her. Greyfriar's Abbey was his home, wasn't that what Justin was always saying? That made Neville something like a host to her. And there was nothing untoward in being hospitable. "The library. I…I can fetch it for you."

Chapter Four

Clara stood behind Mrs. Bainbridge's chair, helping to secure a mother-of-pearl pin into her employer's hair. "Is that better?"

Mrs. Bainbridge eyed her reflection in the mirror of the elegant dressing table in her bedroom. She turned her head this way and that, examining her upswept blond curls. "I've so much silver in my hair. I simply can't credit it. Age does have an aggravating way of creeping up on a lady."

"It's very becoming," Clara said. "The silver, I mean. And the hair ornament."

"A gift from my late husband, God rest his soul." Mrs. Bainbridge met Clara's gaze in the mirror. "You don't find it too youthful?"

"Not at all, ma'am."

"I see that you've chosen to go without ornamentation."

Clara lifted a self-conscious hand to the invisible net in which she'd rolled her tresses. "I didn't have anything to suit. Only a coral necklace, and a satin ribbon in my sewing box, and neither matches my gown."

Her silk dinner dress was as plain as her coiffure. Only the color—a shade of golden brown so soft it was best described as champagne—was worthy of remark. It was the newest of all of her gowns, and even then, two years out of date. But it still fit her as perfectly as the day she'd purchased it in London. And it was the fit that counted, as well as being neat and tidy. Trimmings could be dispensed with. *Should be* dispensed with.

No one wanted a lady's companion decked out in flounces and fripperies.

"Fetch my jewel case out of the wardrobe," Mrs. Bainbridge said.

Clara supposed she should be indignant. She wasn't a lady's maid, after all, to be assisting with arranging and adorning her mistress's hair. But there was no point in kicking up a fuss over trivialities. She did as she was bid, all the while understanding that, to many elderly ladies, a companion was little more than a maid of all work. Someone to run and fetch. To retrieve wayward shawls, spectacles, and prayer books.

And Clara wasn't too proud to do so. Not if the position meant a roof over her and Bertie's head, and the necessary coin to pay her brother's school fees.

She found the case on a wardrobe shelf and brought it to Mrs. Bainbridge.

Mrs. Bainbridge opened the hinged lid and sifted through the scant contents. Clara glimpsed the sparkle of garnets, the shimmer of pearls, and a twinkle of something clear and bright, which might have been either diamonds or paste. "Here."

Mrs. Bainbridge withdrew a small topaz brooch surrounded by seed pearls. "Bend your head, my dear."

Clara obliged her.

Mrs. Bainbridge fixed the little brooch to the top of Clara's hairnet. "There."

Clara straightened, gazing into the mirror. The brooch was delicate but striking, the stone a lustrous golden amber that complemented her eyes and hair.

"You see how well it becomes you?" Mrs. Bainbridge gave her a satisfied smile. "You may borrow it for the evening."

Clara fingered the hair ornament. It was the first nice thing her new employer had done for her. Evidence that her initial impression of the lady hadn't been wrong. Mrs. Bainbridge *was* starchy. She was also kind. And generous, too, it seemed. "You needn't—"

"Nonsense. Every young lady must have a bauble to wear at dinner. Especially when in such refined company as this." Mrs. Bainbridge's voice took on a conspiratorial note. "Lady Helena's brother is the Earl of Castleton. He might have joined us for Christmas, but I'm told he returned to India last month. He owns a tea plantation there in the hills of Darjeeling."

"Oh. I hadn't any idea."

"Indeed. Her ladyship's pedigree rivals that of the finest ladies in the land. Of course, my niece isn't at all intimidated. She's known Lady Helena all of a week and already feels quite at home here. I understand her ladyship puts on no airs. Nor why should she? She's married as humbly as my niece has."

Clara didn't know the history of Mrs. Archer's husband any more than she knew that of Mr. Thornhill. She was aware that the two men had been childhood friends—a connection which had prompted the invitation for Christmas. Other than that, she was completely in the dark.

"One wonders how precedence will be handled at dinner?" Mrs. Bainbridge stood. "Where is my wrap? Ah. There on the bed. Fetch it for me, if you please, Miss Hartwright. And don't forget your own shawl. These old houses can be chilly."

After retrieving their shawls, Clara followed Mrs. Bainbridge down the stairs to the drawing room. Mr. Thornhill and Lady Helena were already there, along with Mr. and Mrs. Archer, Mr. Hayes, and a kindly looking elderly gentleman with gray hair and spectacles.

The gentlemen rose to their feet when Clara and Mrs. Bainbridge entered the room. Only Mr. Hayes remained seated, confined to his wheeled chair. His legs weren't completely immobile—not as far as Clara understood. But he couldn't stand without assistance, and he was entirely unable to walk.

She caught his gaze as the other gentlemen stood, and was certain she saw a glimmer of some deep emotion in the depths of his eyes. It might have been frustration, or perhaps even bitterness. She had no chance to grasp it. When next she looked, he'd wheeled his chair closer to his sister and was replying to something she'd said.

"Mrs. Bainbridge. Miss Hartwright." Mr. Thornhill came forward to greet them. He was dressed in a black evening coat and trousers, with a light-colored waistcoat and a cream silk cravat at his throat. "May I present my steward, Mr. Boothroyd?" He directed them to the gray-haired gentleman. "Boothroyd, this is Mrs. Archer's aunt, Mrs. Bainbridge, and her companion, Miss Hartwright."

Mr. Boothroyd bowed. "A pleasure to meet you, ma'am. And you, Miss Hartwright." He offered Mrs. Bainbridge his arm. "Mr. Thornhill tells me that this is your first visit to Devon."

Mrs. Bainbridge permitted Mr. Boothroyd to guide her to a vacant chair by the fire. "It is, sir."

Clara was left standing as Mrs. Bainbridge and Mr. Boothroyd slipped easily into conversation. It wasn't surprising. The two of them were of an age, and Clara could see no evidence of a Mrs. Boothroyd.

Mr. Thornhill looked down at her. "May I offer you a glass of sherry?"

"Please."

"Do come and sit beside me, Miss Hartwright." Lady Helena beckoned from her place on the sofa. Her mink-colored hair was arranged in an elaborate roll at her nape, secured with a pair of diamond combs. The softly draped fabric of her silk dinner dress shimmered in the firelight.

She looked every inch an earl's daughter.

In other circumstances, Clara might have been intimidated, but Lady Helena's manner was neither cold nor condescending. Her expression was warm, her invitation seemingly genuine.

Clara crossed the room to join her, exchanging murmured greetings with Mr. and Mrs. Archer as she passed.

"Cook tells me you visited the kitchens earlier with Mr. Cross," Lady Helena said as Clara sat down.

Clara had a feeling that nothing happened at the Abbey that its mistress didn't know about. "Mr. Cross was kind enough to bring Bertie in from the stables. I went down to the kitchens to retrieve him."

"Bertie? Is that your pug's name?"

"It is. He was given it by my last employer, in honor of the Prince Consort."

Lady Helena laughed. "Goodness, that's a great deal for a little dog to live up to. I trust he's acclimating well?"

"Quite well." Clara failed to suppress a smile. "I found him asleep in front of the kitchen fire with your two mastiffs, as comfortable as you please."

"If Paul and Jonesy have accepted him, he'll have nothing at all to fear," Lady Helena said. "A creature couldn't hope for a more stalwart pair of protectors."

"They're certainly fearsome to look at."

"And sweet as lambs once you get to know them. Isn't that right, my dear?"

Mr. Thornhill handed Clara a small glass of sherry. "I wouldn't go that far."

"I've found them to be friendly enough," Mrs. Archer said. "Though the older one didn't fancy me much when we first arrived here."

"Rubbish," Mr. Archer replied. "It was me he growled at. No doubt he recognized a villain when he saw one."

Mr. Thornhill gave a sympathetic grimace. "Jonesy thinks everyone is a villain, until proven otherwise."

"A wise dog," Mr. Archer said. "One can never be too careful."

Mrs. Bainbridge gave Mr. Archer a stern look. "You're very cynical, sir."

Mr. Archer only grinned. "I won't deny it."

It wasn't the first occasion on which Clara had observed a hint of tension between Mrs. Bainbridge and Mr. Archer. She couldn't discern why. Perhaps Mrs. Bainbridge disapproved of her niece's marriage? But if that was the case, then why had she agreed to join Mr. and Mrs. Archer for Christmas in Devon?

"You must heed my warning about those dogs, ma'am," Mr. Boothroyd said gravely. "They are accustomed to run on the beach in the morning, no matter the weather, and haven't the slightest scruple about jumping up on one's clothing the minute they gallop through the door."

Mrs. Bainbridge responded with a look of horror. "Dogs of that size? My word. They could do one an injury."

"You have nothing to worry about," Lady Helena assured her. "Mr. Cross will be taking the dogs out for their run early during your stay. Any jumping they have to do will be well out of their systems before they return to the house."

"Speaking of Mr. Cross." Mr. Archer stood, along with Mr. Boothroyd as Mr. Cross entered the room. He was in company with a slim gentleman in silver-rimmed spectacles and a lady with magnificent auburn hair.

"We haven't kept you waiting, have we?" she asked.

"Not at all." Mr. Thornhill swiftly dispensed with the introductions. "Mrs. Bainbridge, Miss Hartwright, this is Mr. and Mrs. Finchley. And you've all met Mr. Cross, I trust?"

Clara's gaze drifted to Mr. Cross quite against her will.

Like the other gentlemen, he was dressed in evening black with a cream-colored waistcoat and matching silk cravat. He didn't look at all like a groom or a stable hand. Indeed, he looked every inch a gentleman. Tall, lean, and golden-haired, with the broadest set of shoulders Clara had ever seen. A Galahad of sorts, just as she'd thought in the stables.

But there was nothing of the sophisticate about him. Nothing particularly suave or debonair. He seemed almost shy. If a gentleman so fine-looking *could* be shy.

It was a puzzle. One Clara had little hope of solving. She'd only be in residence through Twelfth Night. How much about a man could a lady learn in so short a time?

Only that he was handsome. That he was kind to dogs and horses. And that he had some form of speech impediment that caused him to turn red about the collar whenever he attempted to speak to her.

And yet he was speaking now, with apparent ease. Saying something to Mr. Archer. The two of them went to the drinks table with Mr. Thornhill, Mr. Finchley, and Mr. Hayes, looking perfectly content in each other's company.

Mrs. Bainbridge and Mr. Boothroyd were equally content, settled at the opposite end of the room, engaged in low conversation.

"Isn't this an unexpected pleasure." Mrs. Finchley sat down in a chair across from Clara and Lady Helena. "I was warned we'd have a lady's companion in our midst. I'd anticipated an aged spinster with a long face and dour disposition. But you're rather lovely, Miss Hartwright."

"Mrs. Finchley is a great proponent of plain speaking," Lady Helena interjected. "A delicate business in company, often as ill-advised as it is refreshing."

Mrs. Finchley gave Clara an apologetic smile. "You must think me abominably forward."

Clara couldn't help but smile in return. "Not at all, ma'am. I've recently learned that you were once a lady's companion yourself."

"You're surprised?"

"A little," Clara admitted.

Jenny Finchley was exceptionally lovely. Tall and slender, garbed in a velvet dinner dress adorned with delicate beadwork, she seemed the very picture of Parisian fashion, as if she'd stepped straight out of a lady's magazine.

Clara couldn't imagine such a lady having ever been subservient to anyone.

"Because I don't look the part?" Mrs. Finchley arranged her glittering skirts. "My former manservant has set up as a dressmaker in London. He's an utter magician with a needle, and has made it his mission to see I'm fashionably turned out. I believe he could make a silk purse out of a sow's ear."

"You're very hard on yourself," Lady Helena said. "I don't recall you ever looking anything less than neat and proper."

Mrs. Finchley's blue green eyes twinkled. "Was it that bad?"

"I think," Mrs. Archer said, "that Miss Hartwright was referring to your temperament, rather than your dress. You're not the quiet, retiring sort one generally associates with the profession."

"Which is precisely why I failed at it. I have a mind of my own, and wasn't afraid to express my opinions."

Lady Helena gave Mrs. Finchley a warm look. "She was an excellent companion. I owe her my very life."

"In other words," Mrs. Finchley said, "I bullied her and made plans for her. Not at all the kind of thing a companion is meant to do."

Mr. Finchley approached with two glasses of sherry in his hands. He gave one to his wife. "What's this about bullying?"

"Miss Hartwright and I are discussing the position of lady's companion."

Mr. Finchley looked at Clara. He had an incisive gaze. Oddly world-weary, and yet too keen by half. It seemed to see straight through her. "Have you been a lady's companion long, ma'am?"

"For four years," Clara said. "Since I turned twenty."

It felt like a lifetime. And it was, really. Most of her adult existence had been spent living in other people's homes and doing other people's bidding. All to earn a meager recompense, the bulk of which she never laid eyes on, let alone spent.

"And before that?" Mr. Finchley asked.

Her heartbeat briefly lost its rhythm. She took a hasty drink of her sherry. It burned the back of her throat. "I was a teacher."

Mrs. Finchley's face lit with interest. "A governess, do you mean?"

"No, I—" For a moment, Clara's words failed her. She reminded herself that she'd done nothing wrong. Not in a legal sense. "I taught at a school."

"Any particular subjects?" Mr. Finchley enquired.

"Reading, writing, and a little ciphering." Clara paused before adding, "It was only a village school. My pupils were the children of local farmers and laborers."

"Miss Hartwright came highly recommended," Mrs. Archer said. "My aunt is lucky to have her."

"Undoubtedly." Mr. Finchley's eyes remained on Clara. "Will you be traveling to the South of France with Mr. and Mrs. Archer in the spring?"

At that moment, a young footman in blue-and-gold livery materialized at the doors of the drawing room. "Dinner is served, my lady."

Clara could have embraced the fellow. Had the servant not appeared, she may have been forced to do something drastic. To swoon or feign a megrim. Anything to put an end to Mr. Finchley's line of questioning.

"Thank you, Robert." Lady Helena moved to rise.

Mr. Thornhill was instantly at his wife's side to help her from her seat. She clutched tight to his hand. It was the only sign that her advanced state of pregnancy was in any way difficult. The two of them exchanged a look—an unspoken question in Mr. Thornhill's eyes.

Lady Helena responded with a nod. "I'll just take your arm, shall I?"

Her husband's voice was a gentle command. "I insist upon it."

"Come everyone," she said. "We needn't worry about precedence."

"We'd have a dashed difficult time figuring it out," Mr. Archer murmured to his wife as they joined Mr. Hayes.

Clara went to assist Mrs. Bainbridge, but there was no need. Mr. Boothroyd was already there, offering his arm. Mrs. Bainbridge took it, allowing him to lead her from the room. Clara was, once again, left on her own.

Well, not quite on her own.

As she followed in Mrs. Bainbridge's wake, she encountered Mr. Cross.

He stopped in the doorway.

Clara stopped, too, looking up at him in frank expectation. A gentleman would offer his arm, or at least say something.

Mr. Cross did neither.

Which meant absolutely nothing. Not when simple words seemed to evade him.

She waited, nevertheless. Far longer than she'd ever have waited for any other man. So long, she feared she was on the verge of making a ninny of herself. "Well," she said. "I suppose I'd better—"

"May I escort you in?" he asked. The words were blurted out with something very like anger.

She stared up at him, her brow drawn. *Was* he angry? His jaw was taut, his throat working on a swallow. Her gaze dropped briefly to his hands. Sure enough, she found one clenched into a fist at his side.

No, it wasn't anger. And if it was, it wasn't directed at her. She suspected it may well have been directed at himself.

A dozen questions sprang into her mind. She yearned to ask them.

But this was neither the time, nor the place. And besides, it was none of her affair. *He* was none of her affair.

This wasn't real life. It was only a holiday interlude. A brief three weeks spent among strangers. She was obliged to be civil, and that was all. To presume anything more would be impertinent. Dangerous.

She took his arm. "Yes. Please."

Chapter Five

Neville took another drink from his wine goblet. He'd never seen the dining room at Greyfriar's Abbey look so fine and festive. The polished mahogany table was adorned with winter flowers, beeswax taper candles, and colorful assortments of red berries and fruit. The silver had been polished until it twinkled, and the crystal glasses sparkled in the glow from the magnificent gasolier that hung overhead.

Wine and champagne flowed freely, a complement to the asparagus soup, braised leg of mutton, and roasted fowl with chestnuts.

He wasn't much of a drinker. Strong spirits only ever served to make him more muddled in thought and speech. Lady Helena had seen that he was supplied with watered wine. It was a kindness—one of many Lady Helena had done him since her arrival in North Devon last year.

Had she thought it a similar kindness to place him next to Clara Hartwright at dinner?

It didn't feel kind. In fact, it felt rather like a torment.

He cast Miss Hartwright another fleeting, sidelong glance. She was slicing into a piece of mutton with her knife, cutting off a delicate, bite-sized portion.

Mr. Hayes sat on her opposite side in his wheeled chair. Neville had heard the two of them conversing about landscape paintings.

It was the way of things at such dinners. Neville had learned that much during Lady Helena's tenure. A guest was expected to speak to the people on either side of him. To make polite conversation. Talking across the table was frowned upon, as was ignoring one's seatmate completely.

Neville didn't mean to ignore Miss Hartwright. Not really. It was just that, every time he tried to say something to her—no matter how innocuous—he couldn't manage to form the words. It was bloody excruciating.

Far better to avoid her, if he could. That had been his plan, anyway.

Until he'd seen Lady Helena's seating arrangement.

He picked up his fork and knife and attacked his roasted fowl.

Miss Hartwright chose that moment to turn her attention away from Mr. Hayes. She looked at Neville, her chocolate-brown eyes shining in the candlelight. "Mr. Cross, I must thank you again for assisting me with Bertie this morning."

Neville lowered his fork and knife back to the table. "Is he…?"

"He's resting in my room." She put down her own fork, giving him her full attention. "I wonder…where do you advise I take him for his evening constitutional? I daren't let him wander too close to the cliffs."

"There's a g-garden at the back of the house." He flinched to hear himself stutter. It was a consequence of his nerves, and of speaking in anything more than short, uncomplicated sentences.

"The rose garden? I saw it from the drawing room window this morning. It looks very formal. You don't suppose Lady Helena would object?"

He didn't think she would. Nevertheless... "You can bring him to the stable yard. Or..." He paused, trying to calm himself enough to speak without faltering. "Or to the beach. In...in the morning."

"With the other dogs?" She studied his face. "I don't wish to make a nuisance of myself."

He wanted to tell her that she hadn't. That she wasn't likely to. But the words wouldn't come. She was looking at him too steadily, her eyes gazing into his.

"In my last position," she said, "I was obliged to take Bertie out every three hours. He could only walk a short distance. Just to the end of the lane and back. It was hardly any exercise at all, but Mrs. Peak thought it my most important duty. She often claimed she hired me as much for Bertie as for herself."

Neville feared he'd lost the thread of the conversation. "Mrs. Peak?"

"My former employer. Bertie was her dog. Like a child to her, really." She reached for her glass. It was half filled with burgundy wine. "What time will you be taking the dogs out for their run?"

"At dawn."

"It will be raining, I expect."

"They won't mind." Paul and Jonesy enjoyed the rain. Or, more specifically, the mud.

"Bertie might. He abhors the cold weather. I suspect he has arthritis."

"Would you?"

"Mind the rain? Not very much, but I mustn't be careless with my health. If I caught cold, I'd be no use to anyone." She raised her wineglass to her lips. "A companion can't become a charge on the very person she's meant to look after."

He glanced down the table at Mrs. Bainbridge. She was seated beside Mr. Boothroyd, nodding energetically at something he was saying.

Was she a difficult lady to work for?

Neville couldn't tell. He knew nothing of Laura Archer's aunt. He'd only met Laura herself a week ago when she'd arrived on the train, newly married to Alex.

Everything was happening so quickly. How was a fellow supposed to keep track of it all?

Until last year, Greyfriar's Abbey had housed only Justin, Neville, Mr. Boothroyd, and a handful of servants. A bachelor household, Justin had called it. It had been a ramshackle place, in a perpetual state of disrepair. Remote. Isolated.

Neville had preferred it that way.

Justin's reputation had kept the villagers away. It still did to an extent. But Lady Helena's presence had done much to dampen local gossip. And it hadn't hurt that, when she'd taken up residence, she'd brought an entire fleet of servants along with her.

Now, the Abbey was always busy. A day didn't pass without Neville having to speak with a servant or a guest. He was lucky if he could find sanctuary in the stables. They had three times as many horses, which meant more grooms and stable lads about, all of them asking questions or otherwise cutting up Neville's peace.

It was easy not to notice his limitations when he never had to face them. The horses and dogs didn't care if he didn't speak. And when he did, they never looked at him askance. Never treated him as a fool or an idiot.

Is that what Miss Hartwright thought when he spoke? That he was some manner of simpleton?

He brought his gaze back to her.

But Miss Hartwright was no longer looking at him. Her head was turned to Mr. Hayes. The two of them were engaged in an animated conversation. One that sounded as though it had been going on for some little while. "Pencil sketches and watercolors are the extent of my artistic skills, sir," she was saying to him. "And those very poorly. I wouldn't dream of using oils."

"Have you ever tried them?" Mr. Hayes asked. "They aren't as intimidating as they may seem."

A pit of anxiety formed in Neville's stomach. He'd looked away from Miss Hartwright for only a moment, hadn't he? At least, it had *seemed* like a moment.

How much time had really passed?

For how many minutes had he drifted off in his head? How long had he appeared blank-faced and unresponsive?

Long enough for Miss Hartwright to have abandoned their conversation and turned back to Mr. Hayes.

Neville stared down at his plate. Frustration roiled within him. He had to force himself to pick up his fork and knife. To cut into his roasted fowl, and to swallow it down.

The chatter of the other guests sounded all around him. Lady Helena speaking with Alex Archer. Laura Archer speaking with Tom Finchley.

"Are you all right?" Jenny Finchley's low voice sounded from the seat on his left.

He glanced at her. She'd lived with them at the Abbey for a short time before leaving to travel the world, and to—later—marry Tom. Neville had come to know her. To like her. "I'm fine. Just…eating."

Her brows knit with concern. "You've gone very quiet."

He shrugged. "Nothing to say."

Clara wrapped her woolen shawl tighter about her shoulders as she stood at the library window. Raindrops streamed down the glass in a haphazard pattern. She could scarcely make out the churning sea in the distance. It was too dark and too wet, the sky and the water appearing to blend together in a continuous storm of gray.

"Do sit down, Miss Hartwright," Mrs. Bainbridge said. "You're making me nervous with all that pacing."

Clara glanced back at her employer. Mrs. Bainbridge was seated by the fire, working diligently at a scrap of embroidery.

Mr. Boothroyd was in the library as well, hunched over a desk in the corner, scribbling away in a ledger with quill and ink.

Clara wished she was as busily employed. "Forgive me." She returned to her chair opposite Mrs. Bainbridge and sat down. "I'm a little restless this morning."

She'd woken at sunrise to the sound of rain pounding on the roof, and after carrying Bertie to the rose garden to attend to his personal needs, had been unable to go back to sleep. There was too much on her mind. Too many plans to form and decisions to make.

It was that dratted duplicate lesson of Simon's. She couldn't stop thinking about it.

What did it mean for her future? And what did it say about her own gullibility? About the confidence she'd had in her brother? The belief that she would one day be able to apply her studies to a profession?

A lady couldn't have a profession of her own—not in the strictest sense. She couldn't attend a proper university, or earn a position in the scientific community. But there was nothing stopping her from being a secretary to a scientist, or a gentleman with an interest in natural history.

Simon had promised to make her *his* secretary. She would write his letters, catalogue his collections, and help to identify rare specimens. And by virtue of proximity, some of his adventures and discoveries might be her own.

Indeed, when school was done, he planned to undertake an expedition. And he'd sworn to take her along with him. To South America or Australia or wherever the next ship was sailing. Mr. Darwin had undertaken such a voyage as a young naturalist, why shouldn't he?

Not that Clara had any great ambition to travel the world. It was the knowledge she craved. The order and method. More than that, she longed for the quiet contemplation inherent in her chosen profession. To sit in a sweet-scented garden somewhere, and silently observe the natural world around her—the flora and fauna in all its wondrous beauty.

Granted, there were some parts of her studies she enjoyed more than others. Sketching honey bees would always be preferable to drawing centipedes. And she'd far rather note the colors and markings of a butterfly's wings than pin the poor creature onto a board.

But that was beside the point.

The point was that she'd believed her brother's promises. Had counted on them. And for four long years, she'd attended Cambridge right along with him—through his letters, notes, and copies of his lessons. She had been a student, too.

She *was* a student.

But now…

Perhaps she'd been mistaken. Perhaps she wasn't a student at all. Had never been a student. Only a hopeful fool, building dreams for a future on a foundation of girlish fantasy and empty masculine promises.

It was a depressing possibility. And one she wasn't entirely ready to accept.

"Have you no needlework of your own?" Mrs. Bainbridge asked. "Nothing that needs mending?"

"Not at present." Clara's own meager wardrobe was already turned and mended within an inch of its life. "I'd be happy to mend anything of yours that requires repair."

Mrs. Bainbridge shot a look in Mr. Boothroyd's direction. She sank her voice. "I have the odd petticoat and stocking that needs attention, but it's best left to when you have more privacy."

"I can attend to them this evening after I retire."

"There's no urgency." Mrs. Bainbridge tied off a thread in her embroidery. The gold carriage clock on the library mantel chimed the half hour. "The morning's getting on, my dear. Should you not be seeing to that dog of yours?"

Clara's spirits lifted a little. She could do with some fresh air. "Will you be all right on your own for a short while?"

"I'm not on my own. Mr. Boothroyd is here. Perhaps he will join me for a cup of tea?"

Mr. Boothroyd looked up from his work. "I would be delighted, ma'am."

Clara rose from her seat. "I'll be back directly."

"Be careful of the mud," Mrs. Bainbridge called after her. "And don't venture too near the cliffs!"

Clara hurried up the stairs to her bedroom. Bertie was still curled up by the fireplace. It took but a moment to put on her outdoor boots and cloak, and gather him up in her arms.

The rain hadn't stopped, but it had lessened significantly. As she stepped out the front door, she pulled her hood up over her hair.

"Keep to the gravel, miss," the butler said. "The footing is better."

"I will. Thank you." She marched down the drive, the wind whipping her cloak all about her. Bertie shivered beneath it. No doubt he'd prefer a sunny climate. Somewhere warm and dry, where it never rained, and where morning frost never gathered on the grass.

She held him tighter. It would be warmer in the stables. And hadn't Mr. Cross said she could avail herself of the stable yard? She hoped he'd meant it, but after how their evening had ended last night, there was room for doubt.

He'd gone silent in the midst of their conversation, staring off into the distance, with a faraway look in his eyes. As if his thoughts were occupied with something far more important than civil chitchat with a dinner companion.

She'd told herself not to be offended. What had she been talking about anyway? Asking advice from him on where her aged pug could relieve himself? No wonder Mr. Cross had stopped listening to her. It was actually rather mortifying, now she thought of it.

But such things didn't matter much. Not in the grand scheme of things. Mr. Cross was a stranger. And Clara would be leaving soon.

It was but seven days until Christmas, and thirteen more until they departed Devon. Not even three weeks altogether. Time passed swiftly when one was employed. It would be over before she knew it. And then she would return to Surrey with Mrs. Bainbridge.

Though, even that wasn't entirely to be relied upon. Not when Mrs. Bainbridge hadn't yet decided whether or not to remove to France. Until she did, Clara's own future hung in the balance.

If she was left unemployed, her small savings would sustain her for a month or two at most. And then what would she do? She couldn't go home, to the small village in Hertfordshire where she'd been born and raised. There was no home there to go back to. No family and no friends. Only a cottage that had long ago been let.

And she couldn't very well travel to Cambridge. No matter her exasperation with her brother, it wouldn't be permissible to inflict herself upon him at his university.

She would have to go to her mother in Edinburgh. And even then, Clara would have no place to lay her head. The school in which her mother taught provided room and board for its teachers, but not for their families.

A gust of wind and rain tore at her cloak. She quickened her pace. Seconds later she arrived, breathless, in the stable yard.

Bertie practically leapt from her arms, snuffling through the mud to relieve himself against a fence post. When he'd finished, he accompanied her into the stable.

An enormous chestnut stallion was tied in the aisle. His coat gleamed like a newly polished penny.

Bertie trotted ahead, and—much to Clara's horror—continued trotting, right beneath the stallion's legs.

"Bertie, no!" She rushed forward.

Before she could reach him, the groom who was standing on the opposite side of the stallion caught hold of Bertie and lifted him up and out of danger.

She exhaled a shuddering breath. "Gracious. That was a very near thing."

Mr. Cross's blond head appeared over the stallion's back. He rose to his full height, holding Bertie in his arms.

"Oh," she whispered. "I didn't know it was you."

His handsome face was impassive, revealing neither irritation nor happiness to see her. He brought Bertie to her from around the back of the horse. "They won't kick him. They're used to dogs."

"Not little ones, surely."

"He's safe here."

She glanced around the stable. A groom had another horse out at the end of the aisle, working on its winter coat with a brush and a currycomb. Nearby, a stable boy diligently swept up the hair. "Are you sure? He's so small. I'd hate to set him down if he—"

"He's fine."

She bit her lip. "Very well. If you're certain."

Mr. Cross put Bertie back onto the ground. Bertie gave a shake of his coat before wandering as far as the next loose box, snuffling the ground as he went.

"Your cloak is wet," Mr. Cross said.

Clara pushed back her hood, running a gloved hand over the damp tendrils of hair that clung to her face. "Yes, I suppose it is. I shall have to hang it in front of the fire when I return to the house."

He held out his hand. "May I?"

"What?"

"Hang it to dry?"

"Where? There's not a fire here, is there?"

"I'll put it over the door of…of—" He motioned to an empty loose box with a jerk of his chin. "There."

She slipped off her cloak and handed it to him. The fabric was damp with rain, the hemline muddied. "Thank you."

He draped it over the door of the loose box. When he turned back to her, his expression was shuttered.

She ran her hands up and down her arms. Her long-sleeved day dress provided little warmth. "I don't suppose there's a place to sit down? Somewhere I can keep an eye on Bertie without getting in your way?"

A flush of red crept up over his shirt collar. "The mounting block."

Clara hadn't any idea what she'd said to make him blush. Was it merely that she was going to stay awhile? She had little choice in the matter. Not so long as Bertie wished to explore. "A dog requires fresh air and exercise. Even an antiquated pug."

"I know that."

"If you object to us being here—"

"I don't object." A long pause. "I…I invited you."

"You did. I thought you'd forgotten."

"I don't forget things." His blush deepened. "Just because I…"

His sentence remained unfinished, but he looked at her in such a way. It was a look that spoke volumes. She felt it, resonating inside of her, as surely as if he'd confessed his frustration to her, and she'd replied with the perfect expression of commiseration. *I know what it is to yearn for understanding. You don't have to explain it to me.*

But she was no more capable of giving voice to such sentiments than he was. Nor why should she? They were fanciful at best. And she was too prone to fancy. It was something she must always guard against, lest she put her reputation in jeopardy again.

"Right," she said, looking all about her. "The mounting block." It was sitting near the wall, a tall, solid block of wood in which a pair of steps had been carved. She went to it and sat down, arranging her skirts. "Please don't stop what you're doing on my account."

Mr. Cross stared at her for a moment. And then, he resumed brushing the stallion.

Clara watched him as much as she watched Bertie. She couldn't seem to help herself. "Is he your horse?"

"He belongs to Thornhill."

"But you help to look after him?"

Mr. Cross nodded. His brushstrokes were firm but gentle. Long, sweeping passes over the stallion's muscled neck, shoulder, and flank.

Nearby, Bertie continued nosing about in the dirt. He showed no desire to return to the house. Quite the reverse. After a life spent confined to a velvet cushion, he appeared to be relishing the straw, mud, and manure. He dug with his front paws, and kicked with his back ones, snuffling and snorting with pleasure.

Clara rested her chin in her hand, once again turning her attention to Mr. Cross. "Mr. Thornhill said that you prefer being with animals. He said you'd stay in the stable all day if you could."

Mr. Cross glanced at her over the stallion's withers.

"But you're not a groom," she said. It wasn't a question.

He answered her nonetheless. "No."

"Is it just a pastime, then? A hobby?"

"It's all I know." His voice was curiously flat. As blank as his expression. "I'm n-not suited for anything else."

She frowned at him. "That can't be true."

"It is." He moved around to the same side of the stallion on which she sat, perched upon the mounting block, and began brushing the enormous beast from neck to shoulder.

He was extraordinarily graceful for such a large man. His muscles flexed beneath the lines of his coat, his every movement a picture of strength and natural physicality. There was no clumsiness about him. No awkwardness or hesitation in his tall, lean frame.

"Nonsense," she said. "A gentleman can do anything he sets his mind to."

"I'm not a gentleman. I'm…I was…"

"I don't mean your pedigree. I mean the fact that you're a man. You could go to university if you wished. You could join a scientific society in London or Edinburgh, and have your papers published in a scholarly journal."

Mr. Cross flashed her an odd look. "My papers?"

"As an example." She smoothed a crease in her skirts. "All such activities are restricted to men."

"Do you… Is that what you want to do?"

"I would have liked to go to university," she confessed. "There are proper schools for girls, in London and Cheltenham, but no way for young women to attend an institution of higher learning. It's rather unfair, to my mind."

She didn't know why she was telling him so much. Perhaps it was simply because he was willing to listen.

But *was* he willing? Or was he merely being polite?

She watched him as he brushed the stallion, busy about his work, just as he'd no doubt be whether she was there or not.

"Forgive me," she said. "I talk too much. It's a terrible habit. Almost as bad as being overly curious. Another fault of mine."

Mr. Cross stopped brushing. His gaze found hers, his throat working on a swallow. He was going to say something—was clearly working up the nerve.

She stared up at him, waiting.

"It's n-not all I know," he said finally.

At first, she couldn't follow the thread. His words hadn't anything to do with their current topic of conversation—no relation to her senseless chatter, or her overt curiosity.

Realization struck slowly.

"The stable, do you mean? The horses?"

His head inclined in mute confirmation. "Sometimes I help Mr. Boothroyd."

"Mr. Thornhill's steward?"

Another nod.

"Help him with what?"

"His ledgers. And…and writing letters." Mr. Cross stroked a hand over the stallion's shoulder, his expression meditative. "I'm to take his place."

She prayed she didn't betray any surprise at his confession. But it *was* surprising. Could Mr. Cross manage sums and business letters? Was he capable? She supposed he must be.

Which meant that his slowness was limited to his speech. That it didn't extend to his intellect.

A flicker of sympathy stirred in her breast. What must it be like? To be thoughtful and intelligent and unable to express it? To have to struggle for every word?

"Is Mr. Boothroyd retiring soon?"

"Someday."

"I imagine he's looking forward to it. He's of an age. And no one wishes to do the same job forever. Unless it is one's profession. One's passion." She searched Mr. Cross's face. "Do you wish to be a steward?"

He shrugged. "It's something."

"Something enjoyable?"

He briefly looked away from her. "Something…useful."

"I understand." And she did, lord help her. "I daresay we're all seeking to be of use. To live meaningful lives, doing something that makes a difference to someone besides ourselves. But it doesn't follow that we must settle for doing work that makes us unhappy. Not in the long term, anyway."

"Do you…?" His question hung, unfinished, in the sweet, hay-scented air of the stables.

"I have no grand ambitions," she said. "Only small ones."

"But you have them."

"Hasn't everyone?"

He made no reply. A long moment passed, during which she expected he would resume brushing the stallion. But he didn't return to his work. He tossed the brush and currycomb into a wooden box nearby. And then he looked at her, his gaze so intent it lifted the fine hairs at the back of Clara's neck.

"Would you like to see something?" he asked. "In the b-back of the barn?"

It was the sort of thing a budding Lothario might say. A means of luring a young maidservant away so he could kiss her—or worse.

But Mr. Cross wouldn't do that, would he? He was too open. Too guileless. She knew somehow that he wouldn't hurt her.

Nevertheless, she hesitated. Her feminine intuition had been wrong before, and she was still paying the price for it. She wouldn't make the same mistake twice. "What is it? Can you not bring it here?"

"No. You have to c-come with me."

Slowly, she rose to her feet. She seemed incapable of resisting. It was that slight, halting stutter of his. That vulnerability. It completely undid her. "Mr. Cross, I—"

"This way." And, with that, he turned and disappeared down the aisle.

Clara glanced at the remaining groom and stable boy. They hadn't batted an eye. Perhaps it was of no account? Mr. Cross wasn't taking her anywhere private, after all. Not that she was aware. There was nothing untoward in walking with him through the stable, surely?

She paused to sweep Bertie up in her arms before following Mr. Cross down the aisle. He led her past the feed room, and around a corner to what looked to be a dead end. There was an empty loose box there.

Mr. Cross went to its door. "Here."

Clara came to stand beside him. "What is it? A horse?"

"Not a horse." Mr. Cross clucked to the creature within. There was a shuffling sound, and then a loud kick that shook the walls of the loose box.

Clara jumped back. "Heavens!"

"Here," Mr. Cross said again. "It's all right."

She slowly stepped forward and peered over the door. Inside stood a stocky brown pony with a thick black mane and tail, and wild, wideset eyes. A mare, by the look of her. She was heavily pregnant.

"Oh," Clara gasped softly. "She's beautiful."

"She's a Dartmoor pony," Mr. Cross said.

Clara leaned against the door, Bertie squirming in her arms. The little mare had a thick bandage on her right foreleg. "Is she hurt?"

"Her leg...it's... She's lame."

"How did she come to be here?"

"I rescued her."

"Rescued her from what?"

"A man passing through the village. I...I bought her." Mr. Cross reached inside the loose box, holding his hand out to the mare. "There aren't many of them left."

Clara didn't know much about wild ponies, certainly not in this part of the world. "What do you mean to do with her?"

"Keep her here until...until she foals."

Clara's brows knit. "She looks as though she might at any moment."

He smiled slightly. "Not for another week."

"And what then? Will you tame her?"

The mare shied away from Mr. Cross's hand. He withdrew it. "Wild creatures can't be tamed. They…they shouldn't be."

"No. I suppose you're right. But if you mean to help her, what else can you do? Will you return her and her foal to Dartmoor?"

A cloud of uncertainty passed over Mr. Cross's face. "I d-don't know."

"I see." Clara hesitated. The loose box was large and clean, bedded with fresh straw. A bucket of water stood in the corner. "Has she been here long?"

"A fortnight."

"And has she a name?"

"Not yet."

"You should give her one. It may help you to make friends with her." Clara regarded the little mare for a moment. "She looks like a Betty to me. A Brown Betty, like my grandfather used to drink in cold weather."

Mr. Cross looked at her, his mouth hitching up at one corner, as if she was talking nonsense.

"Haven't you ever heard of a Brown Betty?"

He shook his head.

"It's made with brown sugar, brandy, and ale, and seasoned with cinnamon, nutmeg, and cloves. My grandfather learned to make it when he was at Oxford. It was his favorite winter tipple." She gave a short laugh. "Oh, but it was ages ago. An ancient memory. Still, I think it a good name for her."

"Brown Betty."

"Don't feel obliged. It's just a suggestion."

"No, I…I like it."

She smiled. "I'm glad."

"Is your grandfather…?"

"Gone, many years hence." She sighed. "And I must go, too. Mrs. Bainbridge will be expecting me."

His faint smile faded away.

"Thank you for showing her to me," she said.

He acknowledged her thanks with a slight inclination of his head. It was strangely formal, all things considered.

Then again, the two of them had only met yesterday.

Perhaps it was *she* who was being overly familiar. It wouldn't be the first time. She privately scolded herself as she made her way back up the aisle. Would she never learn to be quiet? To be more circumspect?

Mr. Cross followed her in silence to the front of the stables.

"I shall bid you good morning," she said, walking to the door. "And thank you again—"

"Miss Hartwright—"

She stopped and turned, her heart thumping hopefully. "Yes?"

"Your cloak."

Embarrassment heated her face. "Of course. How stupid of me."

He took it from the door of the loose box, offering it to her with an outstretched hand.

She had to set Bertie down again in order to take it and slip it round her shoulders. "Bertie, stay!"

"I have him." Mr. Cross picked him up a split second before he ambled off down the aisle. Bertie snorted in protest.

Clara fastened her cloak. "I'll take him now." She lifted Bertie from Mr. Cross's arms. "What a nuisance we are to you."

He didn't deny it, but when she once again turned to leave, he walked with her to the door. "The rain has stopped."

"So it has. But not for long, I expect. The skies are very dark." She pulled up her hood, wary of the coming storm. "I must hurry."

She didn't wait for him to speak. To bid her goodbye, or warn her—as the butler had—to be careful not to lose her footing. He didn't owe her an excess of courtesy. He'd already shown enough this morning, both to her and to Bertie.

The gravel was slippery beneath her boots as she started up the winding cliff road, Bertie held safely beneath her cloak. She looked back only once. A foolish impulse.

Or perhaps not so foolish.

Her heartbeat quickened.

Mr. Cross was still standing in the doorway, his broad shoulder propped against the frame. He was watching her.

Chapter Six

Neville made a final notation in the leather-bound ledger. Everything appeared in order. All the figures had been entered and balanced, each carefully copied from the reports of Justin's quarterly earnings from his railway ventures, cotton mills, and other investments. Neville had been over them twice just to be sure.

He set down his quill, leaned back in his chair, and stretched.

The heavy wine-colored curtains on the bank of library windows had been drawn open, revealing a wide expanse of stormy gray skies over an equally stormy sea. Rain was coming again. It was always coming in Devon. But for now, at least, it had stopped.

Neville longed to be outside. To return to the stables, or to the beach with the dogs. Anything but the stifling interior of the house.

"Let me see." Mr. Boothroyd came to stand over the library desk. He flipped through the ledger, scanning its pages. "Good, good. Yes, that's right. And you've deducted the payments on the new equipment at the mill?"

Neville sat forward again at the desk. He turned the page of the ledger, drawing his ink-stained finger to a column on the left. "Here."

"Excellent." Mr. Boothroyd nodded his approval. "Now, if only you could cease daydreaming and finish the work with greater speed." He closed the ledger and tucked it under his arm. "Never mind. You'll soon master it, I trust. It only wants practice."

Neville wasn't so sure. No amount of practice was going to turn him into an ideal steward. It hadn't thus far, and he'd been practicing for nearly a year.

The truth was, he wasn't as quick as Mr. Boothroyd, nor as organized. And though he was capable enough at writing letters and balancing figures, he had a tendency to drift off in his head.

Daydreaming, Mr. Boothroyd called it. But it wasn't dreaming. It was thought—boring, everyday thought. Only a kind that made him lose time. Minutes spent staring off into space, while someone waited for him to respond to a question or hold up his end of a conversation.

It was the same thing that had happened two nights ago, at dinner with Miss Hartwright.

The same thing that had been happening to him ever since he'd fallen from the cliffs.

The only time it didn't happen was when he was with the horses. Working with them was too physical. Too immediate. It kept him alert.

Mr. Boothroyd departed the library, shutting the door behind him.

Neville would have followed, but there was something more that required his attention. Something far more important, to his mind, than balancing figures in a ledger.

He withdrew a folded slip of paper from the inner pocket of his coat. The barman at the King's Arms had given it to him yesterday.

Erasmus Atkyns
Hadley House
Tavistock

Mr. Atkyns was a vicar, or so the barman had said.

Neville was skeptical. He nevertheless drew out a fresh sheet of paper and sharpened his quill.

He was halfway through drafting a carefully worded letter to Mr. Atkyns when the library door opened with a click, and a soft tread sounded on the carpet.

"Oh, I beg your pardon! I didn't know anyone was working here."

Neville's heart lurched. He stood at once, so quickly he very nearly toppled the inkpot. "Miss Hartwright."

"Mr. Cross. Good morning." She hesitated inside the doorway. "I'm not interrupting you, am I?"

"No."

"I've only come to fetch a book." She crossed the library to one of the bookcases that lined the walls, her wide skirts swaying gently with each step. She was wearing the same plain gray dress she'd worn on the day she'd first arrived in Devon. "It won't take a moment."

Neville didn't care if it took one hundred moments. He hadn't been alone with her since that morning in the stables two days ago. Not truly alone. The weather had been fierce yesterday, and she'd kept to the house. He'd seen her several times but had only spoken to her once, on the way in to dinner. A word of stilted greeting uttered before she withdrew to her seat between Justin and Alex.

Neville had been seated between Laura and Helena. A place of safety. One where he needn't worry about what he said or how he sounded. But he'd been aware of Miss Hartwright for all that. Conscious of her smiles, and the luminosity of her brown eyes in the candlelight.

"What book?" he asked.

"Something suitable for reading aloud to Mrs. Bainbridge." She stopped in front of a row of thick tomes bound in red leather, the spines stamped in gold.

"The classics?" Neville came to stand at her side.

"They won't do." She frowned. "Mrs. Bainbridge doesn't care for anything too intellectual." Her gaze scanned the shelves. "Hasn't Mr. Thornhill any novels? Something by Sir Walter Scott, perhaps?"

"Here." He reached above her head to one of the topmost shelves, plucking out a thin volume. "*Waverley*."

She brightened as she took it. "Oh, yes. This will do nicely." Her eyes met his. A faint flush of color tinted her cheeks. "Thank you."

He gazed down at her. And he knew, quite suddenly, that she was as aware of him as he was of her. That she felt that same sense of warmth. Of connection.

He'd been around pretty girls before. The barmaids at the King's Arms were always flirting with him. Even some of the housemaids at the Abbey. He sensed that he was a figure of fun to them. A good-looking fellow in form and figure, but not a man. They liked to tease him. To provoke his blushes and stammers, as if he were an untried stripling lad.

But Miss Hartwright was different.

She was nice. More than nice. She was sweet, and rather singular. And she had ambitions for her future. Only small ones, albeit, but ambitions nonetheless.

"Hasn't everyone?" she'd asked him.

But he didn't. He couldn't. Ambitions required aptitude. The ability to learn and grow. And there was no fixing his speech. No remedy to the fact that it made him seem slow and stupid.

How was he ever to live or work anywhere outside of Greyfriar's Abbey? He would be lucky if he could one day take Mr. Boothroyd's place as Justin's steward. Anything more than that was a ridiculous dream.

He was content as he was. Or he had been. Until everything started changing.

"How is Bertie?" he asked.

"In fine form. He's presently asleep in my room. He's made himself quite at home there." She smiled. "How is the pony?"

"Very well." He paused, searching for something more he could say. Something that would keep her here a while longer. "Betty let me comb the brambles from her mane."

Her brows lifted. "You've named her Betty after all?"

"I like it."

"So do I." She clutched her book to her bosom. "What will you call the foal when it comes?"

"What do you propose?"

"I don't know. I'll have to give it some consideration. Naming creatures is a great responsibility. Rather like naming a child. It's not something to take lightly." She fell quiet again, but she made no move to leave.

He didn't move either.

"Have you decided yet what you'll do with them?" she asked.

Neville shot a frowning glance back toward the library desk. "I'm writing to someone."

Her face fell. "Forgive me. I've kept you from your work—"

"No. No, it's not..." He raked his fingers through his hair. "I'm writing to a m-man about Betty."

"What man?"

He turned and went to the desk, retrieving his half-finished letter. Miss Hartwright followed after him. "Mr. Atkyns in...in Tavistock." He extended the letter to her. "He helps the wild ponies."

Clara took the letter from Mr. Cross and spread it open. Her eyes flicked over the page as she read the flowing script. The hand was that of an educated man. An eloquent man. One who wrote beautifully.

A lump formed in her throat.

Was this the real Neville Cross? Was this what it was like to be in his thoughts? To hear his words without the impediment of his faulty speech?

She looked up at him when she'd finished reading, hoping her countenance didn't betray her roiling emotion. "How did you learn of this gentleman?"

"He used to breed Dartmoor ponies, and…and sell them at the annual m-market on the moor. They know of him in King's Abbot."

"Tavistock. That's not far, is it?"

"Forty miles."

She frowned. It wasn't an easy distance. But Tavistock was a market town, wasn't it? There must be rail access. "Could you not simply go there? Call on him yourself? It may be more expedient."

"No. I d-don't—" He stopped. "It's difficult."

She didn't enquire as to what he meant. Was it his speech that posed the difficulty? Was it the weather? She supposed it could be either. "What is it you'd like him to do? Do you want him to take the ponies?"

"Not take them, but…they'll need to go back. To the moors."

Her heart swelled. He wanted to return them to the wild. To their home. Hadn't he said there weren't many of them left? "Is it safe for them there? On Dartmoor, I mean? If their numbers are decreasing—"

"I don't know." He shook his head. "I hope…my letter…"

"Yes, quite." She folded it and handed it back to him. "Mr. Atkyns must have some advice on the subject. I shall pray he writes back to you directly."

Mr. Cross returned the letter to his desk. She waited for him to say something more, but he seemed too preoccupied to continue their conversation.

"I must go," she said. "Mrs. Bainbridge is waiting for her book."

A notch worked its way between his brows. He stared down at her. "Will I see you again?"

Clara's stomach gave a responsive quiver. With her imagination, she could almost believe his question to be romantic. It wasn't, clearly. They simply had a few minor things in common. It had nothing to do with romance.

She moistened her lips. "I'd like to visit Betty again if I might."

"When?"

"I don't know. I haven't a moment to myself today. Mrs. Bainbridge requires me until luncheon. And this afternoon will be taken up with gathering greenery in the woods. Lady Helena hopes to take advantage of the brief respite from the rain."

He nodded. "I'll be there."

"To gather greenery?"

"Unless you—"

"I'd like that," she said. "I shall look forward to it."

It wasn't an assignation. Most of the guests at the house party would be in the woods right along with them, cutting branches and gathering holly and mistletoe. Why then did Clara feel as though she'd just arranged to meet a lover?

Her heart pumped wildly as she exited the library. She had to stop a moment in the hall to cool her blushes.

Will I see you again?

It didn't mean anything. And if it did, it was only the beginnings of a friendship. She needed a friend now, far more than a sweetheart. Someone she could talk to. Someone who would listen.

Was Mr. Cross to be that friend?

The prospect did nothing to calm her swiftly beating heart.

She made her way up the main staircase to the drawing room. She'd left Mrs. Bainbridge there, perched on a sofa, stitching at her embroidery. But when Clara entered the room, *Waverley* clutched in her hand, Mrs. Bainbridge was gone.

"Are you looking for my aunt?" Mr. Hayes's voice sounded from near the window. He was seated there in his wheeled chair, an easel set up in front of him. His manservant had been helping to situate him when Clara left, but there was no sign of the fellow now. "Mr. Boothroyd's taken her for an airing in the rose garden."

"Has he?" Clara inwardly grimaced. "I suppose I—"

"You didn't take too long," Mr. Hayes said.

"I beg your pardon?"

"You're thinking that she must have grown tired of waiting."

"Well, I—"

"Don't." Mr. Hayes applied a careful brushstroke to his canvas. "In case you've failed to notice, my aunt and Mr. Boothroyd are rapidly developing an affinity for each other."

Clara hadn't noticed. Or, rather, she *had*, but she hadn't considered it anything more than a certain civility between two people of a similar age. "You sound very sure of yourself."

He shrugged. "I observe things."

"How ominous." She forced herself to smile. "I shudder to think what you've observed about me, Mr. Hayes."

His mouth quirked. "Do call me Teddy. Everyone does."

"Very well," she said. "But you must call me Clara."

"Done." He lowered his brush. "I suppose you're going out with all the rest of them to gather Christmas greenery."

"Would you like to go?"

"Not especially. It's too much trouble in my condition. And I despise making a spectacle of myself." His smile turned wry. "You disapprove?"

"I merely think you shouldn't deprive yourself of the joy of the season."

"Is it joyful to flounder about in the mud with my chair? Or to have my manservant carry me through the woods like a babe? You and I must have a very different definition of joy." He dabbed his brush into his palette, deftly mixing shades of blue and yellow. "Tell me, what do you think of the way I've rendered the light?"

She went to stand at his side. What she saw on his canvas made her catch her breath.

He'd painted the sea—the water as it rose up over the jagged rocks beneath the cliffs. The sky above was a shadowed purple gray, out of which diffuse rays of sunlight appeared to shine down, illuminating patches of water in stormy blues and greens.

"Goodness," she murmured. "It's quite violent."

"Like Turner." A hint of pride echoed in his words.

"I'm not familiar with all of Mr. Turner's work, but…yes, I can see the similarity. Though this seems altogether different somehow. It's the light. The way it seeps through the storm clouds."

"Yes." Teddy nodded eagerly. "Yes, exactly."

She drew back to look at him. He was just a boy, really. So earnest and passionate. "You're very talented."

He didn't deny it. "Alex says there are painters in France who are experimenting with light the way I am. He means to find one who'll teach me." He laid down another brushstroke. "You were a teacher, weren't you?"

She went still. "Excuse me?"

"You said so the evening we arrived. When you were talking with Tom Finchley." He glanced up at her. "You never said so before."

"It hardly seemed relevant. Besides, I wasn't an art teacher."

"Even so, I'm surprised you abandoned the profession to be a companion to elderly ladies like my aunt. You don't seem suited for it."

"You speak with some authority." Clara made her voice light. As if the subject hadn't rattled her. Hadn't caused her pain. "Have you met many ladies' companions?"

"No, but—"

"We're not all alike, you know. Only consider Mrs. Finchley."

"Yes, I daresay you're right. Still, I think you'd have done better to remain a teacher. Who wants to be trailing after old women all day, catering to their megrims? And what's that in your hand? *Waverley*? Good lord. I suppose Aunt Charlotte asked you to read it to her?"

"I don't mind."

"So you claim. And yet…I have the funniest suspicion that you *do* mind."

Clara felt as if he'd shone a harsh light on her. As if he'd exposed her secrets to the world. Ridiculous, really. Teddy Hayes didn't know the first thing about her. "If I've done something to indicate I'm displeased with my position—"

"Nothing significant. But I told you"—he added a dab of sea-green paint to his canvas—"I notice things."

Chapter Seven

The woods that bordered the Abbey were nothing much to speak of. Only a few clusters of hearty pine trees, willows, and oaks, growing as wild as the rest of the landscape. They were set back from the cliffs, further inland. A natural woodland that had never yet been bent to the will of man.

Neville tramped through the trees with the rest of the guests, the rain-sodden ground squelching beneath his boots. In his early days in residence, he'd often ventured into the woods to cut firewood. Now, however, it was the servants who were responsible for gathering fuel for the fire. Neville rarely had cause to go into the woods anymore, but he was still as familiar with them as he was with the rest of Greyfriar's Abbey.

"We're relying on you to guide us," Tom said. "No one knows the property better than you."

No one save Justin. But he'd stayed behind with Lady Helena. He was loath to leave her for any length of time in her present condition. Jenny had stayed behind as well, fussing over Lady Helena with near as much concern. With them were Mrs. Bainbridge, Mr. Boothroyd, and Mr. Hayes, none of whom had any interest in venturing out into the rain and mud.

Only Alex, Tom, Laura, and Miss Hartwright had come. Along with a party of housemaids and footmen, they traipsed through the woods. The servants were in far better spirits about it than the houseguests. Some of them sang carols. Others talked and laughed.

"Careful!" Alex caught hold of Laura a fraction of a second before she slipped in the mud. "Hang on to me, love."

Laura clung to her husband's arm. "Goodness, this footing is terrible."

"What footing? It's a swamp up here."

"You've lived too long in the city," Tom said. "You've forgotten what it's like in Devon during the winter."

"I haven't forgotten," Alex replied. "I merely prefer the snow to the wind and the rain. There's nothing festive about six inches of mud."

Tom cast a look at the group of caroling maids and footmen. "The servants seem happy enough."

At that moment, one of the housemaids—a tall, dark-haired young woman named Mary—fixed her laughing eyes on Neville. "Where might we find mistletoe, Mr. Cross? Is it much farther?"

The other housemaids giggled amongst themselves.

Neville suppressed the urge to tug at his cravat. Mary had arrived at the Abbey a year ago with the rest of the new servants and had been subjecting him to her flirtatious remarks ever since. It never failed to make him uncomfortable. Especially now.

Miss Hartwright was nearby, choosing her steps carefully through the mud. Her flaxen hair was covered with a sensible bonnet, as plain as her woolen cloak. She hadn't talked very much since they departed the house. Not to him.

"It grows on the oak trees," Neville said. "Beyond the p-pines."

"You'll have to show it to me." Mary giggled again. "I'll never find it on my own."

Neville didn't respond.

Tom shot him a questioning look. His voice lowered. "Is she...?"

"No," Neville said emphatically.

"Beware of corrupting the servant girls, my lad," Alex advised under his breath.

"He's doing nothing of the sort," Laura said in equally low tones. "And it isn't polite for us all to be whispering." She raised her voice. "Are you having difficulty, Miss Hartwright?"

Miss Hartwright had one gloved hand braced against a tree trunk. "No difficulty." She sounded a little breathless. "Just trying not to fall."

Neville went to her without hesitation. "Take my arm."

She looked up at him. "I don't want to be a nuisance."

"You aren't. I should have...before. I didn't think."

"It makes no matter. I was faring quite well on my own at the beginning." After a taut moment, she tucked her hand through his arm. "Thank you."

He inclined his head. There was no other way to acknowledge her gratitude. She was clinging to him so tightly, her small shape pressed against his side. He felt an overwhelming surge of protectiveness for her. It stole his words away.

"The pine trees are ahead," Alex said.

Tom squinted up at them through his spectacles. "Taller than I remember."

They were a healthy bunch of trees, with full, needle-laden branches. Last Christmas, Neville and Justin had broken off as many boughs from them as they could carry, and Lady Helena and Jenny had used them to decorate the house. It had been Neville's first Christmas in memory with all of the trimmings—the pine boughs, holly, and tinsel, and the packages wrapped in colored paper under the tree.

In the orphanage, such things had been practically nonexistent.

Christmas morning had meant being awakened at dawn in a frozen dormitory, his breath visible in the air above him. It had meant cracking the ice in the basin to wash his face, and dressing swiftly in threadbare clothes. A sermon had followed in the chapel, where the boys had sat in feeble rows, limbs numb from the cold and stomachs aching with emptiness.

"Let the word of God be thy sustenance," the vicar would intone.

Would that it had been.

Instead, Christmas day had been as miserable as any other. The proprietor of the orphanage hadn't even seen fit to grant them an extra crust of bread for their tea.

Neville couldn't remember a time when he hadn't been hungry. The only extra helpings he ever got were those sacrificed by Justin and Alex. Tom would have given up his food as well, but he'd been the smallest of them. Justin had never permitted him go without.

"Robert!" Tom called to one of the footmen. "Where's that cart of yours?"

"Here, sir." Robert and one of the other footmen brought two carts forward, stopping them near the base of the trees.

"How many boughs do we require?" Alex asked.

Neville struggled to find his voice. "Last year—" He stopped and started again. "A lot."

Mary and the other housemaids broke into titters.

Tom looked at Neville. "Will two carts' full be sufficient?"

"To begin with."

"Well, then," Laura said. "We'd best get started."

Miss Hartwright's hand slid from the crook of Neville's arm. He felt the loss of it more keenly than he'd have expected. But there was no chance to refine upon it. There was too much to be done—and not a great deal of time to do it, if the rain clouds above were any indication.

With the help of several of the footmen, Neville, Tom, and Alex set about their work, breaking pine boughs and heaping them into the carts. Laura and Miss Hartwright helped, snapping off the smaller branches and gathering holly from the shrubs nearby.

When the carts were piled high with boughs, Neville stepped back from the tree he'd been working at and peered up at the darkening sky.

Alex did the same. "A storm is coming."

"How long do we have?" Tom asked. "Minutes? Longer?"

Laura dusted the pine needles from her gloves. "Is there time enough to gather some mistletoe? Helena has her heart set on it for the decorations."

"There's time," Neville said. And there was—barely.

They made their way through the woods, walking at a far brisker pace than when they'd first set out. Miss Hartwright once again took his arm, clutching tight as they navigated the mud.

The oak trees were on the opposite side of the woods. Last Christmas, he'd found mistletoe growing on them. Lady Helena had hung it all around the Abbey.

At the time, Neville hadn't given the tradition a second thought. Why should he have? There had been no one, then, to make the mistletoe worthwhile. Not for him.

That wasn't to say he hadn't been kissed.

Lady Helena had kissed him on the cheek beneath the mistletoe more than once last Christmas. So had Cook, and Jenny. They'd been sisterly kisses, with nothing of romance about them. This Christmas, however…

He glanced at Miss Hartwright. The hem of her skirts and cloak were muddy, and her cheeks were flushed from the cold. She looked back at him, smiling. A smile that lit up her face. That he could feel, igniting an answering light inside of him.

"'God rest ye merry gentlemen,'" one of the footmen began singing.

The other servants joined in with laughs and foolery. "'Let nothing you dismay!'"

By the third verse, Tom, Alex, and Laura were singing, too. And so was Miss Hartwright, in a clear melodic voice. "'From God, who is our Father, a shining angel came.'"

His heart clenched. Having her on his arm, bright and beautiful, and singing so sweetly. There was a rightness to it that was almost painful. He wanted to keep it close. To save the moment forever, like a winter flower pressed between the pages of a book.

But such feelings couldn't last. Miss Hartwright would be gone in a fortnight. And he would be…here.

Always here.

It was no revelation. It was a fact. One he'd accepted long ago. The recollection of it, nevertheless, served to dim the light glowing inside of him.

He felt, all at once, the full weight of his condition. Of being lonely, if not alone. Stuck in the same place while the rest of the world surged ahead at a startling rate of speed.

Miss Hartwright squeezed his arm. "Only five days until Christmas. The holiday will soon be over."

He stared down at her, his chest tight with conflicted emotion. "Yes. But n-not yet."

On returning to the Abbey, Clara hoped to find that the post had come, and with it, a letter from her mother. But though Clara's own letter was sure to have arrived in Edinburgh by now, no reply awaited her.

It wasn't entirely surprising.

As efficient as Mama was in other respects, she was woefully inadequate when it came to attending to her personal correspondence. Amid the chaos of lessons, and other professional responsibilities, her family was inevitably prioritized dead last.

An unfortunate fact, and one that Clara had little time to dwell upon at present.

The rest of the afternoon and evening was taken up with preparing the pine boughs, holly, and ivy to be hung. Footmen arranged card tables in the drawing room on which the maids set out ribbons, tinsel, and bowls of murky white liquid.

"We've all been lamenting the lack of snow," Lady Helena said, "so we shall make our own." She guided them to their tables. "The mixture in the bowl is boiled water and alum. We'll use it to frost the leaves and branches."

"It's very thin," Mrs. Bainbridge remarked as she sat down.

"At present." Mr. Boothroyd took a seat next to her. "But by tomorrow it will have dried to crystals."

Lady Helena smiled. "Quite right. And then we can begin to decorate the house."

"A daunting proposition." Mr. Archer joined the table at which Mrs. Archer and Teddy were seated. "Have we enough pine boughs?"

Mr. Thornhill pulled a chair out for his wife at a table by the hearth. The two mastiffs lay stretched out nearby, dozing in front of the fire. "We don't decorate every corner of the Abbey. If we did, we'd need more than five days to do it."

Lady Helena sat down, settling her skirts about her. "We'll focus on the main rooms. The drawing room of course, and the dining room, and library. And then there are the halls, and the stairs."

"And the corners and the alcoves." Mrs. Finchley sat down beside her husband. "Lots of hidden places to hang mistletoe."

Everyone laughed. Clara, too, albeit a little self-consciously. She was glad Mr. Cross wasn't present. He was busy helping the servants to carry in the remainder of the pine boughs. She supposed he'd join them shortly to decorate the leaves and branches, though it was difficult to imagine him engaged in such delicate work. He seemed the sort of man who was more comfortable out of doors, performing physical labor.

"I shall leave that to you and Tom, my dear," Lady Helena said, provoking more laughter. She glanced across the room at Clara. "You must bring your pug down to join us, Miss Hartwright."

Clara looked to Mrs. Bainbridge for permission.

"Go on, my dear," Mrs. Bainbridge said. "It will do no harm."

Clara was up in a flash. She thanked Mrs. Bainbridge, and Lady Helena too, as she made her way from the drawing room and out to the hall beyond. She'd gone as far as the main staircase, leading up to the third-floor bedrooms, when she encountered Mr. Cross.

He was coming up the stairs from the main hall, his arms full of pine boughs. He stopped when he saw her, the two of them meeting on the landing.

He took a step toward her, only to halt again. Hesitating, as if he was uncertain of her. "Are you leaving already?"

He was close enough that she could touch him if she wished. So close she could feel the warmth emanating from his large frame. The scent of fresh pine tickled her nose, and the scent of *him*—horses, leather, and the wild fragrance of the sea.

Butterflies unfurled their wings in her stomach. A delicate motion. Not a flutter in and of itself, but the beginning of one. "Oh, no. I'm only going to fetch Bertie from my room. Lady Helena says he may join us."

Mr. Cross didn't reply.

Clara couldn't be certain that he would. "Will you be sitting down with us to decorate the greenery?"

"Yes." He paused. "You'll be back?"

"As soon as I see to Bertie."

It was assurance enough. He inclined his head to her, and then continued on his way to the drawing room.

Clara stood there a second longer, looking after him, before turning to climb the stairs to her room. She was puzzled by Mr. Cross. Puzzled, intrigued, and very much in danger of becoming enamored.

She recognized the signs in herself. The tendency to idealize someone. To attribute to them qualities that they didn't have. Feelings they didn't have. To spin a romance out of whole cloth.

It wouldn't do.

She was no longer a sheltered country schoolteacher. A gullible young miss susceptible to the blandishments of well-to-do gentlemen, and to the yearnings of her own young heart.

"You foolish, stupid girl," Mama had said. "You've ruined us all, do you realize that?"

Clara *had* been foolish. And stupid, too. But not now. Not for a good long while, in fact. She was older. Nearly five and twenty. And she knew better of men—and of herself.

She entered her room to find Bertie curled up in his usual spot in front of the fire. He didn't hear her advance, only waking when she scooped him up in her arms. She murmured to him in an encouraging voice. "Do you want to go downstairs, Bertie? To see Paul and Jonesy?"

Nearby, her carpetbag sat upon the dressing table in silent reproach.

There were no new lessons from Simon, it was true, but that was no reason she couldn't be going over her old lessons, or studying on the subjects she'd already learned about. Perhaps Mr. Thornhill had books on natural history in the library? Something to do with the classification of butterflies or beetles?

Her brother had always nattered on about collecting beetles in his earlier letters. He'd been accustomed to sharing everything then. The sights and sounds of Cambridge, and all that he was learning there.

What had changed?

Had he simply grown tired of sharing his work with her? Or had he grown tired of the work itself?

Clara sighed as she exited her room, shutting the door behind her.

She supposed that most of life's endeavors began with good intentions. Each person trying to do their best. To honor their agreements. There were few who entered into an arrangement intending for it to go bad. Yet arrangements went bad nonetheless. People lost interest. Lost heart.

But if Simon thought he could change his mind about university—or about the promises he'd made to her—he was in for a very rude awakening. She had no intention of giving up her education. And hers was inextricably tied to his. Like mistletoe growing on an oak. A parasitic organism obliged to derive nutriment from its host.

Not a particularly flattering view to take of her situation, but there it was.

It was essential that Simon stay the course.

As for herself, a few days of holiday revelry could do no harm. And then she must get back to her studies. To making lists, and sorting things into neat rows and columns. To being quiet and sensible, her thoughts as orderly as her emotions.

There was contentment to be found in such pursuits. More than that, there was security. And security was no small thing for a woman. Especially a woman like her.

Chapter Eight

The next day passed in a whirlwind of activity. While the storm raged outside, the guests decorated the Abbey from top to bottom.

Clara helped to hang holly and mistletoe and to twine pine branches with ribbons and secure them on the banister of the main staircase. It was time she could have better spent on her studies, but she didn't begrudge the loss of it. Indeed, she was grateful for a momentary distraction from the worries about her future—and her past.

Teddy Hayes made no more mention of her former life as a teacher. He was too busy laughing and teasing with his aunt and sister. The three of them sat together at a low inlaid table in the drawing room, making wreathes out of crystal-encrusted pine boughs.

Nearby, Mr. Archer was up on a ladder, fixing boughs over the windows. Mr. Thornhill was similarly occupied with the arches over the doors. Lady Helena stood below him, offering direction.

"Can you not bend the branch a little further, my love?" she asked. "So it follows the outline of the arch?"

"Like this?"

"Yes, but with the bulk of the bough at the apex. It should fade to nothing as it curves on either side."

As Clara passed up and down the stairs with her own decorations, she saw Mr. and Mrs. Finchley attaching mistletoe to the bottom of the large gasolier in the hall. She saw them using it, too.

Wary of interrupting such intimacy, she turned back the way she'd come, ducking into the library. Mr. Cross was there, along with Mrs. Bainbridge and Mr. Boothroyd. The two gentlemen were nailing pine boughs around the bank of windows, and Mrs. Bainbridge was arranging crystallized holly and ivy on the bookshelves.

Mr. Cross glanced at her as she entered.

She looked away from him, conscious of the warmth rising in her face.

"Have you finished already, Miss Hartwright?" Mrs. Bainbridge enquired. "Come, you can help me awhile."

The dogs were in the library too. All three of them, curled up in front of the fire. Jonesy raised his head when she passed him, but he didn't growl. She flattered herself that he was growing accustomed to her. Yesterday evening, after dinner, he'd even taken a biscuit from her hand without snapping off her fingers.

"You've been running up and down those stairs too much today," Mrs. Bainbridge said. "Your cheeks are flushed."

"Are they?" Clara helped herself to some of the crystallized holly from Mrs. Bainbridge's basket. "I suppose I *am* a little overheated."

"When the rain relents, you must take a turn in the garden. A proper airing will set you right."

Clara busied herself on the library ladder, placing holly on the shelves that Mrs. Bainbridge couldn't reach. It didn't seem as if the rain would ever relent. But as the hour ticked by, the skies gradually lightened and the rain slowed to a drizzle.

By that time, the library was finished. Mrs. Bainbridge and Mr. Boothroyd sat down to enjoy a cup of tea, and Mr. Cross was putting away his tools.

She walked by him to set down the now empty basket of greenery.

"I have to see to the horses," he said quietly. "Do you want to c-come?"

The butterflies quivered their wings in warning. It was a warning Clara ignored. At least, for the moment. "Yes. Of course." She raised her voice. "Mrs. Bainbridge? May I take Bertie down to the stables for a run?"

"With Mr. Cross?" Mrs. Bainbridge frowned. "Is that wise?"

Clara's stomach knotted at the subtle reprimand. Did Mrs. Bainbridge think—?

"It's rather wet out there," Mrs. Bainbridge went on. "You might hurt yourself."

Clara pressed a hand to her waist. She prayed her relief didn't show on her face. Her employer was talking about the rain, not about Clara's reputation.

"She'll be safe enough with Neville," Mr. Boothroyd said. "As long as she doesn't wander out of his sight."

"I won't wander," Clara assured him,

"I'll look after her," Mr. Cross said.

Mrs. Bainbridge settled back in her chair. "Then I see no reason why not. But don't dally, Miss Hartwright. The weather is very changeable here."

"Yes, ma'am." Clara swiftly gathered Bertie into her arms, and along with Mr. Cross and the mastiffs, exited the room. "I'll have to fetch my cloak. Will you wait for me? And will you hold Bertie?"

Mr. Cross agreed to both counts. And when she returned from hastily donning her cloak, bonnet, and gloves, it was to find him standing by the doors, cradling Bertie in his arms.

Her heart turned over.

How kind he was. Genuinely kind. He must be to treat animals with such care and affection. Not all gentlemen were as honorably disposed. Men often whipped their horses or kicked their dogs. More than most, Clara feared. But not Mr. Cross. He could easily harm a lesser creature, but instead he treated them with gentleness and respect.

"Are you warm enough?" he asked

"Quite warm." She took Bertie back from him, settling the little pug under her cloak. "Shall we go?"

He held the door for her, and she preceded him down the steps. It was too cold and wet to stroll and talk, even if they'd had a mind to. Instead, they made their way down the cliff road at a quick clip, Paul and Jonesy loping ahead of them, barking.

By the time they reached the safety of the stable, Clara was wet and breathless, raindrops streaming from her bonnet and cloak. She deposited Bertie on the ground with the other dogs before reaching to untie her bonnet. "Gracious. If Mrs. Bainbridge could see me now."

Mr. Cross gazed down at her. A second passed, and then he moved to assist her. She dropped her hands, permitting him to unknot her wet bonnet strings, as if she were the veriest child. It took him but a moment. Less than a moment.

But he didn't stop there.

The strings untied, he reached up and very gently lifted her bonnet from her head, revealing her rumpled hair, pinned in its haphazard chignon.

And Clara no longer felt breathless. She felt as if she had no breath at all. No lungs. Only a rapidly beating heart, and those dashed butterflies, who had chosen this inauspicious moment to open their wings and give an honest to goodness, full-bodied flutter.

"Mr. Cross," she objected. "I really don't think you should—"

"You're very…"

"What?" Her voice was a whisper of sound. "What am I?"

His neck reddened faintly above the line of his cravat, but he didn't look away from her. This time, when he spoke, he didn't falter. "You're beautiful, Miss Hartwright."

Neville gazed down at Clara Hartwright, her wet bonnet held loose in his hand. He was riveted by her. By her eyes, soft and shimmering, like rich, chocolate brown satin. By the graceful arch of her dark, winged brows, and the damask rose hue of her half-parted lips.

All day he'd been aware of her. As she'd moved about the Abbey, twining pine boughs on the banister, and arranging alum-frosted holly and ivy on the shelves in the library. He'd been conscious of her soft voice, and her gentle, competent manner. Of the rustle of her woolen skirts over her starched petticoats as she walked past him. Aware of her to the point of distraction.

She *was* beautiful, though no one else seemed to notice but him.

She was also plainly shocked at the liberty he'd taken with her person.

"Thank you, Mr. Cross. That's very kind of you. But…I must say, I'm not feeling very clever at the moment." She cast an anxious glance down the aisle. There were no grooms standing about. No stable boys or other servants to have witnessed his brief breach of decorum. "I suppose I've ruined it."

"Ruined what?"

"My bonnet. I'd have fetched an umbrella, but it didn't seem necessary. It was only a light drizzle when we left the house." The words tumbled out more quickly than was her habit. It was the only sign that he'd flustered her. That and the heightened color in her face. "Is there somewhere you can hang it to dry? And my cloak, too?"

"On the…on the door of the loose box."

Her fingers moved to unbutton her cloak. Her hands were trembling.

Neville felt a stab of guilt. Was she afraid of him? Had he crossed some sort of line—not only in terms of social decorum, but in regard to her sense of personal safety?

They weren't alone together. Not in the strictest sense. The grooms and stable boys might appear at any moment. But a gentleman could still pose a threat to a lady, even in the most public of settings.

"I d-didn't mean—"

"Here you are." She handed him her cloak. "I hope it will be dry enough by the time I return."

He privately cursed his stammer as he took her wet things and draped them over the door of an empty loose box. If only he were more eloquent, like Alex or Tom. If only he were as confident as Justin. None of them ever seemed to have difficulty when speaking to their ladies—or to any ladies, for that matter.

Paul and Jonesy nosed about nearby, Bertie snuffling right along with them. Neville gave the dogs a cursory look before turning back to Miss Hartwright. He made an effort to speak slowly and calmly. To avoid the difficulties that plagued his speech whenever he got anxious.

"Would you like to see Betty?" he asked.

A look of relief came over Miss Hartwright's face. "Oh, yes. I was hoping we could. Should I bring Bertie, or—"

"Leave him. They won't run off." He led her through the stables to the loose box at the back. It was ideal for a wild pony. She needed to feel safe and protected. And she needed to rest her injured foreleg. Her life, thus far, had been one of tumult. Captured from her home on the moors to be sold at the annual horse sale, she'd been manhandled and beaten—though never into compliance.

The first time he'd seen her had been in the coaching yard at the King's Arms. A horse peddler had had her trussed up with ropes, and was trying to force her to follow his wooden cart. Betty had been limping badly, but her injury hadn't stopped her from kicking and snapping her teeth, thrashing about with such violence that she'd shaken the peddler's cart on its wheels. That's when the peddler had begun striking her with his stick.

Neville related the story to Miss Hartwright as they walked. He halted and stuttered over the worst bits, his anger rising as he recollected Betty's mistreatment.

Miss Hartwright listened, brows drawn and mouth compressed into a frown. "It sounds as if *he* was the one who deserved a beating. I know it's not very Christian, but I wish you'd given it to him."

Neville had been hard pressed not to. "I took his stick. I broke it."

"I'm glad."

"He'd been st-starving her to weaken her. To make her… submit. I gave her some oats. It's how I g-got her here."

"The poor dear. She must have been exhausted." Miss Hartwright stepped up to the loose box.

Neville stood next to her, both of them peering inside. Betty looked out at them, one ear twitched forward, listening.

"Here, Betty." Neville extended his hand.

Betty took a cautious step forward. She stretched her head out, nostrils quivering. Neville brushed his fingers over her muzzle. She flinched, but she didn't run off. He trailed his fingers down to her whiskery chin and gave her a gentle scratch.

"She likes you," Miss Hartwright said. "I'm not surprised."

"She's learning to trust me." He paused, adding, "I feed her."

Miss Hartwright laughed. "Food is a powerful motivator. I know. I've been winning Jonesy over with sugared biscuits."

He gave her an amused glance. She was good with the dogs. And not in the way of some people. She wasn't merely being polite. He often heard her speaking to Bertie, and to the mastiffs, too. As if they were people. Friends, not dumb animals. "Good morning," she'd say. "How are you today?"

It was enough to melt Neville's heart.

"Will you brush her again?" she asked.

"I can try," he said. "I'll fetch some grain."

It took him but a moment to make up a bucket of warm mash. He carried it to the loose box and unlatched the door.

Miss Hartwright stood back. "Shall I—?"

"Wait here. It's…safer."

"Very well."

He stepped inside the box, shutting the door behind him. Betty immediately showed him her haunches. It was a warning that she'd kick him if he came too close.

Neville clucked to her softly. "Easy, Betty." The handle of the bucket jingled, a recognizable sound to the Abbey's horses.

Betty's swollen sides expanded on a deeply indrawn breath.

"Here, girl." He approached on her left. When Betty moved her haunches, he rested a hand on her rump, letting her know he was there. She gave an anxious hop, one of her back hooves lifting in unmistakable threat.

Neville didn't let it deter him. He simply continued around her, touching her side, and then her shoulder as he went. Gentle, reassuring touches that told her she was safe. That she had nothing to fear from him.

All the while, Miss Hartwright remained at the door, silent. He suspected she was holding her breath. A wild pony was less dangerous than a wild horse, but a well-placed kick from one could still do significant damage.

"Easy, Betty," Neville murmured again. "You're all right." He stopped at her shoulder. It was up to her now. If she wanted the mash, she'd have to turn her head to take it.

He'd been through this with her every day since she arrived. She knew what she must do, and as each day passed, she became a little more willing to do it.

Today was no different.

After several minutes of cringing away from him, she finally worked up the courage to face him. A few limping steps, and another flare of her nostrils, and then she was lipping the rim of the bucket.

Neville clipped it to a metal hook on the wall. Betty thrust her head inside to eat her mash.

"I can brush her while she eats," Neville said. "And check her…her bandage. If you'll pass me that box?"

Miss Hartwright retrieved the wooden box of brushes. A roll of cotton gauze, and a small bottle of liniment were tucked inside of it. She smiled as she handed it to him. "You've charmed her, utterly."

He took the box, his bare fingers brushing hers. The brief contact sent a jolt of heat through his belly. "It's nothing."

"Indeed it is. You have a way with animals, Mr. Cross. I admire it very much."

He didn't know quite what to say to that. He'd always been good with animals. But since his accident, being with them had become even more meaningful to him.

Since his accident.

He still thought of it as if it had happened recently. But it was decades now. In truth, he scarcely recalled what his life had been like before.

"It's easier with them," he replied at last. "They don't expect me to…to talk."

"But you do speak to them."

He shrugged. "Nonsense words."

"I like a bit of nonsense. So does she. Don't you, Betty?" Miss Hartwright crooned. "What a handsome girl you are."

Neville's mouth twitched. Gauze and liniment in hand, he crouched down beside Betty's front leg. She gave one half-hearted stamp of her hoof. After that, she was too consumed with eating her mash to pay him much mind.

"You said there weren't many of them left. Do you know how many?"

"On Dartmoor?" He slowly removed the old gauze from Betty's leg. "Hundreds, probably."

"So few? I wonder if they're in danger of going extinct? Like the creatures Mr. Darwin writes about in his book."

He shot her a questioning look.

"Charles Darwin. The naturalist. He calls it natural selection. It's nature's way of winnowing out the weak creatures and fostering the bloodlines of the strong."

Neville massaged liniment into Betty's leg. "The ponies are strong enough. It's the people who won't…who won't leave them alone."

"Do you believe they'll die out?"

"Not if something's done to help them."

"Such as what?"

"Such as…" Neville faltered. He had ideas, of course. A surfeit of them. But there was nothing he could do directly. Not while remaining at Greyfriar's Abbey.

What the ponies required was an advocate. Someone who could help to protect them, and replenish their numbers. It's what he hoped Mr. Atkyns had been doing in Tavistock. The bar man at the King's Arms had said as much.

Old Atkyns is keen on preserving the breed. You should speak with him.

But Mr. Atkyns hadn't responded to Neville's letter. Not yet.

"I don't know." He rolled a fresh bandage over Betty's leg. "But the ponies need…someone."

Miss Hartwright folded her arms on the top of the door, resting her chin on her hands. "Has it occurred to you that that someone might be you?"

Chapter Nine

It *had* occurred to Neville. And it occurred to him again the following afternoon when he received Mr. Atkyns's letter. Only it wasn't from Mr. Atkyns.

It was from his widow.

"He's dead," Neville said blankly, the letter held open in his hand.

Tom glanced up from his chair near the fire. "Who?"

He was in the library along with Justin, Alex, Mr. Hayes, and Mr. Boothroyd. They'd gathered there for brandy and cigars while the ladies occupied themselves in the drawing room.

Jenny's former manservant, Ahmad Malek, had come down from London for the day. Now a dressmaker of growing renown, he'd made the trip specially to perform the final alterations on Jenny's and Lady Helena's Christmas gowns.

"Erasmus Atkyns," Neville replied. "He died last month."

"Who the devil is Erasmus Atkyns?" Justin asked. "Not that vicar in Tavistock?"

Neville nodded. "His widow has written. He's… His property is…"

Tom stood and came to join him. "Do you mind if I have a look?"

Neville handed him the letter, waiting while Tom read through it. The other men resumed their conversation. Something about the feasibility of improving the cliff road. A tedious subject, and one that Justin had been rather keen on since first learning of his impending fatherhood.

"When the heavy rains come, the road washes out, and we're isolated here for days at a time," he was explaining to Mr. Hayes. "It won't do when there are children in residence. If one should become ill or injured, there would be no way to summon the village doctor or the surgeon."

"I'm surprised you haven't removed to town for the winter," Alex said. "With your wife expecting, it seems only sensible. You'll want her under a doctor's care."

"She won't go," Justin replied grimly. "She insists on remaining here for Christmas. Besides which, she has a well-founded mistrust of doctors. Our child's to be delivered by a village midwife."

Neville was only half listening. He couldn't focus on anything fully at the moment. The news of Mr. Atkyns's death had thrown his thoughts into chaos. Sensing his distress, Paul and Jonesy milled about nearby, too concerned for him to lie down.

"Mrs. Atkyns is very civil," Tom murmured as he read. "But it seems her husband was in some financial difficulties. He must have been for them to be having the estate sale so soon after the funeral." He looked up from the letter. "Will you go?"

Neville's stomach tightened with apprehension. Mrs. Atkyns had invited him to attend the sale. Had said she wished to speak with him further on the matter of the Dartmoor ponies. But it would mean leaving Greyfriar's Abbey. Traveling to Tavistock, and staying a day or two, at least. "I d-don't—"

"It sounds as though she's eager to speak with you in person."

"Yes, but..." Neville felt the bitter urge to laugh. Speak with him? Wouldn't that be a charming conversation. Him stopping, starting, and stammering, and her trying to make heads or tails of what the devil he was saying. "I don't want..." He took a breath. "It isn't..."

Tom's eyes were keen, as always. Seeing everything. "You needn't decide this very moment. The sale isn't until after Christmas. There's plenty of time yet to determine the best course."

Neville took back the letter. He folded it carefully.

"If you require any help," Tom said, "any advice, I'm here. You need only ask me."

"I know that." Neville was grateful to him. Tom never pressed. Never attempted to exert his will. "Thank you."

Tom smiled. "Won't you join us? God only knows how much longer the ladies will be with Ahmad."

"I can't. I..." Neville cast a look at the door. He wanted to get out, not only of this room, but of his own head. To walk, or to work with the horses. Something physical. "I need...I need some air."

Tom inclined his head in understanding. "Of course. I'll make your excuses."

Neville ducked out without another word, Paul and Jonesy at his heels. The voices of his friends quieted to a dull murmur as he shut the door behind him. It was wet out and growing colder by the minute. But he preferred it to the stifling feeling of being trapped indoors.

He'd never liked being inside, not even as a boy. During lessons in the orphanage schoolroom, he'd often lost himself gazing out the window, falling into a pleasurable daydream—until the teacher had roused him with a vicious box to the ears.

"Will you never pay attention, Cross? Do you aspire to a permanent state of stupidity?"

The nuns at St. Crispin's in Abbot's Holcombe had been slightly kinder. After his accident, Mr. Boothroyd had arranged for them to take Neville in. They'd never expected much of him. Once he'd recovered from the fall—as much as he *could* recover—he'd been given simple work. Washing up in the convent's kitchens, or mucking out soiled straw in the convent's stables.

"Silent obedience, Cross," the Reverend Mother had often said. "That's what the Lord demands of us."

It had been permission to refrain from speech. To cease the mortifying struggle of trying to form words. A blessing, really.

Not that he'd thought so at first.

In the days following his accident, he'd felt only frustration. The desire to speak—to be *heard*—and the anger incumbent in realizing that he couldn't express his thoughts or feelings with any degree of eloquence. In the beginning, even short sentences had proven difficult. His fists had clenched, and perspiration had risen on his brow. The struggle had, at times, driven him to tears of rage and bitterness.

It would have been easier to have given up. To have refrained from speech altogether. But he was no mute. He'd frequently had things he wished to say. Questions to give voice to, and opinions he longed to express.

What he'd wanted—*needed*—was someone to be patient with him. To understand.

When Justin had returned from India and bought the Abbey, Neville had been glad to come and live with him. Now, it had seemed, his life could at last begin.

But life at Greyfriar's Abbey hadn't been so very different from his life at St. Crispin's.

There was Justin and Mr. Boothroyd, and occasionally Tom. They were a family of sorts. The closest thing to one that Neville had ever known. But when it came to his own identity, separate and apart from them, nothing much had changed at all. Indeed, it felt that nothing ever would.

He ran a hand over his hair as he passed through the main hall. He'd gone no more than a few steps when he stopped short, his attention arrested by movement on the stairs.

Miss Hartwright was descending, garbed in her cloak and bonnet, with Bertie in her arms. When she saw him, her mouth curved into a smile. "Mr. Cross. Good afternoon." She stepped down into the hall. "Are you going to the stables?"

"I'm… I was…" His hand curled into a fist at his side. "I was going for a walk."

Her gaze dropped briefly to his clenched hand. Her brows knit as her eyes met his, her smile fading. "Is something the matter?"

"No." He looked away with a grimace. "Yes."

"What is it?"

He didn't answer. Everything was getting too jumbled. And he was too aware of her, curse it. He couldn't think straight, let alone speak.

"I must take Bertie out," she said. "But if you'd like to talk, I'm happy to listen." She searched his face. "Would you like to talk?"

To talk.

A surge of resentment rose within him. But something else rose in him, too. It was a swell of longing. An ache so bittersweet it tightened his throat and pricked at the back of his eyes.

He swallowed hard, abandoning his pride. "Yes, I…I would."

"Very well." She waited while he fetched his hat and coat, and then again for him to hold the door open for her. As she passed through it, he caught the orange blossom fragrance of her hair.

His fingers tightened on the doorknob, drawing it shut behind them. They exchanged not a word as they started down the winding cliff road, Paul and Jonesy trotting ahead.

It wasn't raining at the moment, but the wind was icy sharp. It ruffled Miss Hartwright's skirts, and the long ribbon ties of her bonnet. She wrapped her cloak tighter around Bertie.

Neville was silent, his head bent against the cold, and his hands thrust into the pockets of his black woolen coat. In the distance, storm clouds gathered over the sea. "Mr. Atkyns is dead," he said at last.

"The gentleman you wrote to?" Her brow creased. "Oh, dear. How unfortunate. Was it very recent?"

"Last m-month. Part of his estate is being sold. The livestock and…and…" He took a breath. "There's a public sale in January. His widow wishes to m-meet with me to…to talk about the wild ponies."

She seemed to comprehend the difficulty. "And you don't feel you can go? That you can speak to her?"

He shook his head, a muscle working in his cheek.

She was quiet for a long moment. Their steps down the cliff road were slow and measured, nothing like their hurried pace the previous day. He heard her take a breath. "May I ask…forgive me if I'm being too bold, but…what caused your speech impediment?" She paused. "It is an impediment, isn't it?"

He didn't answer straightaway. He couldn't. It wasn't the sort of thing he'd ever imagined himself discussing with her.

"Were you born with it?" she asked. "Or—"

"I fell," he said gruffly.

"From a horse?"

"From there." He pointed to the cliffs in the distance, the ones that curved along the sea some miles away. They were different from the cliffs beneath the Abbey. No jutting outcroppings of stone existed to aid someone in descending to the beach. The cliff face was stark and sheer, dropping straight down to the violently frothing surf below.

"*There?*" The whistling wind nearly stole her voice. "But how?"

"We were climbing down, and…and I fell. I hit m-my head and I dropped…into the sea. Alex saved me."

They'd been joking with each other as they went, spirits high on the thrill of it all. Neville had turned to say something. A clever, laughing remark. In that same instant, the rock had crumbled beneath him.

"Mr. Archer?" She slowed to a halt. "When?"

He came to a reluctant stop in front of her. "Long ago. When I was a boy."

"What in the world were the two of you doing up there? Surely you must have known it was dangerous."

Of course they'd known. But the climb down the cliffs had seemed worth the risk. It had been the only way to access the beach below, and the boat that was docked there. They'd used it to row down the coast to Greyfriar's Abbey.

At the time, the Abbey had been the home of Sir Oswald Bannister. He was the orphanage's foremost patron—and rumored sire of several of its inmates.

Justin was one of them. Alex was likely one too.

Add to that, the lure of legends that spoke of buried pirate's treasure, and the four of them could scarcely resist venturing onto the Abbey's grounds several times a week. Sometimes they made mischief for Sir Oswald. Other times they searched for the treasure.

In the end, only Neville's fall had been able to stop their pursuits.

"Thornhill and Finchley were there, too," he said. "We d-didn't care about the danger. We weren't afraid."

"Boys never are when it comes to foolish schemes. My own brother might have broken his neck a dozen times over if my mother and I hadn't taken him in hand."

Neville's gaze lifted to hers. There was a storm in his breast, as tumultuous as the one brewing over the sea. "I didn't have a…a m-mother. Or a sister. None of us did. We were p-parish orphans."

"*All* of you?"

He didn't say anything.

It was reply enough.

Miss Hartwright absorbed the information in silence. "I'm sorry. I didn't realize."

His throat contracted on a swallow. His gaze flicked out to the sea. To the treacherous cliffs beyond. The ones he'd fallen from so long ago.

"What happened afterward?" she asked.

"I don't remember." His mouth flattened. "For a long while, I…I didn't even remember falling. Only waking up in…in the orphanage."

It was only later that it had come back to him. First in nightmares, and then in waking memory. The terror when he'd fallen and hit his head. The rush of salt-damp wind as he'd plummeted down, sucking away his breath before he'd ever hit the water. And the sea itself. A living organism—cold, dark, and relentless. It had swallowed him whole in the seconds before he'd lost consciousness.

He remembered those early nights in the orphanage, coming awake all at once in his narrow bed, his sheets soaked with sweat. "I c-can't breathe," he'd gasped, when he could speak at all.

But there had been plenty of air. It had been compassion the orphanage lacked.

"They sent me away," he said.

"To where?"

He resumed walking toward the stables. "A…convent."

Clara readjusted Bertie in her arms as she followed at Mr. Cross's side. The little pug was used to being carried about like a valuable parcel, and made no objection to being held warmly under her cloak. "A sort of hospital, do you mean? Here in Devon?"

He shook his head. "St. Crispin's in... Abbot's Holcombe. Mr. Boothroyd arranged it. The sisters n-nursed me."

His words were slow, and drawn out, as if he were retrieving each one from the bottom of a murky well. Clara gathered that it was difficult for him to speak in long sentences. To explain things to her with any degree of complexity. His frustration at the process was palpable. Were his hands not in his pockets, she was certain she'd find that one of them was again clenched into a fist.

"You knew Mr. Boothroyd as a boy?"

"Yes." He looked straight ahead, his jaw set. "The orphanage... It was a b-bad place. He... he helped us."

Clara fell quiet again. It was all very complicated. Far more than she'd have guessed from her first, or even second, impressions of the residents and guests assembled at the house party.

And yet, she wasn't entirely surprised.

There was an element of darkness to the group. Of lingering tragedy. She'd felt it from the moment she arrived at the Abbey, so high atop the cliffs overlooking the sea. At the time, she'd attributed it to the Gothic architecture of the place, and to the wind and rain that stormed all about it.

But it was the people that created the atmosphere. Mr. Thornhill with his burn scars. Mr. Finchley with his world-weary blue gaze, so much older than all the rest of him. And even Mr. Archer. The way he looked at his wife. The way he stayed close to her and held her hand. It was love, of course. But there was something else there as well. The thirst of a man too long deprived of water.

And what of Mr. Cross? The most mysterious gentleman of all.

He wasn't like the others. And she began to understand why.

"How long did you remain at the convent?" she asked.

"Until I c-came here. When Thornhill...bought the Abbey. Nearly f-four years ago."

Four years?

She couldn't hide her dismay. "Do you mean to say you've only lived at the Abbey for four years? That you've spent most of your life living in a convent?"

He gave her a wary look.

"But you're a grown man. At least thirty, by my guess."

"One and thirty," he said. "I lived at the c-convent for... for sixteen years."

She gaped at him, so stunned she nearly lost her footing on a patch of loose stones. His hand shot out to grasp her elbow, steadying her before she could fall. Clara's heartbeat surged into a gallop. For all his shyness and halting speech, he was a strong, capable man. Quick enough to catch her before she could come to harm.

"Careful," he said.

"Yes, thank you." She was breathless, and sounded it. "I wasn't paying proper attention." His touch sent a pleasurable shiver through her veins. Was it possible to feel the warmth and weight of his hand all the way through the folds of her cloak and the sleeve of her woolen bodice? Or was she imagining it?

She suspected the latter.

Another incidence of romanticizing things, no doubt. And who wouldn't succumb to such? She was alone with a handsome gentleman on a cliff top above the sea. A gentleman who had just saved her from falling. And who had been raised in a convent, of all places.

"Like Sir Galahad," she blurted out.

A look of bewilderment passed over Mr. Cross's face. "Who?"

Clara closed her eyes briefly against a swell of embarrassment. She wished she'd kept that particular thought to herself.

But there was no unsaying it.

"Sir Galahad." Her arms tightened around Bertie. "A knight of King Arthur's Round Table. The one who found the Holy Grail. He was raised in a convent, too."

"I don't read fairy stories."

"Sir Galahad isn't a fairy story. He's part of Arthurian legend. Mr. Tennyson wrote a poem about him some years ago." She recited the first lines from memory:

"My good blade carves the casques of men,
My tough lance thrusteth sure,
My strength is as the strength of ten,
Because my heart is pure."

Mr. Cross stared at her, an emotion in his eyes that was hard to read.

Heat rose in her cheeks. "Forgive me. I used to be rather fond of that sort of poetry. It's silly. And utterly irrelevant to the matter at hand."

"You don't like it anymore?"

"No. It was a girlish fancy of mine, and one best left in girlhood. Now I've grown up, I prefer to expend my energies on more practical matters. Science and natural history. That sort of thing." She cleared her throat. "I believe we were discussing your letter. Your hesitation to visit Mrs. Atkyns."

He exhaled heavily. "You see why it's d-difficult."

"It needn't be. That is, I can appreciate that you're self-conscious about talking, but—"

"It's not only that. How can I... How would she understand?"

"I don't have any difficulty understanding you."

His eyes met hers. "You're different."

The butterflies in her stomach fluttered to life. She was acutely reminded that only yesterday he'd called her beautiful. It was a precious jewel of a compliment. One she'd immediately locked away in her heart. In the coming years, she could take it out again whenever she was feeling plain and invisible. She could remind herself that once a handsome gentleman had called her beautiful, and meant it.

No one had ever done so before.

"On the contrary," she said. "I'm exceedingly ordinary. Ask anyone."

"I don't need to ask. I c-can judge for myself."

His matter-of-fact words warmed Clara to her toes. "My point is, if I can understand you, then I don't see why Mrs. Atkyns should have any trouble."

"Mrs. Atkyns isn't you. Some people..." He left the sentence unfinished as they approached the stables. The two mastiffs were already there, milling about the yard.

Clara dropped her voice. "How much do you want to be part of helping the ponies?"

"I want to, but..." He looked away from her. "I c-can't go there."

"Then what will you do?"

"I'll send Finchley in my place. Or Boothroyd. It's...easier."

Clara wanted to press him further but knew she hadn't the right. His limitations were his own business. She wouldn't presume to manage him. "It's your decision, of course. You must do what you think best."

Inside the stables, a groom was busy cleaning a harness. Another had a carriage horse out in the aisle, painting its hooves with turpentine. The caustic scent lingered in the air, along with the fragrance of saddle soap, silver polish, and fresh hay.

"Afternoon, Miss Hartwright," the older groom said. "Come to see that wild Dartmoor mare again?"

"You'll never make a saddle pony of her, miss," the younger groom remarked. "Best look elsewhere."

Clara forced a smile, greeting the two men as she set Bertie down onto the ground with the other dogs. The grooms thought her frequent visits were because of Betty. That she was besotted with her and had hopes of making her into a suitable mount. Clara didn't bother correcting their misapprehension. She went along with it, pretending both to them and to herself. It was easier than admitting the truth.

She *was* fond of Betty. But it was Mr. Cross she'd been coming to the stables to see.

Not because she was setting her cap at him. Not because he was tall, and handsome, and like a golden knight from Arthurian legend. But because he'd been kind to her. He'd been kind to Bertie. And there wasn't enough kindness in the world. Not in *her* world, at least. Not from gentlemen like him.

That was all there was to it. Kindness. A possibility of friendship. Not attraction. Certainly not romance.

She must take care not to make more of it than it was. If she did...well. The consequences of such foolishness wouldn't be to her liking.

They hadn't been the last time.

Chapter Ten

Clara stood outside the gates of the village churchyard in King's Abbot, waiting while Mr. Boothroyd assisted Mrs. Bainbridge into the Abbey's black-lacquered carriage. The horses stamped their impatience, snorting clouds of steam in the frigid December air.

Clara felt rather like stamping, too. She'd spent the last two hours in an ice-cold church, seated at Mrs. Bainbridge's side on a hard wooden pew, listening to a sermon that was more hellfire and brimstone than tidings of Christmas joy. Her hands and feet had turned to blocks of ice and showed no signs of thawing.

No wonder Mr. Thornhill and Lady Helena hadn't wished to attend Sunday services in the village.

And they hadn't been alone in refraining. Mr. and Mrs. Finchley hadn't come either. Nor had Teddy or Mr. Cross.

Only Mr. Boothroyd had been willing to accompany them. A sacrifice which had endeared him to Mrs. Bainbridge all the more.

"Miss Hartwright?" He offered Clara his hand.

She took it, permitting him to help her up the carriage steps and into the warmth of the cab. With a murmur of thanks, she squeezed in next to Mrs. Bainbridge.

Mr. Boothroyd climbed in after her, shutting the door behind him.

"We're obliged to you for escorting us, sir," Mrs. Bainbridge said as the horses sprang into motion.

"Make no mention of it, ma'am." Mr. Boothroyd settled in the green velvet and leather-upholstered seat across from them. He wore a heavy woolen coat, with a worsted muffler wound around his neck. "I couldn't in good conscience permit you to travel into the village alone."

Mrs. Bainbridge pursed her lips. "I'd anticipated Mr. Archer would escort us, but my niece's husband has a will of his own." She withdrew a handkerchief from her jet-beaded black reticule. "I'm sure he had good reason to stay behind—and to keep Laura with him. Mind you, he's not irreligious. He often attended services with us in Surrey. But he's not a particularly reliable sort of gentleman, if you take my meaning."

Clara shrank back into her corner of the carriage, clutching her Bible in her lap, and fervently wishing she was somewhere else. Her previous employer, Mrs. Peak, had often gossiped with friends and family, talking to them as if Clara wasn't even in the room. But this was the first time Mrs. Bainbridge had done so. It was never a comfortable experience. Indeed, it felt rather like eavesdropping.

"The gentlemen do have their reasons for staying away, ma'am," Mr. Boothroyd replied. "It's very much a matter of conscience. The churches hereabouts weren't always as charitable to orphan boys as they should have been."

"My niece tells me that you've known Mr. Archer and his friends for some time. Since they were small children. I must confess, I was puzzled. Were you affiliated with the orphanage in some way?"

"I was secretary to its patron, Sir Oswald Bannister, the former owner of Greyfriar's Abbey. He was a particular villain to the boys. They would often come to the Abbey to make mischief for him. It was then I first encountered them."

"And took them under your wing?"

"I tried to redress a great wrong. In many respects, I fear I was too late. By the time I recognized the type of man I was working for, considerable damage had already been done."

Mrs. Bainbridge dabbed at her nose with her handkerchief. "You make it sound rather dreadful."

"Not for me, no. But for them—the four boys—dreadful doesn't begin to describe it." He frowned, as if at an unpleasant memory. "I've long wondered why any of them wished to remain in these parts. Far better to start anew in some other locale. I daresay Mr. Archer had the right idea."

"I'm constrained to admit that Mr. Archer's life has been, thus far, ignoble." Mrs. Bainbridge lowered her voice. "A gambler, sir. On the continent. And not, I fear, of the honest variety."

"Yes." Mr. Boothroyd's frown deepened. "I'd heard something to that effect."

"My niece is having a favorable influence on him, naturally. But they've not been married overlong. Such things take time."

"Marriage has vastly improved the lives of Mr. Thornhill and Mr. Finchley," Mr. Boothroyd said. "I trust it will have the same effect on Mr. Archer. Though, I admit, he was always somewhat of a mystery to me as a boy."

"And Mr. Cross? Do you anticipate his marriage?"

"Ah. As to that..." Mr. Boothroyd looked out the window a moment, his countenance grave. "I don't believe Mr. Cross will ever leave the Abbey. If he marries at all, it will be to a maidservant there, or perhaps a village lass. Someone who has no great expectations of life—or of him."

Clara's fingers tightened around her Bible, a spark of indignation flaring in her breast. How dare they speak of Mr. Cross in such an unfeeling fashion? As if he was less deserving of happiness than the other gentlemen were. As if he'd stay at the Abbey forever, aspiring to nothing more than marrying a maidservant.

Not that there was anything wrong with maidservants. She might have been one herself, given less opportunity. But the very thought of Mr. Cross consorting with a pretty housemaid—like the brazen girl who had flirted with him in the woods—made Clara feel vaguely ill.

"I daresay it's a kindness. We must protect the weaker among us. Only consider my nephew. He believes himself fit enough to accompany my niece to France, but I truly don't know, Mr. Boothroyd. I truly don't know."

Mr. Boothroyd reached to take one of Mrs. Bainbridge's gloved hands. He patted it, giving a murmur of sympathy. "There, there, madam."

Clara averted her gaze from the intimacy. She affected to be riveted by the passing scenery, feeling very much like an intruder on some private romantic scene.

A growing affinity for each other? It was something more than that, surely.

She was happy for Mrs. Bainbridge, of course, but—at the same time—Clara fretted over what such a relationship might portend for her own future. If Mrs. Bainbridge was to wed, would she have need of a lady's companion any longer? Clara didn't expect so.

And then what? Another round of employment agencies and interviews?

Clara didn't think she had the stomach for it.

She continued to gaze out the window as Mrs. Bainbridge and Mr. Boothroyd talked. The carriage clattered up the narrow, winding cliff road to the Abbey, rolling right along the dangerous edge. Bits of earth and stone crumbled beneath its wheels, falling down into the frothing surf below.

"We didn't care about the danger," Mr. Cross had said. "We weren't afraid."

She could almost see them, four boys climbing down the cliff's face, three with dark hair and one with fair. Neville Cross. He couldn't have been more than eleven at the time. Just an orphan lad with his friends. She imagined him falling and hitting his head, dropping into the sea to disappear beneath the waves. And when he'd come out again—when he'd been rescued and nursed back to health—he'd been irrevocably altered.

But Mr. Cross wasn't weak. That much she understood absolutely. How could his friends not see it? How could they have underestimated him so?

Back at the Abbey, Mrs. Bainbridge retired to her room for a short rest. "You may have a little time to yourself, my dear," she said. "A walk, perhaps. Or a visit with that pony you've grown so fond of."

Clara helped Mrs. Bainbridge onto her bed. "I believe I'll take Bertie to the rose garden."

"As you please." Mrs. Bainbridge lay down atop the quilted counterpane, still clad in her black crepe dress. "But see that you're back and changed by half past one. Mr. Boothroyd says the gentlemen have gone to cut the Christmas tree. And Lady Helena intends us to spend the afternoon gilding walnuts and who knows what else."

"Yes, ma'am."

After leaving Mrs. Bainbridge's room, Clara retreated to her own. She fetched Bertie from his place in front of the fire. A quick visit to the rose garden so he could relieve himself, and then she was back in her room, fishing the key to her carpetbag out from within the bodice of her gown.

Bertie ambled to the warm hearth and curled up again, promptly falling back asleep. He'd be awake and asking to go out again soon. But not yet. She had ample time for a little quiet study.

Too many days had passed without reviewing her old lessons. She had begun to feel guilty. Since becoming a lady's companion, her studies had been the single focus of her free time. It should take more than a week of Christmas revelry and the friendship of a gentleman to break that focus.

She unlocked her carpetbag and withdrew a handful of the large, overstuffed envelopes inside. Sitting down at the dressing table, she opened the oldest of them and spread the folded papers out before her.

Simon's handwriting was distinctive. He had a peculiar habit of adding a curling loop to the bottom of some letters and the top of others. It was so much a part of his script that she hardly noticed it anymore.

She reread his notes on Carl Linnaeus's system of taxonomic nomenclature, and on Aristotle's *History of Animals*. She refreshed her memory on species, genus, class, and order. On the classification of plants, minerals, and insects.

In his earliest letters, Simon had often drawn pictures of insects or flowers, labeling things he'd observed under the microscope, such as pockets in the knees of bees, and the hooks on the feet of flies. He'd also posed questions to her, or directed her to books she might read to supplement her learning.

When in London with Mrs. Peak, Clara had had a subscription to the circulating library, and had borrowed what volumes she could. Unfortunately, most of the books her brother was reading at university weren't available to her. Or—if they were—it was only to purchase, and then in a daunting ten or twelve book series, which far exceeded the meager limits of her income.

Clara had made do as best she could. But she always had the feeling she was missing far more than she learned. That some essential component was absent from her experience. Some cask of information that would fill in all the gaps and render her knowledge complete.

But of course something was missing. She wasn't *there*, at Cambridge. She didn't have access to lectures, to books, and to tutors. To the university's enviable collection of fossils, and insects preserved in amber.

She was learning everything secondhand, via letters sent from a great distance away.

It was rather akin to listening to a symphony orchestra with cotton wool packed in her ears. She could feel the music's vibration, and sense the swelling rhythm. It was sufficient to stir her spirits and to make her hunger for more. But it was never enough for her to discern the melody. To recognize what piece was being played.

It was an altogether frustrating experience.

She folded away her brother's old notes and opened his most recent batch. The ones in the oversized envelope that had been waiting for her the day she arrived in Devon.

As she read through them, a niggling sense of uneasiness stirred within her.

Before all other things, man is distinguished by
his pursuit and investigation of TRUTH.

A direct quote from *Herschel's Preliminary Discourse*. She recognized it, along with the wording in the rest of Simon's notes. A duplicate lesson, to be sure. But there was something else wrong with it. Something she couldn't quite put her finger on.

After long minutes reading and rereading, she stood and went to her carpetbag. She fished out another handful of packets, and returning to the dressing table, began to go through them page by page.

It was in the final packet that she found it. A packet sent six months ago. The same scrawled apology from Simon was in the top right-hand corner, and the same quotes from *Hershel's Preliminary Discourse* were in the notes. The notes she'd received from Simon on Monday were, indeed, a duplicate.

She laid the pages side by side, comparing them.

Gooseflesh rose on her arms.

They were more than a duplicate in content. They were an actual, physical copy, identical right down to the curling loops on the letters.

It was as if Simon had traced over his own writing.

Or someone else had.

Neville hoped the Christmas tree would meet with the ladies' approval. It had taken the greater part of the morning to find and cut it. A majestic fir, with full, sappy branches, he helped the servants lift it onto a cart, and then walked along with the horses, offering them encouragement, as they hauled it back to the Abbey.

Justin went ahead of them, leaving as soon as the tree was cut. He was anxious to return to Lady Helena. It didn't matter that she had Jenny and Laura to look after her, he never seemed to feel at ease until he was back in her company.

"Does he anticipate difficulty?" Alex walked alongside the cart, keeping a watchful eye on Teddy, who was seated atop the box next to the driver. Teddy's wheeled chair had been placed in the back.

Tom trailed behind. "Justin always anticipates difficulties. It's one of his most endearing qualities."

Neville glanced back at them from his place at the horse's head. "Lady Helena is strong."

"He knows that," Tom said. "But he still worries about losing her. And now that she's nearing her confinement—"

"He must be bloody terrified." Alex's expression turned grim. "I know I'd be if it was Laura. I'm not sure an infant would be worth the risk to her health."

Tom's mouth hitched. "Your wife may have something to say on that score."

"Does yours?" Alex retorted.

"Jenny and I have no interest in children at present. We have other plans. But one day..." Tom shrugged. "I suppose we'll settle down eventually."

"I know one thing," Alex said. "Christmas is a dashed inconvenient time to be expecting a child. Justin will be too distracted to enjoy himself."

"On the contrary," Tom replied. "He's enjoying himself very much—in the company of his wife."

"What about you?" Alex looked up at Teddy. "Are you glad you came?"

Teddy gave his brother-in-law a sheepish smile. "I still think it's too much trouble."

"No trouble at all," Alex said. "Unless you'd rather have remained back at the Abbey? Or perhaps you'd have preferred to attend church with your aunt and her companion?"

"No, no," Teddy objected, laughing. "This is much preferable." He gripped the seat of the cart. "Though I do wonder how Clara is managing."

Neville shot Teddy a narrow glance. He'd gotten to know him a little better since his arrival, enough that they'd advanced to using each other's Christian names. He seemed a confident lad, often talking or laughing with his sister.

Or with Miss Hartwright.

Clara.

Had she given Teddy permission to call her that? The very idea of it made Neville's chest constrict with jealousy.

It was a new sensation, and one he didn't much care for.

"Miss Hartwright will be fine," Tom said. "She strikes me as an adaptable lady."

Neville scowled at him. "What is that supposed to mean?"

"Only that I suspect she's capable of conforming herself to a variety of settings. Of doing what's required of her. I mean it as a compliment."

"It doesn't sound like one."

Alex and Tom exchanged a glance.

Neville affected not to notice. As the cart approached the back of the Abbey, it slowed to a lurching halt.

Alex was instantly at Teddy's side, one hand on the padded seat of the cart. "Steady."

"I'm all right," Teddy said. "I'm not made of glass, you know."

"Humor me. If anything happens to you, I have to answer to your sister." Alex helped Teddy down from his seat as one of the footmen brought around his wheeled chair.

The housekeeper, Mrs. Quill, emerged from the back door of the Abbey. "Oh, this is a fine one." She walked around the cart, giving the tree a thorough once over. "It must be rinsed off." She directed two of the footmen, and one of the maids to the task. "I'll have no mud in this house."

Neville cast a look at his clothes. He had cut the tree himself, and his coat and trousers were all the worse for it. "I have to go wash."

"As do we all." Tom removed his spectacles and cleaned them with his handkerchief. During the felling of the tree, he'd somehow got sap on his lenses. "I'll see you at tea?"

Neville nodded before turning toward the cliff road. He had rooms in the house but rarely used them except for sleeping and changing into dinner dress. The rest of the time he preferred his room over the stables. He had an iron bedstead there, a writing desk, and a humble wardrobe in which he kept most of his clothing. As an added enticement, there was a washstand that had been plumbed for hot and cold running water.

It was an improvement Justin had insisted on for the horses in the stable below. Routing some of it to the rooms above had been no trouble at all.

"Just don't use it as an excuse to never come up to the house," Justin had said at the time. "You're not a groom, however much you may like playing at one."

Neville didn't care what his title was, as long as he could do what he wanted. At the convent he'd been under the head groom, and had often wished he could take the top position for himself. But the Reverend Mother would never have permitted it. It would have violated her stricture that Neville be seen and not heard.

He climbed the stairs to his room and shut the door behind him. It took no time at all to wash and change into a clean pair of trousers, a white linen shirt, and dark cloth waistcoat. He looked at himself in the mirror above the washstand as he tied his cravat.

Miss Hartwright had compared him to Sir Galahad. Neville supposed it was a compliment. A roundabout way of calling him handsome. And perhaps she thought he was.

The idea filled him with an uneasy warmth.

As a boy, he'd frequently been praised for his good looks. Though, after the accident, such sentiments had often been tinged with regret. *Such a shame*, people would say. *Such a waste.*

He'd be lying to himself if he said it hadn't hurt.

What man wished to be thought of in such terms? It wasn't how he thought of himself. His world might have been limited, but his life after leaving the orphanage hadn't been so terrible.

Not as bleak as the years he'd spent within that grim institution.

Delivered to the place as an infant, he'd lived eleven years inside its walls. Eleven long years being subjected to ice-cold dormitories, spoiled food, and beatings for infractions both real and imagined.

But such hardships hadn't mattered overmuch. Not when he'd had Justin, Alex, and Tom to rely on. They'd been his friends. His *family*.

After Neville's accident, they'd all gone their separate ways. Justin had been apprenticed to a blacksmith, and then later joined the army. Tom had moved to London to begin his legal training. And Alex had vanished, seemingly into thin air.

Only Neville had remained. He'd been removed to the convent forthwith. Provided for, but otherwise forgotten.

Alone for the first time in his life, he'd spent many a night in tearful anguish over the loss of his friends, and many more over the loss of his speech. It had taken the better part of a year for him to settle into his new routine. To acclimate himself to silence and solitude.

It hadn't been easy. But in the end, when grief had at last given way to acceptance, he'd found a measure of contentment at St. Crispin's. More than contentment. He'd been happy working in the convent stables, and happier still when he'd come home to Greyfriar's Abbey.

He knew he could find that level of happiness again, given the chance.

This feeling of restlessness—of melancholy—that had plagued him of late was sure to pass. Miss Hartwright would be leaving soon. And he would be getting back to his work. To his life, here at the Abbey.

He shrugged on his coat, swept up his beaver hat in his hand, and departed for the house. It was a cold and dreary morning, though not a rainy one. He was grateful for the warmth of the Abbey. It enveloped him as soon as he crossed the threshold into the main hall.

He stopped in the middle of the carpeted floor to remove his hat and coat. The butler wasn't about. No doubt he'd joined Mrs. Quill outside to oversee the preparations for bringing in the Christmas tree. It was an undertaking that affected his domain as much as hers.

"Mr. Cross!"

Neville's head jerked up at the sound of the familiar laughing voice. It was Mary, the housemaid. The one who got such pleasure in teasing him. He was hard-pressed to conceal a grimace.

She crossed the hall with a bouncing step, stopping directly in front of him. "Just look at where you're standing, sir. Almost as if you'd planned it so."

He gave her a blank look.

She giggled and pointed upward. "You're under the mistletoe, ain't you?"

His gaze shot up. Sure enough, there was a cluster of yellow-green leaves and white berries above him, suspended from the gasolier with a red velvet ribbon. He felt the unholy temptation to snatch it down. "This isn't the time. I'm in…n-no mood to—"

"Ah, listen to you stammer," she teased. "Don't be nervous. Everyone kisses under the mistletoe at Christmas. It's bad luck not to."

"It's not—"

Before he could finish his sentence, she jumped up, flung her arms around his neck, and kissed him hard on the mouth.

He pulled back immediately, setting his hands at her waist to keep her from falling against him. Mary was a tall girl, but not anywhere near as tall as he was. She'd practically had to leap on him to kiss him.

Her arms still twined around his neck, she gave him a cheeky grin. And then she looked up at the landing. "Sorry, miss. Didn't mean to shock you."

Neville stomach sank. Somehow he knew who it was even before he turned to find Miss Hartwright standing at the top of the stairs.

His hands fell from Mary's waist. He drew away from her, forcing her to release his neck.

"Privilege of the season," Mary said, giggling. She dropped a curtsy and darted out through the door to the servants' stairs. As it shut behind her, she and another maid burst into raucous laughter.

Neville stared up at Miss Hartwright. His heart pumped in a heavy, desperate rhythm. For the life of him, he couldn't think of anything to say.

Very slowly, she descended the steps. Her face was a mask of genteel composure. Her eyes downcast, her lips compressed.

"Miss Hartwright—"

"Mr. Cross." There was a faint tremor in her voice. So faint, he wasn't sure he didn't imagine it. "Forgive me for interrupting you. Do you perhaps know if—"

"You weren't interrupting—"

"It's quite all right. I've only come down to ask if you know whether there's a way I might send a telegram?"

He blinked. "To where?"

To whom? he wanted to ask.

"Edinburgh," she said. "I can pay for it."

The telegraph office in King's Abbot was only open until noon on Sundays. Neville knew that well enough. He'd sent messages there as part of his duties for Mr. Boothroyd. "You c-can write it out. Someone will…will have to t-take it down to…to the village."

She pressed a hand flat against her midriff. It was the only sign that she was upset. "How soon can they take it?"

And suddenly he knew he'd do anything to remove that worried expression from her face. "I'll take it. I can…at once."

She nodded. "Very well. Give me a moment to write the message down. It's rather private."

He stood there, unable to formulate another word, as she slipped into the library.

A kiss under the mistletoe was no great thing. It was a Christmas tradition, that was all. Why then did he have the decided impression that he'd done something wrong? That he'd broken some part of the friendship he was forging with Miss Hartwright?

Broken it. Ruined it.

He didn't understand the why of it. All he knew was that, somehow, he had to make it right.

Chapter Eleven

Clara stood from her chair and walked to her bedroom window, stretching her arms as she went. She'd been up since dawn attending to Mrs. Bainbridge's basket of mending. Her back and neck ached, and her fingers were cramped from needlework.

Outside, the sky was gray but it wasn't raining. It was too cold for rain. The sort of heavy, ice-infused weather that promised a flurry of snow.

Did it snow in Devon?

Clara hadn't any notion. She hardly cared. Since sending a telegram to Mama yesterday, she'd merely been going through the motions. Trying to keep herself busy. So busy she wouldn't have time to dwell on that unsettling duplicate lesson—or on the kiss she'd interrupted between Mr. Cross and his pretty housemaid.

She felt like a fool on both counts. It was a familiar sensation, if not a pleasant one. She'd been a fool before. Not only with her studies, but with a man. She'd vowed never to repeat the experience.

And she hadn't. Not publicly, at least. Outwardly, she was resolved to comport herself with as much dignity as she could muster.

When Mr. Cross had returned from the telegraph office, she'd thanked him as civilly as if she'd never seen him kissing someone under the mistletoe. She'd been equally civil in the drawing room, when they'd all gathered to gild acorns and walnuts, and all through dinner, though her elegant meal tasted like sawdust in her mouth.

After dinner Mrs. Finchley had played carols on the piano, and they'd eaten fresh baked gingerbread and drunk mulled wine. Everyone had been merry. Even Clara, who had pasted a smile on her face so determinedly that by the time she retired to bed, her cheeks were aching.

Mama hadn't wired her back as yet. Perhaps she wouldn't respond at all. Perhaps, as had happened in the last crisis, Clara was entirely on her own.

The prospect weighed heavily on her heart.

She rested her forehead against a frozen pane of glass. The household still slept, but the servants were up and about. Outside, a groom was leading a horse up the drive, and one of the housemaids was smiling and laughing with a roguish young footman. The two mastiffs, Paul and Jonesy, trotted by them, heading toward the stables.

Mr. Cross followed. His blond head was bent, his hands shoved into the pockets of a heavy woolen coat. As he passed her window, he glanced up.

Their eyes met for an electric instant.

She took a hasty step back, one hand lifting reflexively to her throat to close the opening of her lawn wrapper. A rush of scalding heat swept up her neck and into her face.

What had she been thinking to stand so brazenly at the glass? Her hair was unbound, for heaven's sake, and she was wearing naught but her nightgown and wrapper.

No wonder Mr. Cross had stopped to gape at her.

He already felt awkward enough in her company after she'd interrupted his kiss with the maid. He'd avoided talking to her through most of the afternoon and evening, and when he *had* managed a few words, they'd been produced with even more difficulty than usual. He'd plainly been embarrassed.

And he was sure to feel doubly so now.

Had she the luxury of time, Clara would have remained hidden in her room with Bertie for the rest of the morning, nursing her mortification. But her time wasn't her own. She shook off her humiliation and went to the washstand, filling it from the pitcher of cold water that stood near the bowl.

In short order, she was washed and dressed, her hair arranged in a thick roll at her nape. She stuck her stocking feet into a pair of slippers and went to the adjoining room to look in on Mrs. Bainbridge.

"Ah, there you are, Miss Hartwright." Mrs. Bainbridge was propped up in her bed, a frilly cap atop her disheveled curls. She held a book open in her hand. "I reckoned you for an early riser. Have you been up long?"

"Since sunrise," Clara said. "I've been doing the mending."

"Excellent." Mrs. Bainbridge turned the page of her book. "Look here. Did you know that Barnstaple is the oldest borough in England?"

"Er, no. I don't know anything about Barnstaple, I'm afraid."

"Mr. Boothroyd has a house in the valley there. He means to take up residence when he retires from his role as steward to Mr. Thornhill." Mrs. Bainbridge read aloud from her book. "'As a place of abode, Barnstaple is healthful, pleasant, and convenient.'" She looked up. "What do you think of that, my dear?"

"It sounds very..."

"'Healthful,' the writer says. Do you imagine it's true?" Mrs. Bainbridge closed her book, setting it on her bedside table. "I've never heard such a thing about any town hereabouts. Except for Bath, of course." She moved to rise.

Clara hurried to her side. "Let me help you."

Mrs. Bainbridge waved her away. "My niece has the notion that I'm an invalid, but I'm not yet at my last prayer. Do bring me my dressing gown, won't you?"

Clara retrieved the voluminous garment from the back of a nearby chair and held it open for Mrs. Bainbridge. "Shall I call for hot water?"

"Not yet. I mean to breakfast in bed, and then I shall wash and dress." Mrs. Bainbridge slid her arms into the sleeves of her dressing gown. "Now, all I require is a bit of privacy. You may come back for me at ten o'clock."

"Yes, ma'am." Clara withdrew from Mrs. Bainbridge's room and returned to her own. If she had an hour or two to herself, she might as well use it to attend to Bertie.

She slipped on her cloak and boots and gathered him up in her arms. He was warm and heavy against her chest. She held him tight. "Are you ready to go out?"

He blinked up at her, exhaling a snuffling breath.

She pressed a swift kiss to his forehead as she walked to the door. "Good boy, Bertie."

The hall outside her bedroom was empty. She headed toward the main staircase, her footsteps silent on the thick carpet. Only when she reached the entry hall did she encounter any servants. The elderly butler was there, appearing as if by magic, to open the door for her.

"Good morning, Miss Hartwright," he said. "Mind how you go."

"Thank you. I will." She went past him out the door and down the front steps. The frigid morning air bit at her face. It smelled of the sea—wild and salty sharp. She inhaled a deep breath of it.

If she had any sense of modesty, she'd avoid the stables. After her exhibition at the window, it would save her untold embarrassment. Then again, avoiding Mr. Cross would only serve to make their future interactions more awkward.

No. It was better to act as normal. To do precisely what she would have done if he hadn't spied her in a state of undress.

She began to descend the cliff road but had gone no more than a few steps when a thunderous noise sounded behind her. Turning sharply, she was very nearly knocked over by two galloping mastiffs.

"Look out!" Mr. Cross shouted. The wind whipped away his voice.

She clutched Bertie tight as Paul and Jonesy ran by, disappearing over the side of the cliffs.

Mr. Cross came after them to stop at her side. He looked more concerned with her safety than he was with theirs. "Are you…?"

"I'm fine," she said. "Are *they*?"

He followed her startled gaze to the cliff's edge. "It's the path to the beach."

"Is it? My goodness." She exhaled the breath she'd been holding. "I thought they'd leapt over the side."

He looked back at her, his gaze holding hers.

She was reminded of how he'd stared up at her as she stood at her window. There was warmth in his eyes. Wariness, too. Her stomach performed a disconcerting somersault. "Are you going with them?"

"Yes."

"Oh." She couldn't hide her disappointment. "I was bringing Bertie to the stables. I thought—"

"He can come."

"Down there?"

"Why not?"

"Is it safe? The path, I mean. It doesn't look as if it is." She took an unconscious step backward. "And it's very cold. Bertie won't like it."

"Let him down."

"What? Here?"

"He'll follow the other dogs." Mr. Cross gave a low whistle. Seconds later, one of the mastiffs loped up over the side of the cliff, his tongue lolling. "See? There's Paul."

She bit her lip. "Very well." Reluctantly, she set Bertie down on the mud and gravel road. At the sight of Paul, the little pug barked twice—a high, hoarse yip—and trotted off.

Paul ducked and weaved, bowing to Bertie once before turning and clambering back over the cliffs. Bertie followed without hesitation.

"Well." A slow smile crept over Clara's face. "It seems I've been making a mountain out of a molehill."

Mr. Cross's mouth curved up slightly. "He's a dog."

"I suppose he is, at heart. Though he hasn't lived like one for most of his life."

"He knows what he is."

"It seems he does." She gave a sudden laugh. It was tinged with rueful awareness. "Would that we all had the same self-knowledge."

He stared down at her. His jaw was clean-shaven, his golden hair rumpled from the wind. He was ridiculously handsome by any measure. But it wasn't his face that captivated her attention, nor even his tall, strapping frame, standing over her like some Arthurian hero come to life. It was his eyes. The look in them was strangely intent.

An image of him kissing the housemaid sprang into her mind.

She moistened her lips. "You may take Bertie—"

"You can come—" he began at the same time.

She bent her head, nearly laughing again at the sheer awkwardness of it. But when she raised her eyes back to his, she saw no humor in his gaze, only the same peculiar intensity. It made her heartbeat stutter. "Do you mean it? It wouldn't be an imposition? Or a—"

"No."

She cast another wary glance at where the dogs had disappeared over the side. "You're certain I won't tumble down and break my head?"

Mr. Cross didn't answer, merely walked to the cliff's edge. She trailed after him, craning her neck to look over the side. There *was* a path there, albeit a dangerously steep one. It wound in a narrow, haphazard fashion to the beach below.

He looked back over his shoulder. "I'll go first. Like on the stairs."

She nodded, waiting as he ventured down ahead of her. He'd gone no more than a few steps when he turned and offered her his hand.

Clara swallowed hard. And then she took it.

As he led her down the path, loose stones skittered beneath her boots. But it wasn't fear that made her pulse leap and her palms grow damp beneath her gloves. At least, not *only* fear.

"Is there no other way to the beach?" she asked.

"None easier."

"How unfortunate. Though it appears as if the dogs— *Oh!*" Her foot slipped straight out from under her. She pitched forward.

Mr. Cross caught her about the waist with his left arm, his right hand still holding tight to hers. "I have you."

She hung onto him for dear life. "Heavens. I very nearly—"

"I won't let you fall."

"That's all very well, but…what if *you* should fall?"

"I won't." His voice was a deep rumble near her ear. "I'm not clumsy."

His blunt statement startled another laugh out of her. "Nor am I, sir. Not under usual circumstances."

Mr. Cross's arm remained around her until they reached the bottom. There, he released her and leapt down to the beach. He turned and reached for her, his hands closing about her waist to lift her gently onto the sand.

He hadn't asked for permission. It was a courtesy, nothing more, and one he didn't push beyond its limits. He released her as soon as her feet touched the ground. Nevertheless, her heart pounded like a trip-hammer. As she straightened her cloak and skirts, she fancied she could still feel the heat of his touch all the way through her woolen gown and corset.

Thank goodness for the dogs. No sooner had she and Mr. Cross appeared than they all galloped toward them, barking and yipping like mad, the wet sand churning beneath their paws.

Mr. Cross bent to pick up a large stick from the beach. He threw it for them in a wide arc. The dogs immediately gave chase. Even Bertie—who looked to be having the time of his life.

Clara smiled. "How happy he is."

"He belongs in the country."

"He hasn't much choice in the matter. No more than I." She strolled along the edge of the water, her eyes fixed on the dogs playing in the distance. "If Mrs. Bainbridge decides to go to France with Mr. and Mrs. Archer, I shall have to find a new position."

"You won't go with her?"

"I can't. I have to remain close to my mother and brother. They rely on my employment." She paused before explaining, "My brother, Simon, is at Cambridge. My grandfather left a small sum for his education, but it isn't enough on its own. My mother and I make up the rest with our wages. It's a very near thing."

A vast understatement.

It took nearly every penny she made, and every penny Mama made, to pay Simon's fees. A university education was expensive. And she owed it to her brother. If not for her, he'd have been blessed with a scholarship, or perhaps even a patron.

"I can't just go off to France without a by-your-leave," she went on. "If something were to happen there—if I lost my position, or became hurt or ill—what on earth would I do? How could I afford passage home? And how would I manage to travel all the way back to England alone? It isn't at all feasible. Not with my family depending on me."

Mr. Cross was silent.

She folded her arms. "I daresay you think it strange that I must work for the benefit of my brother. In most circumstances it would be the other way around, with him helping to support me. But he's doing so, in his way. When he's finished at university and begins his profession, he'll take me on as his secretary. I'm to catalogue his collections and compile research for the articles he'll write."

"What collections?"

"Beetles, butterflies, and suchlike. He finds them on field trips with his schoolmates. His rooms are filled with them." A flash of uncertainty made her hesitate. "Or so he tells me in his letters."

The younger mastiff, Paul, loped forward with the stick in his teeth. Mr. Cross took it from him and threw it again. Paul galloped after it. Bertie and Jonesy ran along with him, barking their encouragement.

Mr. Cross dusted the wet sand from his hands. "Do you like insects?"

"Not especially. But Simon intends to be a natural historian, like Mr. Darwin. And I do enjoy sketching butterflies, and painting them in watercolors—though I'm not very skilled at it." She frowned. "No. It's not the insects I like. It's the organization of it all. Categorizing things and sorting them into neat little columns. It's orderly work."

"Like keeping ledgers."

"Yes, I suppose." She cast him a glance. "And you? Do you enjoy balancing ledgers and keeping accounts?"

He walked at her side, so close that his leg brushed against her skirts. "It's work, not pleasure."

"The two aren't mutually exclusive, you know. One can enjoy one's work. Why else do you think gentlemen take up certain professions? They have a true interest in law or medicine. A calling for the church, or a yearning to join Her Majesty's Navy."

"It isn't always a choice."

"No. I suppose not." She wondered how much choice Mr. Cross had been given when living in the orphanage. Or later, in the convent. She wondered how much choice he had now. "But all the same, one needn't be miserable."

"I'm not miserable."

"I was speaking in generalities. I wouldn't presume to voice any opinion on your work. Not this early in our acquaintance. We don't know each other well enough."

Paul brought the stick back to Mr. Cross and he threw it again with uncommon strength. It spun over itself, round and round, as it sailed through the air. The dogs followed with a storm of barking.

He looked at her. "But...you do have an opinion?"

"Not an opinion. I only wonder—"

"About what?"

"About you." Warmth seeped into her cheeks. "Just...you."

Chapter Twelve

"What about me?" Mr. Cross asked.

"I don't know. All sorts of things, I suppose." A cold gust of wind over the sea whipped at the ribbons of Clara's silk bonnet. She brushed them back from her face. "When I first arrived here, I couldn't tell if you were a groom, or a guest, or even a gentleman."

He didn't reply. But his head was bent, listening to her as they walked.

"And now I wonder why, when you're so happily disposed toward animals and outdoor work, you'd wish to take up a position that ties you to a desk and ledger."

He absorbed her words in stony silence. A long moment passed, and then: "I wonder about you," he countered.

Her eyes met his.

"I wonder why you were...upset...yesterday. And why you sent that t-telegram."

"It was to my mother. In Edinburgh."

"I know that much."

"Yes, well..." Clara generally preferred to keep her own counsel on family matters. But it wasn't as if it was a secret. "My mother rarely answers the letters I write to her, not as a matter of course, and never in a timely fashion. If I want to learn anything about my brother, it seemed more expedient to wire her." She kicked at a small rise of wet sand. "There's a chance she's aware of things that haven't yet been made known to me."

"Such as?"

She sighed. "I don't know. It may very well be nothing, but...I can't seem to rid myself of the feeling that something is wrong."

Mr. Cross fell quiet again as they walked.

It prompted her to confide even more. "He sends me his notes from his lectures and readings, and from the sessions with his tutors."

"Why?"

"So that I might learn what he's learning. His notes permit me to attend Cambridge, too, after a fashion. It's unconventional, to be sure, but there's nothing so shocking about it."

She knew her words to be false as soon as she uttered them.

It *was* shocking. And grossly unladylike. She was stealing knowledge meant only for her brother. Presuming to raise herself to the level of a gentleman, even if only to a lesser degree. A lady wouldn't aspire to such. And if she did, she'd have the good sense to restrict her studies to their proper milieu. A ladies' society, or better yet, the tutelage of an indulgent husband.

She waited for Mr. Cross to condemn her. To meet her confession with a cool remark, or a look of masculine condescension.

He did neither.

"I don't think it's shocking," he said. "It's...it's good to learn things."

Some of the tension left her shoulders. His words were an unexpected balm to her frayed nerves. "That's certainly how I've always viewed it. When he was at home, Simon often shared his lessons with me. Until—" She stopped herself, realizing too late what she'd almost said

Mr. Cross looked at her. "Until what?"

A familiar chill threatened at the edges of her wellbeing. It was a bad memory, nothing more. Sometimes she could almost convince herself that it hadn't happened at all. Or else that it had happened to another person.

"My brother used to be tutored at home by our local squire's son. He was a Cambridge man himself and was helping to prepare Simon for university. But then...four years ago, Mama decided it was best if Simon went away to school. She sent him to a proper boy's school in the north. A year later, he left for Cambridge."

It was the truth, though not the whole of it. She'd omitted her own part in the matter. The conduct that had lost Simon his tutor, and Clara her place as teacher at the village school. It was her own cross to bear. Her secret shame. And besides, it was long ago. Years and years now. It had no relevance to her conversation with Mr. Cross.

"And you continued your studies by post?"

She nodded. "I've been accustomed to receiving Simon's packets of notes twice a month. But lately, some have begun to seem similar. And on Monday, when I arrived, I received an actual word-for-word copy of an earlier lesson. I can't even be sure it was my brother who wrote it."

"If he didn't, then…?"

"I haven't any notion. It's all exceedingly strange. I begin to think I'm mistaken or have imagined it all in some fit of fancy."

"What will you do?" he asked.

"I don't know. I pray my mother will advise me when she replies to my wire."

If she replied.

And there was the rub of it. Mama had always put her own work ahead of the demands of her family. Clara admired her for it. Had even sought to emulate her. But in times of crisis, it was rather hard.

"I'm sure there's a simple explanation. There usually is where one's brother is concerned. It's ridiculous to fret. But I haven't seen Simon since he left for university. He spends all of his holidays with his friends. Goodness knows what he might be up to." She could imagine all sorts of terrible things having gone wrong, from masculine pranks and mischief to broken limbs—or worse. "And here I am, fretting nonetheless. I've been anxious over it since yesterday."

Mr. Cross looked out across the sea, his expression inscrutable. "I thought…" He struggled for his words. "I thought it was…because of…of Mary."

Mary?

"Is that her name?" Clara couldn't keep the note of dryness from her voice. "She's very pretty."

"The mistletoe..." He scrubbed his jaw with one hand. "*She* k-kissed *me*."

"So I saw." Sea foam rolled up onto the sand, frothing near her half boots. She stepped away from it without thought, focusing on the dogs playing up ahead. Bertie was right in the thick of things, snapping at the stick Paul still carried in his mouth. "Did you truly think that was why I was upset? Because I encountered you kissing a pretty maidservant?"

"It wasn't..." His brows lowered. "Mary is... She..."

"She likes you. It's plain enough. Who wouldn't?"

He thrust his hands into his pockets. "Do you?"

It was a simple enough question. Yet there was an undercurrent to it. Something imbued in those two short words that made his enquiry feel weighty. Important.

She answered carefully. With honesty, though not, perhaps, with soul-baring candor. "I like you very much. I hope we've become friends."

His footsteps slowed. Again, he looked out at the sea, his gaze fixed at a point over her head, and past it. A muscle tightened in his jaw. "Friends."

"Friendship is a precious thing."

"I have friends."

"One can have several. An infinite amount. There's not a limit that I'm aware of."

"Is that all?"

She wanted to pretend she didn't understand him. That she'd lost the thread of their conversation. But that would have been a lie. "Was it only the mistletoe?" she asked instead.

His gaze slid back to her face.

"That is..." She stopped on the wet sand, arms still folded at her waist. "I understand there was mistletoe. And kissing someone you encounter under it is practically obligatory. What I wonder is...was it *only* that?"

He came to a halt in front of her. "I don't..."

"Would you have kissed Mary in the stables? Or here, on the beach?"

"Of course not."

"I see." Her stomach trembled. She told herself to be quiet. To change the subject or make her excuses and return to the house. Such warnings proved useless. The words tumbled from her lips nonetheless. "Is there anyone you *would* wish to kiss outside the presence of mistletoe?"

He gave her a wry look.

Her heart thumped hard. She was standing on the precipice. It wasn't too late to step back. To choose a different course. But for all her feminine resolve—all her determination never to repeat past transgressions—she seemed powerless to stop herself.

"You're very tall. I shall have to stand on something." She glanced about the beach, trying to ignore the fact that a scalding blush was burning its way from her throat all the way to the roots of her hair. "Is there a boulder hereabouts?"

Mr. Cross was staring at her, his expression intent. His throat contracted on a swallow. And then he turned his head, scanning the beach. "There."

A few yards from the path, a rock formation as high as her knees protruded from the base of the cliffs. She crossed the sand and climbed atop it, her skirts clutched in one gloved hand.

Mr. Cross came to stand in front of her. He continued to regard her with that same intent gaze. Alert. As if she were a wild Dartmoor pony who might bolt at any moment.

She was assailed by a surge of self-doubt. "You did mean me, didn't you? That I'm the one you wish to kiss? I wasn't imagining it, was I?"

His neck had gone faintly red, and twin banners of color stood out on his cheekbones. He was still taller than her, despite her stance on the boulder. "I meant you."

Her lips trembled on a faint smile. "That's a relief."

She waited, but he didn't move to embrace her. He merely looked at her. Watchful and patient, just as he was with Betty. So she did precisely what she most yearned to do. She took his face in her hands, cradling it tenderly. And, stretching up, she pressed a soft kiss to his mouth.

His arm came around her waist then, and he bent his head to hers. He kissed her back, gently, ever so gently. A sweet, lingering kiss that made her knees go weak.

When at last their lips parted, it was her turn to be at a loss for words.

Mr. Cross loomed over her. He was still slightly red about the collar but otherwise appeared in complete command of the situation. "May I call you Clara?"

"If you like." She was appalled to hear a quaver in her voice. Goodness' sake, it was just a kiss. It had scarcely lasted five seconds—a fact which hadn't seemed to matter to the butterflies rampaging in her stomach. She dropped her hands from his face.

He helped her down from the boulder, and when the dogs came, barking their eagerness to return to the house, he assisted her back up the cliff path, one hand holding hers, and the other guiding her at the small of her back with a touch that was vaguely proprietary.

And she had the sinking suspicion that she'd underestimated him. Or, at the very least, mischaracterized him. That she'd painted him in her mind as some innocent gentle giant who was too good for this world. A handsome, golden Galahad.

And perhaps he *was* innocent.

But Neville Cross was no boy. He was a man. A great, healthy male, as potentially dangerous to her virtue as any other.

Good lord. What had she begun?

Chapter Thirteen

Neville held the basket of tree candles up so Tom could reach them. He stood on a high ladder, wiring them to the topmost branches.

Jenny was similarly occupied with the branches at the bottom. Her silk skirts pooled all about her as she knelt on the floor. "Will there be enough?"

"There's more in the kitchens." Lady Helena tied a frosted glass ornament to a branch with a bit of red velvet ribbon. "We have plenty of everything. Don't feel obliged to stint."

Neville exchanged a look with Justin. Last year, with their dutiful assistance, Lady Helena had managed to cover most of the surfaces inside the Abbey with greenery, ribbons, and tinsel. There was no question of stinting on anything. She'd been determined to give them a Christmas to remember. And it had been, for both Justin and for Neville.

But this Christmas, he suspected it would be even more so. Not because the celebration was grander in scale, but because all of them were together. Neville, Justin, Tom, and Alex. Reunited for the holidays for the first time in two decades.

And because of *her*.

Clara.

"It's a splendid tree." Mrs. Bainbridge helped herself to one of the candles from Neville's basket. "The largest I've ever seen."

Clara was beside her, with a handful of gilded acorns and walnuts. Each had a long tack hammered into the end, which she was using to string them into the branches.

"We had a tree in Surrey last Christmas," Mrs. Bainbridge went on. "A frail little thing that could scarcely hold its ornaments. Our cat, Magpie, was intent on destroying it."

"You may thank Mr. Cross for the size of this one." Tom secured another candle with a bit of wire. "He cut it himself. The rest of us only helped to get it into the cart."

Clara glanced at Neville. Their eyes met for a moment. She swiftly looked away, the faintest of blushes darkening her cheeks.

He was viscerally reminded of their kiss. How she'd cradled his face so gently between her palms. How her lips had clung to his so sweetly. It had sent a rush of heat through him. Had prompted him to put his arm around her waist and to kiss her back.

It had been only a brief moment. A few seconds of soul-stirring tenderness while the raging sea crashed on the shore and the wind whistled all about them.

But it had changed everything.

Not only for him, but for her. He'd seen it clear as day in her face. A notch had worked itself between her brows as she gazed up at him. As if she were seeing him with new eyes.

He hoped that she was.

Though for what purpose, he didn't know. Their time together was rapidly coming to an end. Tomorrow was Christmas. And then, in twelve more days, she'd be gone. They had no future together.

A fact that hadn't stopped him from replaying their kiss over and over again in his mind as he'd gone about his work.

The warmth of it still hadn't dissipated.

He felt, rather fancifully, as if it never would.

"Who will put the star on top?" Laura asked, approaching the tree.

Alex caught her hand as she passed, and pressed a discreet kiss to her palm. Her fingers curled to brush against his cheek in an affectionate caress.

Neville looked away. With all three couples in residence, it was impossible to avoid such displays. Justin and Lady Helena could scarcely be out of each other's sight, and Tom and Jenny were forever making excuses to touch each other.

Alex and Laura were the worst offenders. Though the two newlyweds tried for discretion, one would have had to be blind not to observe their stolen kisses, clasped hands, and molten glances.

Neville didn't begrudge any of his friends the affection they shared with their wives. All the same, it was dashed awkward at times.

Was it any wonder Mr. Boothroyd was making such an effort with Mrs. Bainbridge? He was probably tired of being one of only two unattached people in residence, and sought to strike up a romance of his own. Either that or he'd developed a genuine affection for Laura's aunt.

"Tom's already on the ladder," Jenny said. "Shall he do it?"

"Justin must do it." Lady Helena handed the large tinsel star to her husband. "It's our tradition."

Tom climbed down from the ladder. "I won't argue with tradition."

"I've done it all of one time." Justin took Tom's place. The ladder creaked beneath his weight. "I'm hardly an expert of longstanding."

"Expertise is not required," Lady Helena said. "Only that you be the master of the house."

Justin set the star atop the tree. It tilted precariously to one side. He leaned against the branches, stretching out a hand to straighten it. The ladder swayed.

"Have a care, sir!" Mr. Boothroyd exclaimed.

Neville came forward to brace the ladder. Lady Helena stepped back, permitting him to take charge.

"It's perfect as it is, Justin," she said. "Do come down now."

Justin descended with ease. He drew Lady Helena to him. "What do you think?"

She leaned into his side. "I think it's beautiful. But…"

"But?"

"The tree needs a bit more tinsel."

Jenny laughed. "There's plenty of that."

A footman carried out the wassail bowl, and another the bowl of cider. Two maidservants brought trays of spiced ale and cake. The tree trimming continued in earnest as the guests drank, and ate, and laughed.

"Clara," Teddy said. "What happened to all of that fruit we wrapped in gold foil?"

"It's here." Clara fetched one of the baskets and brought it to him.

As she crossed the floor, Neville helped himself to a golden apple. Her eyes met his again as he took it.

She gave him an uncertain smile, the blush still high in her cheeks. "I haven't seen you since this morning."

"I've been at the stables."

"With Betty?" She handed the basket of golden fruit to Teddy.

"Is that the wild pony?" he asked. "Laura mentioned there was one in residence."

"There is," Clara said. "And there will be another soon. She's expecting a foal."

"Oh?" Teddy appeared only mildly interested. He began tucking the fruit into the branches he could reach from his wheeled chair. "Alex? Come and put some of these near the top, will you?"

Alex joined his brother-in-law. "Is the lack of symmetry bothering your artistic sensibilities?"

"As a matter of fact," Teddy said, "it is."

Clara drifted away from the conversation, and Neville followed. "How is Betty?"

"Restless."

"Can you walk her yet?"

He shook his head. If Betty were a lame saddle horse, he'd lead her up and down the drive for a bit of gentle exercise. But she was only now becoming accustomed to letting him lead her out of the loose box. Anything more would likely result in her thrashing about and re-injuring her leg.

"I mean to turn her out. In the p-paddock behind the stables."

Clara's brows lifted. "When?"

"In the morning." It would be quieter then. Lady Helena was giving most of the servants the early hours off with their families, and the guests would be occupied all day with feasting and opening gifts.

He wondered if Clara could be persuaded to steal away from the Christmas festivities long enough to see Betty in the paddock.

Would she even want to?

He knew now that what she felt for him was more than mere awareness. More, even, than friendship.

It gave him confidence. And yet…

At the same time, he found himself feeling more uncertain than ever. Not only of her, but of himself. He couldn't dismiss their kiss as a Christmas tradition. There had been no mistletoe on the beach. When their lips had met, he'd known in his bones that it was significant. That it could be the beginning of something.

Which was precisely why a gentleman wasn't supposed to kiss a lady, or meddle with her affections. Not unless his intentions were honorable.

And how could Neville have any intentions, honorable or otherwise? He was in no position to do so. He *knew* that.

The whole of it was a futile enterprise, which would only result in her being hurt or compromised in some way. He resolved to behave better in future. To act the gentleman with Clara, even if it killed him.

"I'd like to be there," she said.

He gave her an alert look. "Tomorrow?"

"At the paddock. Unless I'd be intruding. I wouldn't wish to upset Betty."

And just like that, all of his gentlemanly resolve flew right out the window. "You wouldn't," he said. "I...I want you to come."

Christmas morning dawned gray and wet. Outside, the storm was still raging, the rain falling in a continuous drumbeat against the windows and roof. Clara expected that any plans for turning out Betty would be scuttled. However, when she brought Bertie down to the kitchens for his breakfast, it was to find Mr. Cross sitting at the long wooden table.

He was garbed in a heavy wool coat and trousers, his blond hair rumpled in a most attractive fashion. His gaze was fixed at the entrance to the kitchens. When he saw her, he sprang to his feet.

"Are you waiting for me?" she asked.

His face fell. "Have you changed your m-mind?"

"No, but I'd assumed, given the weather..." Clara set Bertie down with Paul and Jonesy, who were milling about nearby. "You're not going to turn Betty out, are you? Not in this maelstrom?"

"She's a wild pony."

"Yes, but—"

"A *Dartmoor* pony. She's used to the rain."

"I suppose." She hadn't thought of it that way. "May I have a moment to drink a cup of tea? I feel I'll need one if I'm to go out in all that."

"I'll make it."

She opened her mouth to object, but Mr. Cross forestalled her.

"Sit down," he said. "I know what I'm doing."

Reluctantly, she sank into one of the straight-backed wooden chairs at the table.

He lit the stove and put on the kettle. A tin of tea leaves was produced from one cupboard, and two cups and saucers from another. He placed them on the table, along with a pitcher of milk.

"You're very efficient," she said.

"Anyone c-can make tea." He added leaves to the pot, and when the kettle whistled, he poured in the boiling water.

Clara expected Cook to appear at any moment and scold him for making free with the tea things. But there was no sign of her, nor of any of the other servants. The curtains in the house remained drawn, and the fires unlit. Clara supposed Lady Helena had given the servants Christmas morning off.

She drank her tea, while Mr. Cross fed the dogs their breakfast.

"We'll leave them here," he said. "They bark when...when they get excited. Betty won't like it."

"I can well imagine that." Betty wasn't much bigger than the two mastiffs. If the pair of them were barking at her, it would make coaxing her into the paddock that much more difficult.

After finishing her tea, Clara fetched her cloak and bonnet and bundled up as best she could against the rain.

Outside, the cliff road was the muddiest she'd ever seen it. She was obliged to take Mr. Cross's arm and cling to it all the way down, the two of them huddled beneath a sturdy umbrella.

"Good heavens!" she exclaimed, laughing, as they entered the stable. "What a tempest!" Her fingers were numb inside her gloves. She fumbled with the buttons at the neck of her cloak, struggling to open them.

Mr. Cross tossed aside his hat and coat before coming to assist her. Gently batting her hands away, he unfastened her cloak and stripped it off of her arms.

She shivered. "Is winter always this way in Devon?"

"It is at the Abbey."

"Because it's so near to the sea?"

"Probably." He untied the strings of her bonnet and lifted it from her head.

Her heart skipped a beat. She remembered what had happened the last time he'd removed her bonnet. How he'd looked at her, and what he'd said.

You're beautiful, Miss Hartwright.

He was looking at her the same way now, his blue eyes intent. She held her breath, expecting she knew not what. But he didn't compliment her again. He turned away to shake out her wet things and hang them up alongside his own.

"I'll have to put them on again when we go out to the paddock," she said. "They'll have no time to dry properly."

"They'll be dry enough." He might have said more, but at that moment, Mr. Thornhill's chestnut stallion thrust his head out of his loose box and whickered. Another horse echoed the greeting.

Mr. Cross went to them, offering each a soft murmur and a few firm pats on the neck. "They want their mash."

"Let them have it, by all means. I don't mind waiting." She didn't have to be back to the house for several hours. Mrs. Bainbridge never rose before nine. Clara was becoming accustomed to having the early morning to herself. And no one could begrudge it to her. Not on Christmas, surely.

She perched on the mounting block, her chin propped in one hand, while Mr. Cross took a hot bucket of mash to the stallion, and another to a dainty bay gelding. A third bucket was given to a dappled gray horse that Clara had never seen before. He was of a truly impressive size, with a thick mane and tail, and a nose that was slightly Roman.

"Who does he belong to?" she asked

"He's mine."

"Yours?" She couldn't conceal her surprise. "I didn't know you had a horse here. You never said."

"He's been in pasture. I brought him in...when the storm worsened."

She stood and went to join him. There was no question of petting the great gray beast. His nose was firmly ensconced in his bucket of mash. She leaned against the door, admiring him nonetheless. "What's his name?"

"Adventurer." There was a trace of irony in Mr. Cross's tone. "I b-bought him at...at auction in the summer."

He had bought him?

Clara hadn't given Mr. Cross's personal wealth—or lack thereof—much thought, except to note that he dressed rather humbly most of the time, and spent his days with the horses, engaged in menial tasks. She'd assumed he didn't have a great deal of money.

But if he could afford to purchase a horse of such quality, he must have some manner of income. Perhaps Mr. Thornhill had settled something on him? Clara wouldn't put it past him to have made provisions for his childhood friend. Especially given Mr. Cross's injury.

"He was meant to be a race horse," he said. "But he didn't have the heart for it."

"Or the build. He's enormous."

"He has to be."

She gave a short laugh. "I suppose it does make sense. You'd dwarf a smaller mount."

"Do you ride?" he asked.

"Only a little, and not very well. I'd never dream of attempting to handle a horse of this size." She drew back from the door. "In case you hadn't noticed, I'm not very big."

The corner of his mouth curved up. "I've n-noticed."

"Given my height, I don't wonder that all the grooms think I'm keen to make a saddle pony out of Betty." She cast a glance about her. "Are none of them here today?"

"Not this m-morning. Not yet." He made his way back to the feed room, and she followed. "Danvers is here...somewhere. He'll feed the rest of them."

Clara looked on while Mr. Cross made up another bucket of mash. She'd met the coachman, Mr. Danvers, the day she'd arrived, and then again during some of her visits to see Betty. He was a weather-beaten man in his middle forties. Civil enough, but she didn't relish encountering him when she was in company with Mr. Cross, alone and unchaperoned.

The stable was open on either end. A public place. It wouldn't be the same as being caught alone with a gentleman in a private room or a closed carriage. Still...

She knew she was playing fast and loose with her reputation. And at a time she could least afford to do so.

Mr. Cross hoisted the bucket of mash. Water sloshed over the rim. "The rain is slowing."

Clara cocked her head, listening, as she walked with him to the back of the stables. "I wish it would cease altogether."

As they approached Betty's loose box, a low groan emanated from within. The unsettling sound made Clara stop short. "What in heaven?"

Mr. Cross brushed past her to open the door. She caught a brief glimpse of Betty before he shut it behind him. The little pony was lying down on the straw, her tail raised, and her sides heaving.

A shiver of foreboding quickened Clara's pulse. She came to lean over the door of the loose box. "Is she foaling?"

"Trying to." Mr. Cross knelt down beside Betty on the straw. He talked to her in a low, soothing voice as he examined her.

"But it's too early, isn't it?"

"Yes." His hands moved slowly over Betty's swollen belly. "Something's wrong."

Clara's mouth went dry. She knew little about physicking horses, and even less about assisting in a difficult equine labor. But as she looked at Betty's trembling body—and at Mr. Cross's somber expression—her spine stiffened with resolve. "What can I do to help?"

Mr. Cross's eyes met hers over the door. "Find Danvers."

Chapter Fourteen

Neville murmured to Betty as he palpated her belly. He'd helped to deliver foals before, and knew enough to recognize that this particular one wasn't in the right position. It was turned the wrong way around in the womb, and would have to be righted if Betty was to have any hope of a safe delivery.

How long had she been in this condition?

He cursed himself for not having gone to her first. For having wasted time preparing mash for the other horses. But she'd seemed well enough when he'd checked on her last night. She'd been restless of course, but he'd attributed that to her confinement. To her need for exercise.

There had been no other symptoms of impending labor. None that he'd noticed. A mare usually exhibited signs. A distended udder, or the appearance of a yellowish wax on her teats. Betty had shown evidence of neither, which had led him to believe it would be another week, at least, before her foal would come.

Had he missed something important? Had he been so distracted by his burgeoning feelings for Clara that he'd failed to see what was right in front of his eyes?

Betty groaned again, her head moving restlessly on the straw.

Neville stroked her neck. "Easy girl," he murmured. "You'll be all right."

He prayed to God that she would be.

After everything Betty had been through, all the obstacles she'd overcome, surely she couldn't die in labor. A wild pony, breathing her last in a dratted loose box of all places. What sort of end was that for such a majestic creature? To die in captivity?

Footfalls sounded softly outside in the aisle. Seconds later, Clara's face appeared over the door, her cloak fastened at her neck. She was breathless. "I can't find Mr. Danvers. I've looked everywhere."

Neville's stomach sank. He needed someone to hold Betty while he turned the foal. He couldn't do it alone. "The Abbey—"

"I've already been there. It's what took me so long." Damp tendrils of flaxen hair framed her face. She pushed them back from her forehead. "Cook was up, but there was no sign of Mr. Danvers. She said he must have gone into the village last night, or up to one of the tenant cottages. She expects he'll be back in time for feeding the horses."

Neville muttered an oath under his breath.

"Is he the only one who can help her?" Clara asked.

"I can help her, but I n-need…I need someone to hold her head and neck." It would have to be Justin. He knew something of horses, at least, though certainly not as much as Danvers. "You'll have to fetch Thornhill."

"You want Mr. Thornhill to hold her?" Clara gave him a doubtful look. "But she doesn't even know him. If he suddenly appears and attempts to subdue her, she's bound to find it distressing. Especially after her experiences with that dreadful horse peddler."

It was the truth. Betty wasn't going to appreciate the presence of a strange man at her head. It would likely cause her to thrash about. To fight. Making the entire procedure that much more difficult.

Neville gritted his teeth. "There's no other choice. I…I have to turn the foal. She won't like it."

"You're going to press on her belly?"

"No. I…" He could think of no delicate way to describe it. "I have to…to reach inside of her."

Clara's gaze flicked to his hands. Her face paled. "Have you done that before?"

"Once."

"With a pony?"

"A c-carriage horse." He knew it didn't compare, but what else was he to do? "There's no other way."

Her delicate features hardened with feminine determination. She stripped off her gloves. "I'll help you."

He felt an unexpected rush of affection for her. And something more than that. A feeling of respect. Of deep admiration. Clara was small but mighty. She didn't quail from anything. "I…I'm…"

Humbled.

Besotted.

Halfway to falling in love with you.

"I'm grateful," he managed to say. "But…you're n-not strong enough to hold her."

"I'm stronger than I look."

"I know that. But this—"

"And if I'm not, I'll do the other bit." She removed her cloak. "You can guide me through it."

The other bit?

He stared at her. Was she suggesting that *she* would be the one to reach inside of Betty? That *she* would turn the foal? No lady would ever contemplate such a thing, let alone propose to do it. "Clara…"

"Indeed, it makes even more sense than my trying to hold her."

"I d-don't see how."

"Betty recognizes you. She's come to trust you. Who better to have at her head to soothe her?" A crimson blush rose in her face. "And besides," she said. "I have smaller hands."

Clara had no illusions about her abilities. She was small and slight and—though she loved animals—had little practical experience with them. Add to that, her woolen dress didn't exactly lend itself to equine midwifery. Her bodice was too tight, her skirts too cumbersome, and her sleeves far too long.

A willing disposition could only get one so far.

The best she could do was to listen to Mr. Cross. Not that he seemed particularly keen to accept her assistance.

"We haven't much time," he said.

"How much?"

"In the n-normal course of things?" He grimaced. "Thirty minutes. Less."

Her heartbeat quickened. "Tell me what to do."

"There's t-toweling in the feed room. And... we'll n-need hot water. A bucket of it."

She hurried off to do as instructed. It didn't take long. The Abbey stable was arranged in an orderly manner. She found clean towels folded in a feed room cupboard, and empty metal buckets stacked near the stores of grain.

After filling one of them with hot water at the tap, she raced back to Betty's loose box.

"Come inside," Mr. Cross said. "Quietly."

Clara unlatched the door and let herself in. Water sloshed over the rim of the bucket and onto the straw as she sat it down, closing the door behind her. "Where do you want me?"

"At her head," he said, matter-of-factly.

Clara wasn't surprised. The look on his face when she'd suggested reaching up inside of Betty to turn the foal had been one of gentlemanly horror. As if Clara was too lady-like to be subjected to the nether regions of a female animal.

Honestly, did he think she was made of spun sugar? That she didn't realize where it was babies came from? Some ladies might be ignorant of such matters, but she was a student of the natural world. She knew that animals and humans gave birth, and she understood the rudiments of how they did so. It was simple biological science.

"Shall I bring the towels?"

"Leave them."

She dropped the stack of towels next to the bucket of water. Her boots crunched on the straw as she made her way to Betty's head. The little pony's eyes rolled wildly at the sight of her.

"Easy, Betty," Clara whispered. "We're going to help you."

Mr. Cross held out his hand to her, and Clara took it, permitting him to assist her in kneeling down on the straw. Her skirts pooled around her in a heap of petticoats and crinoline. She'd never before felt so frustrated by the present fashion. It wasn't at all conducive to a crisis.

"Hold her neck," Mr. Cross said. "And…be c-careful of her teeth."

"She won't bite me." Clara stroked Betty's sleek brown neck. "Will you, girl? I'm not going to hurt you."

"Be careful," he said again. His tone was stern. "She might lash out."

Clara nodded. "I shall remain on my guard."

Mr. Cross rose and went to the bucket. He removed his jacket, revealing a plain black waistcoat and white linen shirt. Rolling up his sleeves, he wet his hands in the hot water.

"Is hygiene very important?" she asked.

"Warmth is." A long pause. And then: "My hands were t-too cold."

"Oh." Heat rose in Clara's face. She endeavored to ignore it. A scientist wouldn't blush.

Mr. Cross moved to Betty's hindquarters and sank down onto the straw. He spoke to her in a deep, low voice, giving her a reassuring pat on the flank, before he reached beneath her upraised tail. "She m-might struggle," he warned Clara before he proceeded further.

"I have her." Clara didn't look to see what Mr. Cross was doing. She concentrated on holding Betty's neck, murmuring to her gently. "Never mind, my dearest. It's only a brief indignity, and then all shall be well."

Betty tried to raise her head, as if to look, but Clara held her tighter. "Easy." She shot a glance in Mr. Cross's direction. "Can you feel anything?"

His brow was creased in concentration. "The head. And… one of the…of the legs."

"Only one?" She cast him another worried look. "Where's the other leg?"

He reached further inside of Betty. "Here. I feel it. It's… It's b-bent backward."

"How do you mean?" she asked. "Where should it be?"

"Both legs should be…straight out under the head. The foal c-comes out with its front hooves f-first."

"Can you straighten the bent leg?"

"I'm going to try." His gaze lifted to hers. "Clara…"

"Don't mind me," she said. "I'll put my whole weight on her neck and shoulder if I have to."

He gave her an unreadable look.

She had no time to ponder it. As soon as he resumed his task, Betty began to struggle in earnest, raising her head, and thrashing her legs.

Clara did just what she'd said she would. She draped herself over Betty's neck and shoulder, holding her tight, even as she whispered to her, begging her to please be still. "Only a moment longer," she promised.

When next she could spare a glance for Mr. Cross, she saw that his features were taut, and his hairline damp with perspiration. Whatever he was doing to straighten the foal was taking as much skill as it was strength.

The reality of the situation hit Clara all at once.

Betty could die, and her foal along with her.

What had Clara been thinking to offer her help? She was no horsewoman. No groom or stable lad with the requisite masculine strength. She was only a woman. A lady's companion, for goodness' sake.

What if she failed?

It was a real possibility. One that made Clara sick to her stomach. She feared she'd acted without thinking. That she'd been more concerned with proving herself than with respecting her own limitations.

And now, here she was. In her third best day dress, lying across the neck of a wild Dartmoor pony. Only inches from being bitten, kicked, or otherwise mauled about. She'd told Mr. Cross she was strong, but she wasn't as strong as she wished to be. As she *needed* to be.

"Are you any closer?" she asked.

"Almost. Just...a little...m-more." Mr. Cross's eyes lit with triumph. "There!" He withdrew his hand from Betty. The little pony gave a heaving groan, and then, before Clara could blink, the foal's head and front hooves appeared. The rest of it followed in a mighty rush—aided by a great deal of bodily fluids.

Mr. Cross rose swiftly to his feet. After washing and drying his hands, he caught Clara around the waist and lifted her up as well, drawing her away from Betty, and back to the door of the loose box.

"She c-can do the rest," he said. "We mustn't get in the way."

Clara nodded mutely. She could think of nothing to say. Despite all her scientific study—all those hours spent poring over dry passages in books—she'd never actually witnessed nature at its most miraculous.

It was dreadfully untidy.

And so wondrous that it brought tears to her eyes.

The foal was as sleek and brown as his mother, his impossibly long limbs folded beneath him as he lay on the straw. Remnants of after-birth clung to his motionless frame like a shroud.

Betty stood and went to him. She nuzzled him with her nose, lipping at his wet coat, and nudging him to respond.

The foal's small mouth opened and closed, as if he wished to suckle.

Clara exhaled with relief. "He's alive." She paused. "It is a he, isn't it?"

"It is."

"I thought so." Mr. Cross's arm was still settled around her—a warm, reassuring weight. He hadn't removed it after hoisting her up from the straw. She wasn't certain she wanted him to. "You must choose a name for him."

"You do it."

"Truly?"

"I…I want you to."

"Hmm." Clara examined the little creature. "He's very small. And though he's brown, his coat has a great deal of red in it. What about Firefly?"

"Firefly," Mr. Cross repeated. "I like it."

"You saved his life, you know. And hers, too, I have no doubt."

"With your help."

Pride bloomed within her. She *had* helped, hadn't she? She'd been useful in a practical, tangible way. Not only to Betty, and Firefly, but to Mr. Cross. It was a giddy feeling, and one she was careful not to indulge.

"Nonsense," she said. "Anyone could have done my part. But you…" Her voice softened. "What a blessing it was that she encountered you that day at the King's Arms."

"I wish I c-could have done more."

"You've done more than most would. More than anyone I've ever known. It's easy to see an injustice and to feel grieved by it, but most people pass on. To actually do something—to speak out against a wrong and make an effort to right it—is a rarity. How many gentlemen would have cared for the plight of an injured wild pony? Most don't even care for the plight of a poor injured child."

"They should."

"Yes, I daresay." Firefly continued mouthing the air, but he made no other effort to move. "When will he stand?"

"Within the hour." Mr. Cross's arm fell from her waist. "We'll have t-to prepare."

She looked at him in alarm. "For what? There's no other difficulty, is there?"

"Betty hasn't any milk yet. Until she does...I'll have to give him c-cow's milk."

"How?"

"With a tea kettle. You'll see." A flicker of uncertainty clouded his brow. "Unless... Do you have to go?"

"I believe I can stay another hour." She smiled. "It *is* Christmas, after all."

His mouth curved slowly. "I'd forgotten."

"I haven't." She stared up at him. And the moment was so perfect—*he* was so perfect—that she raised her hand to touch his cheek. "I shan't ever forget the events of this morning. Not for as long as I live. And I mean to live a good long while, Mr. Cross."

Warmth heated his face—and his eyes, too. As if her touch had kindled a fire within him. "Please...call me Neville."

Her pulse fluttered. It hadn't occurred to her to address him by his given name. Not even when he'd begun using hers. She was that wary of making assumptions. Of presuming an intimacy that didn't exist. "Are you certain?"

"Yes."

She drew her fingers along the rough plane of his cheek in a brief caress. He went still at her touch. Holding his breath, just as she held hers. Relishing the moment. Waiting to see what might happen next.

Who was she fooling?

This *was* intimacy. The two of them, alone together. Sharing such an experience. There was no way to mistake it. "Neville it is, then."

Chapter Fifteen

Clara returned to the house with Bertie in her arms, a growing storm not far behind her. The weather had worsened since Christmas, dark clouds gathering ominously over the sea.

She hardly noticed them. Indeed, she scarcely noticed anything of her surroundings at all. She passed through the hall in a state of pleasurable distraction, only vaguely registering the servants milling about.

It had been two days since Betty delivered her foal. Two wonderful days during which Clara had spent her every free moment at the stables.

She'd learned how to make Betty's mash, and how to feed Firefly warm cow's milk from the cloth-wrapped spout of a small teakettle. She'd laughed with Neville, and shared whispered conversation. Had marveled with him as Firefly took his first wobbly steps.

It had been a much-needed reprieve from her worries about Simon. A chance to cease studying old lessons, and to engage with nature directly. Simon referred to such activities as fieldwork. But it hadn't felt like work. It had been pure pleasure. Not only because she enjoyed being with Betty and Firefly, but because she enjoyed being with Neville.

Spending so many hours together with the ponies had accelerated their friendship like nothing else. It had made them easier in each other's company. Had brought them closer.

It had also wreaked havoc on Clara's wardrobe.

She cast a rueful glance downward. The hem of her skirts was muddy from traipsing up and down the cliff road, and her bodice was streaked with dirt. She'd vowed to be more careful of her appearance today, but had been no more successful at it.

Swiftly ascending the stairs, she went straight up to her room to change into a fresh dress.

Winter in Devon, as a whole, was rather hard on one's clothes. That is, unless one remained forever indoors. An unappealing prospect, especially now. Clara had never enjoyed being shut up in the house for hours on end.

She was just stepping out of her soiled crinoline when a knock sounded at her door. "Yes?"

"Miss Hartwright?" The Abbey's housekeeper, Mrs. Quill, entered the room, closing the door behind her. "The post came early today from the village. You received another parcel."

Clara's fingers froze on the tapes of her petticoat. "A parcel?"

The housekeeper handed Clara the large, overstuffed envelope without further comment.

"Thank you," Clara said as she took it.

It was smaller than the packets Simon usually sent. On closer inspection, she discovered the reason why.

It wasn't from her brother at all. It was from her mother in Edinburgh. And it was postmarked four days ago.

She looked up at Mrs. Quill. "Is this all I received?" she asked. "There's not a wire for me from the telegraph office?"

"No, miss. Only the parcel."

Clara's spirits sank. She needed an answer to the wire she'd sent her mother, not a packet of who knows what that had been sent days before. "Is it too late to send a reply by return post?"

"We don't get the post but once a day here, Miss Hartwright. Not like London. Not with the cliff road being dangerous as it is." The housekeeper paused, one hand resting on the doorknob. "I suppose, if it's urgent, I could send someone down to King's Abbot. The post comes there morning and evening—as late as five o'clock most days. But given the weather..."

A clap of thunder shook the windows. Outside, the storm clouds were no longer gathered over the sea. They'd moved up the cliffs, blanketing the Abbey in a fog of damp gray darkness. Rain fell again, hard and fast.

Clara was reluctant to subject a servant to such vile conditions. "It may not be necessary. I shall soon know if it is."

"Very good, miss."

Clara waited until the housekeeper was gone before tearing open the envelope. The topmost paper in the enclosure was a brief letter from her mother, but it wasn't in response to the letter Clara had sent last Monday. It appeared to have been written many days earlier.

13 December 1860

Dear Clara,

Simon has encountered some manner of trouble at school. I am not in receipt of all the particulars, but understand that it is of a grave nature. It would behoove one of us to go to there and to lend him such assistance as we may, lest the situation result in his being sent down.

I advise you to make the journey as soon as possible after Christmas. I am unable to go myself. We have ten boarders at school, and Mrs. Ginch cannot manage them alone.

While you are in Cambridge, please attend to the enclosed tradesman's bills, and bills from the university for various necessities of Simon's academic life. The bulk of these I have paid myself. The remainder, you must pay out of your savings. As for the rest, you shall have to negotiate terms.

Be mindful of your duty.

Faithfully,
Mrs. A. Hartwright

A growing sense of dread built in Clara's breast. Simon was in danger of being sent down? What in heaven had he done? She'd never heard of anyone being sent down from Cambridge, except in cases of gambling or public brawling. And even then, the conduct in question had to be egregious.

She set aside her mother's letter to examine the sheaf of bills beneath. As she paged through them, one by one, her dread rapidly gave way to anger.

Necessities of academic life?

There were bills from the bedmaker, the shoeblacker, the cook, and the laundress. And those were merely the bills from university. She found a bill from a bootmaker, a tailor in Bond Street, and a jeweler who had sold Simon a pair of engraved cufflinks. There was even a bill from a smithy, who had apparently shod a horse for her brother in early November.

Simon didn't even *have* a horse.

Clara thrust the stack of bills back into the envelope, her hands trembling.

The contents of her savings were meager. Only the pittance she'd managed to save during her time as a teacher, and the few pounds she'd set by each year since becoming a companion. It would pay some of Simon's bills, but not all of them.

How in the world was she supposed to negotiate terms?

She could hardly promise to pay the balance of Simon's debts at a later date. She had no means to find the money for them, either then or now. Her quarterly wages weren't due until next month, and she had nothing she could sell, or spout. No valuable family heirlooms, or expensive jewelry.

"Cufflinks," she muttered to herself as she changed her clothes. "Horseshoes."

Her crinoline required washing, and her gown needed to be sponged and pressed, but there was no time for it. Mrs. Bainbridge expected her back in less than half an hour.

Clara supposed she could take a few minutes to dash off a letter. But to whom could she write? Another letter to Mama would be fruitless. A letter to Simon even more so.

She was, again, completely on her own.

And now Mama expected her to go to Cambridge. To upend her life, and endanger her new position. To drop everything in order to rush to Simon's aid.

Would it have been this way if things had passed differently so many years ago in Hertfordshire? If Clara had not insinuated herself in on her brother's lessons? Had not turned a few acts of kindness into something more?

Her brother had said he'd forgiven her, but Clara knew the truth. A lifetime of servitude—of orderly thoughts, and orderly habits—would never make up for her having damaged Simon's prospects. She had been expected to pay for her sin, and would be expected to keep paying, for as long as she lived.

But she couldn't afford to let her guilt and bitterness consume her. She didn't have the luxury. Not with a looming crisis to contend with.

After smoothing her hair and giving one last shake of her skirts over her petticoats, she went to Mrs. Bainbridge's room.

The door stood open. A maidservant was inside, making the bed. The very same maidservant who had kissed Mr. Cross under the mistletoe.

When she caught sight of Clara, she stopped and stood at attention. She was a tall girl, with dark hair and laughing, sherry-colored eyes.

"Good morning," Clara said. "Mary, isn't it?"

"Yes, miss."

Clara had too much on her mind to reflect overlong on the flicker of jealousy that tickled down her spine, or on the knot of melancholy that tightened in her stomach as she recalled Mr. Boothroyd's words in the coach.

I don't believe Mr. Cross will ever leave the Abbey. If he marries at all, it will be to a maidservant there, or perhaps a village lass.

"Are you looking for Mrs. Bainbridge?" Mary asked.

"I am."

"She left not ten minutes ago, miss. She was asking after you."

Clara spirits sank even further. "Do you know where she's gone?"

"Down to the kitchens, she said."

Clara thanked the maid before returning to her room to collect Bertie. He'd already eaten this morning, but Cook was generous with the dogs, always handing out bits of bread or bacon. And Bertie could do with fattening up.

She carried him down the main staircase until she reached the hall, and then descended another flight by the servants' stairs to the kitchen, hugging the curving stone wall with her body as she went.

She wished Mr. Cross was there to lend her his hand.

How lovely it would be to lean on someone. Not only on steep, curving staircases, but in life. And Mr. Cross was the sort of gentleman one *could* lean on. He was protective. Dependable. And strong enough to shield those he cared for from any ill.

But Mr. Cross was nowhere in sight.

Which was for the best, really. She mustn't become used to relying on other people.

She stepped down into the kitchens. Paul and Jonesy were on the opposite side of the room, lounging in front of the fire. At her arrival, Jonesy raised his head. He didn't growl. He merely looked at her, as if gauging whether or not she might have a biscuit in her pocket.

"There you are, Miss Hartwright." Mrs. Bainbridge stood at the stove next to Cook. A pot of some boiling substance steamed in front of them. "I'd begun to despair of you."

Clara crossed the stone floor to join them. "Is everything all right?"

"Indeed." Mrs. Bainbridge took a scrap of paper from Cook and tucked it into the wide sleeve of her crepe gown.

"Cook has given me a recipe for that marvelous gingerbread she served us on Christmas. Was it not delicious? We all remarked on it."

"It's the treacle, ma'am," Cook said. "There's some who substitute in dissolved loaf sugar and potash, but I don't hold with that."

"The old ways are the best," Mrs. Bainbridge agreed.

Clara set Bertie on the ground. He shuffled over to plop down beside Paul and Jonesy.

"You leave that dog here, miss." Cook returned to stirring her pot. "I've got some marrow bones for the lot of them." She shot a brief glance at Bertie. "He's got all his teeth, hasn't he?"

"Most of them," Clara said.

Mrs. Bainbridge gave Bertie a look of sympathy as she and Clara left the kitchen. "What a trial it is to be old."

Another clap of thunder sounded outside.

"And in this weather. The dampness, you know. Not but that it isn't pleasant enough inside." Mrs. Bainbridge started up the stairs. She didn't appear to have as much difficulty navigating them as Clara did. "The dogs certainly prefer it to the out-of-doors. Which brings something to mind."

Clara followed after her, one hand braced on the wall. "Yes, ma'am?"

"I do hope your pug is tolerant of cats. Magpie won't stand for being chased or snapped at. He's put many a dog in its place."

The two of them emerged through the door from the servants' stairs and crossed the hall to the main staircase. Clara ascended at Mrs. Bainbridge's side. "Bertie hasn't had many encounters with cats. Mrs. Peak didn't have one, and we rarely saw them in the street."

"If he meddles with Magpie, you will have to confine him, or keep him on a lead."

"He won't be any trouble, Mrs. Bainbridge," Clara promised. "You have my word on it."

Voices sounded from the drawing room as they approached. There was a clink of porcelain teacups and the rustle of starched petticoats. Someone was tinkling the keys of the piano, as if preparing to play.

Clara slowed her step. "Mrs. Bainbridge, might I speak to you a moment?"

Mrs. Bainbridge gave her a distracted glance. "Yes, my dear?"

"It's rather private."

Mrs. Bainbridge's expression turned wary. "This hasn't anything to do with that wild pony, has it? I can permit a small dog at the cottage, but I haven't the wherewithal to—"

"It's not about the pony, ma'am. It's about my brother."

"A family matter? Ah. I see." A small room stood empty along the hall to the drawing room. Mrs. Bainbridge motioned for Clara to enter. "Your brother's at university?"

The room was dark and cold, the heavy curtains drawn shut over the windows and most of the furnishings concealed beneath white Holland covers. Clara could just make out the shape of a low chair and a settee.

"At Cambridge." She waited for Mrs. Bainbridge to sit down before taking a seat herself. "I received a letter from my mother today. She informs me he's in some difficulty, and that I must go there. She bids me leave at once."

"Today?" Mrs. Bainbridge looked appalled.

"No," Clara said quickly. "Not today, nor tomorrow. But perhaps the following day? After arrangements have been made?"

"I can hardly forbid you. Not if it's a matter of urgency. But I shall have to speak to my niece. She may have something to say on the subject."

At that very moment, a soft tap sounded at the half-open door. Mrs. Archer poked her head in. "Aunt Charlotte. I thought I heard your voice." She looked to Clara. "Is everything all right?"

"Do come in, Laura," Mrs. Bainbridge said. "Miss Hartwright must leave us for a time. Her brother is in trouble at university."

Mrs. Archer's ebony brows lifted as she sat down next to her aunt on the cloth-draped settee. "Nothing serious, I trust?"

Clara folded her hands in her lap, feeling herself under painful scrutiny. She'd only just taken up her position. To leave so soon—and at such a time—would put Mrs. Archer to great inconvenience. Without a companion in residence, she'd be obliged to look after her aunt herself. "I don't know, ma'am. I must go there and find out. I hope it won't take more than a few days, and I shall come back directly, but I—"

"Of course you must go," Mrs. Archer said. "But not this very moment, surely?"

"She plans to leave day after tomorrow." Mrs. Bainbridge's mouth flattened into a line. "There will be no point in her coming back."

Clara's stomach dropped all the way to her slippers. Was she being dismissed?

"Quite," Mrs. Archer agreed. "It makes no sense for you to travel all the way back to Devon, Miss Hartwright. If your business with your brother takes longer than a day or two, you may go straight to my aunt's cottage in Surrey. The housekeeper, Mrs. Crabtree, will look after you until we return."

It was all Clara could do to disguise her relief.

Mrs. Bainbridge addressed her niece. "Someone must accompany her."

"Oh no," Clara protested. "I don't require an escort."

"Cambridge is rather far," Mrs. Archer said.

"I'm more than capable of making the journey. I've traveled all over England by rail. And I don't wish anyone to make a fuss. I only..." Clara steeled herself. "I only would ask that you—if it's at all possible—see fit to advance me my wages. I'll need money for my fare, and for my board and lodging."

Mrs. Archer nodded. "I'll speak to my husband."

Clara suppressed a swell of unease. Before nightfall, everyone in the house would know she was leaving. "I'm sorry to put you in this position."

Mrs. Archer stood. "We shall manage. Won't we, Aunt Charlotte?"

"We managed well enough before you insisted on hiring a companion for me." Mrs. Bainbridge rose to join her niece. "I've told you, Laura, I'm not an invalid."

Mrs. Archer took her aunt's arm. "It makes me feel better to know you have someone nearby to look after you. If you should have palpitations—"

"A maid will suffice in Miss Hartwright's absence. If her ladyship can spare one."

Clara walked with them from the room, feeling guilty and anxious and rather infuriated with her brother. It was all she could do to keep her countenance.

She hadn't lied. Since leaving Hertfordshire four years ago, she'd crossed most of the country by rail and coach. Long, solitary journeys to take up employment in London, in Kent, and even as far as Yorkshire. She'd become accustomed to managing on her own. To dealing with porters, coachman, and innkeepers. A companion didn't need a companion, Mama said. And it was true enough.

Clara nevertheless quailed at the prospect of the long miles to Cambridge. It would be cold and wet, and her welcome when she reached journey's end was uncertain.

The starkness of the situation was only beginning to sink in. With it came a depressing realization.

She would be unable to take Bertie with her.

Neville crossed the drawing room to join Clara, feeling a little out of his element. He'd seen her at dinner, seated across the table between Tom and Alex. She'd appeared oddly subdued, just as she appeared now, sitting apart from the others on a small velvet-upholstered settee near the window. Her hands were folded in her lap, her champagne-colored skirts arranged neatly about her.

He glanced to the space beside her on the settee. "May I?"

"Please," she said.

He sat down carefully. The settee was a delicate piece, made for equally delicate ladies. It gave a creak of protest at his weight. He inwardly winced.

Across the room, Jenny played the piano. A sprightly tune in keeping with the festive feeling in the air. Tom was beside her, dutifully turning the pages of her music.

Nearby, Teddy sat at a card table with Mrs. Bainbridge, Mr. Boothroyd, and Laura. Alex stood at Laura's shoulder. He bent and whispered in her ear.

"Unfair!" Teddy protested. "You're not allowed to get help."

Laura's eyes widened with exaggerated innocence. "Not even from my husband?"

"Your husband," Teddy replied dryly, "is a sharper."

"Come children, enough bickering." Mrs. Bainbridge laid down a card. "Direct your attention to the game."

Alex and Teddy grinned at each other, and Laura stifled a laugh. "Yes, aunt," she said.

To look at them—and at Justin and Lady Helena holding hands by the fire, the three dogs dozing at their feet—one wouldn't think Christmas was over. They were still aglow with the spirit of the season. All of them merry and bright.

Neville supposed he should be merry as well. But Twelfth Night was fast approaching. Only eleven more days, and Clara would be gone.

He wanted to prolong his time with her. To make it last forever. But try as he might, the brief moments they shared only seemed to pass that much more quickly. He could feel them slipping through his fingers like so much North Devon sand.

Even her scent—that bewitching hint of orange blossom that clung to her so sweetly—there was no preserving the magic it wrought on his senses. The fragrance evaporated from the air the second she left his presence.

"Are you going back to the stable this evening?" she asked.

He nodded. "I must."

Betty's milk was beginning to come in, but Neville wasn't taking any chances. He intended to continue feeding Firefly warm cow's milk from a teakettle for the next several days, until the foal was nursing successfully.

"I wish I could come with you," she said.

"Can't you?"

"Not this evening, no." Her features settled in a pensive frown. She seemed distracted. Not entirely herself. As if something wasn't quite right.

His old insecurities rose to the surface. Had he done something to upset her? Said something wrong? Something stupid?

He tugged at his cravat. His evening clothes were perfectly tailored. They nevertheless left him feeling awkward and constricted. He didn't belong in a black evening suit with a cream silk vest and matching neckcloth, no more than he belonged hunched over a desk all day. He'd far rather be with the horses.

And she would too, he had no doubt.

Beautiful as he found her, she never shone so brightly as when she was helping him with Firefly. She smiled and laughed—finding humor in her missteps and fairly glowing at each small accomplishment.

"Perhaps in the morning?" she suggested. "Before Mrs. Bainbridge wakes?"

"At dawn?"

"We can meet in the kitchens again. Or I can come straight to the stable if you'd rather not wait."

His heart pounded. "I'll wait."

There was something exciting about arranging to meet her. It felt illicit. Thrilling.

Though their time together was hardly a secret.

The entire household knew that Clara had been visiting Betty and her foal whenever she had a chance. No one had so much as batted an eye.

Which was a bit depressing, really.

Neither Mrs. Bainbridge, Mr. Boothroyd, nor even Justin seemed to suspect that there was anything going on between Neville and Clara. As if Neville could pose no possible threat to her virtue. As if the thought of romance would never enter his mind.

But it *had* entered his mind, almost from the moment he'd first laid eyes on her—and every moment since. Scarcely an hour passed that he didn't think of her, whether in the house, the stables, or alone in his bed.

Last night he'd even dreamed about her. One of those hazy dreams that disintegrates upon waking. All he could recall of it now was the feeling of deep contentment it had left him with. A warm sense of rightness.

Only eleven more days.

The rain beat heavily against the drawing room windows. If not for the blazing fire and the gasolier, and countless lamps and taper candles flickering on the marble mantelpiece and the inlaid side tables, the room would be swathed in darkness.

Normally, Neville wouldn't have given a thought to the oncoming storm. The elements hereabouts had always been fierce and unforgiving. As brutal as the cliffs sheering down to the sea. One simply got on with things. Acclimating to the climate—just as one acclimated to every other cruelty.

Clara didn't belong here.

It pained him to acknowledge it. But it was the truth. One that became more evident with each passing day. Despite her eccentricities—her aspirations for education, and employment—she was made for a gentler world. She *deserved* a gentler world.

"I never noticed the storm," she said. "Not until I returned to the house this morning."

"It isn't so b-bad."

"No? I shudder to think what could be worse."

He replied without hesitation. "When the rain c-comes sideways. And when…when the road washes away."

"Does that happen often?"

"Once a year. Sometimes m-more."

"You've never considered moving someplace more hospitable?"

"I like Devon."

"Yes, but Devon consists of more than this strip of coast. It's a large county, I believe. Surely there must be places that are less volatile."

Neville frowned. He didn't know what else there was. He'd never been farther than Abbot's Holcombe. "Sometimes…I imagine a f-farm."

Her face lit with interest. "A horse farm?"

"With p-paddocks, and a barn, and…lots of room."

She tilted toward him ever so slightly. "With acres of clover, and rolling fields for the horses to run and to graze?"

He looked into her eyes, very much in danger of losing himself in their satiny depths. "Yes. All of that."

"And more," she said.

"What else is there?"

"A snug little farmhouse. And…a butterfly garden."

His brows lifted in question.

Her cheeks turned a delightful shade of pink. "A garden planted in such a way as to attract butterflies, with lavender, heliotrope, and the like. The butterflies come to sip honey from the flowers. One can sketch and paint them—if one has a mind to."

His mouth curved. "But this is m-my farm. My dream."

"Is it?" she asked. "Your dream, I mean? Something you want just for yourself?"

"Sometimes," he admitted. "But…" No dream was worth giving up his friends. He shrugged. "I belong here."

"I suppose you do." Clara's gaze drifted over his face. Fondness shone in her eyes—and a faint sadness, too. "You're a part of this landscape, as much as anything. It's how I shall remember you. Walking along the cliffs with Paul and Jonesy. And in the stables, with Betty and Firefly."

There was a finality to Clara's words. It settled in his chest, extinguishing the warmth that had bloomed there as she spoke of clover fields and butterfly gardens.

But this wasn't the end. They had eleven more days together, didn't they?

He studied her face. It revealed nothing more to him.

Perhaps this wasn't the place for it. He needed to get her alone. To speak with her frankly. *What shall we do when you go? Shall we write to each other? Shall you come back and visit next Christmas?*

He knew he would live for every letter. For every visit, even if it was only once a year.

And yet…that wouldn't be living at all, would it? It would be heartbreak. It would be misery.

He swallowed. "I'll turn them out in…in the m-morning."

Her face brightened. "Oh, I long to see that. But what about—" She broke off. A sheepish smile edged her mouth. "I won't make the mistake again of pointing out the inclement weather. Except to say that, though Betty may be a Dartmoor pony, Firefly has known nothing save that loose box."

"Dartmoor is in his blood."

"Perhaps, but he's still bound to be frightened by all the rain."

"He'll t-take his…his c-courage from his mother."

"Is that how it works? Each of us learning to be brave from the example set by our parents?"

His mouth quirked. "I wouldn't know."

Her own smile evaporated. "I'm sorry. I didn't think—"

"It's all right. I d-don't mind it."

"I mind it for you. You shouldn't have had to be all alone."

"I wasn't," he said. "I had Justin, Alex, and Tom. And now…"

And now I have you.

But he didn't say that. He couldn't. Not here.

Not yet.

Chapter Sixteen

Clara was awakened at dawn by the sounds of rain on the rooftop, and thunder breaking over the sea. She was glad, for once, that Bertie was hard of hearing. Asleep beside her in the bed, he hadn't been at all bothered by the storm. He'd snored straight through the night.

She let him sleep while she washed and dressed, and then gathered him up to carry him down to the kitchens.

Neville was waiting for her there, as promised—along with a steaming mug of tea and a thick slice of bread and butter. "I thought you m-might be hungry."

Clara smiled her gratitude. "Oh, thank you. I haven't had any breakfast."

He fed the dogs while she ate, and then the pair of them made their way down to the stables. It was a familiar path by now, though no less treacherous. She clung to Neville's arm.

She hadn't yet told him that she was leaving. There had been no opportunity last evening. None save the few moments they'd shared in the drawing room, sitting together on the settee. And she hadn't had the heart to ruin that.

Stupid, really. They might have already discussed the matter. But she knew, once they did, everything would change. Besides, she was too busy savoring his every word, and every gentlemanlike gesture. Storing it all away. Cataloging every minute with him so she could call it back again in future. Labeling this, and cross-referencing that. A whole file of memories to carry her through the difficult times ahead.

But she owed him the truth. And she knew better by now than to make an entire drama of it. They weren't Romeo and Juliet for heaven's sake. They were two sensible adults.

Even so, there was a part of her—a weak, cowardly part—that had hoped he might already have heard the news from Mr. or Mrs. Archer. But as the evening progressed, she'd realized that the Archers had been in no hurry to enlighten the other guests. Nor why would they be? The employment status of their elderly aunt's companion was hardly food for gossip.

No. It was up to Clara to tell Neville. And she must do it today. This very morning.

And she would.

Just as soon as she could find an appropriate moment.

He helped her remove her cloak and bonnet, shaking the raindrops from them before hanging them to dry.

Clara smoothed her hair, feeling a bit self-conscious. The stable was eerily empty. Even the horses were quiet. "Where is everyone?"

"A tree fell at…at the b-bottom of the cliff road last night. They've gone to…to help clear it."

"Mr. Danvers, too?"

"He fed the horses early so he c-could go." Neville was silent for several long moments. "I d-didn't go. I…I'd rather b-be here. With you. Is that…"

"It's fine." She took a step toward him. "I'm glad you didn't go to help them. I'd have been terribly disappointed not to see you. And Betty and Firefly, of course. I've grown quite attached to them."

He regarded her intently. And she knew—she simply knew—that he understood. That it was him she was attached to. Deeply attached.

Drat the entire situation!

She hadn't come here meaning to develop an affection for anyone. There was no place for such things in her life. Nor in his, she'd wager.

She turned abruptly toward the feed room, her voice artificially bright. "Shall we make their breakfast?"

Neville followed after her without a word.

He let her take charge of Betty's mash, mixing the bran, grain, and hot water. And he permitted her to assist him in heating the foal's milk and wrapping the spout of the teakettle with soft toweling. But it was he who carried the bucket. He always sought to spare her a burden. To make the way smooth for her.

Yet another admirable quality to file away in her box of memories.

She walked alongside him down the aisle. As they approached Betty's loose box, she poked her shaggy head out over the door. When she saw Neville and marked the bucket he was carrying, she gave an impatient whinny.

"Here, Betty." He let himself inside the loose box, shutting the door behind him. "Easy."

Clara cradled the teakettle in her hands as she watched over the door. Betty was still a little wary of Neville, but she no longer cringed away or threatened to kick him. Taking his cue from his dam, Firefly stepped forward to bump Neville's arm with his tiny muzzle, demanding his attention.

It was one of the sweetest things Clara had ever beheld. "Is it safe for me to come in yet?"

Neville clipped the bucket to the hook on the wall. Betty thrust her head into it without hesitation. "Now it is."

Clara crept inside. Betty didn't pay her any attention, but Firefly was ready and waiting. He nudged her with his nose, and pushed her hard with his shoulder. "He's getting strong!"

"He wants his milk." Neville held Firefly's neck, keeping him still. "Remember...you have to p-pour it."

"I remember." She offered Firefly the padded spout of the teakettle, tilting it so the milk slowly streamed into his waiting mouth. He drank deeply. A smile spread over her face. "He's getting better at this."

"So are you," Neville said.

She didn't know about that. It was impossible to keep the milk from spilling. At least now, however, after three days' practice, she was confident that more was ending up in Firefly's stomach than on the straw-covered floor.

"Good boy," she murmured. "How clever you are."

When the teakettle was empty, she stepped outside the loose box again. She was careful not to press her luck with Betty. It was Neville who must win the ponies' trust, not her.

He remained inside with both of them. His hands moved over Betty while she ate, stroking along her neck, shoulders, and flanks. It was as if he was speaking to her. Gentling her and reassuring her. Persuading her to trust him.

Firefly wandered along with him, mouthing at Neville's sleeves with tiny, experimental nips.

Neville glanced at Clara. "Fetch your bonnet and cloak."

She quickly did as he bid her, retrieving her things from the front of the stables and slipping them on as she returned to the back. By then, he'd managed to put a rope halter over Betty's head and was leading her from the box.

Clara stood back, well out of kicking range. "What about Firefly? Doesn't he need to be haltered?"

"He'll follow her."

Sure enough, Firefly ambled along at Betty's side as Neville led her through the arched doorway at the back of the stable. It opened to a series of long paddocks with white wooden fences. The smallest was closest to the stables. A pen, merely, with an even footing of mud and grass.

Neville walked Betty into it. Her nostrils flared, and her sides heaved like a bellows. "Will you shut the gate?"

Clara closed and latched it behind him. Her heart was halfway in her throat, her stomach clenched in both fear and anticipation. She didn't know what to expect. At only twelve hands, Betty couldn't do much damage, could she? She was just a pony.

But when Neville slipped the rope halter from her head, Betty managed to make herself look as big and dangerous as a full-sized horse. She reared up on her hind legs, shaking her neck and striking out with her hooves.

Clara's hand flew to her mouth. "Oh, do be careful!"

Neville didn't seem at all alarmed. He backed away from Betty slowly. When he reached the fence, he climbed over it with ease.

Betty cantered wildly around the pen, Firefly leaping and kicking at her side. She whinnied, high and shrill, tossing her head and quivering all over.

"She'll hurt herself," Clara said.

Neville came to stand next to her. "She won't."

Clara wished she could feel as confident. Instead she felt cold and wet and quite certain she was about to witness either Betty or Firefly break one of their legs. "Is there nothing you can do to calm her?"

He shook his head. "She'll c-calm on her own."

Clara supposed she'd simply have to trust him. He knew horses far better than she did. And he was the last person on earth who would let an animal come to harm. "I hate to see her so frightened."

"She's not afraid."

Eventually, Betty slowed to pace the perimeter of the pen, examining the fence and what lay beyond it. She stopped to snatch a bite of grass, and again to paw at a mud puddle. And then, all at once, her front legs folded beneath her and she seemed to collapse to the ground.

Clara was on the verge of another worried exclamation when, much to her surprise, Betty rolled straight over.

And then she rolled over again, back and forth on her back, until she was covered with mud.

An involuntary gurgle of laughter rose in Clara's throat. "My goodness. She's certainly enjoying herself."

Neville smiled. "She is." He turned his head. "Are you?"

"Yes. Very much." The rain streamed from Clara's bonnet. "I only regret that it's not a bit sunnier."

"You should come back in…in the summer."

"I doubt Mrs. Bainbridge could be persuaded to return. She's had difficulty acclimating to the dampness." Clara hesitated. "And I don't know if I'll still be employed by her in the summer. Or even in the spring."

His smile faded.

"I have to go away, you see. And I've only just taken up this position. It isn't very well done of me, to abandon my post so soon after being hired. I wouldn't be surprised if Mrs. Bainbridge decides she's better off without me."

"What are you..." He visibly struggled over his words. "I d-don't understand."

"I wanted to tell you yesterday evening, but there was no opportunity. And then, later, I thought you might have already heard something about it from Mr. or Mrs. Archer."

"I haven't heard anything." He searched her face. "What d-do you mean you have to...to go away?"

"Just that." An unexpected tremor of emotion seeped into her voice. "I'm leaving Devon day after tomorrow. And I don't expect I'll be coming back."

Neville listened in numb silence as Clara explained about her brother, and how she must depart Devon. She didn't know for how long. There was a good chance she wouldn't come back at all, that she'd instead return directly to Mrs. Bainbridge's cottage in Surrey.

In which case, he'd very likely never see her again.

A chill settled around his heart. He hardly noticed Betty and Firefly wandering in the pen, or the rain soaking his hair and seeping through his coat. He could only stare at Clara, a mass of emotion knotting itself inextricably in his chest.

He'd thought he had ten more days with her. But now...

"You can't go," he blurted out. A grimace followed. He hadn't meant to put it so bluntly. So unartfully. "You just… you c-can't."

"I must. I'd have gone sooner if I could. Heaven knows what's going on with my brother." A deep shiver ran through her. "Cambridge wouldn't threaten to send someone down for no reason." Her teeth began to chatter. "It must b-be very b-bad."

Neville's brows lowered. Her cloak and bonnet were dripping, and her face was pale as marble. He cursed himself for failing to notice it before. "You're freezing."

"I am, rather. I think I'd b-better go inside."

"Wait for me," he said. It wasn't a request.

She nodded again before turning back to the stables, picking her way around the puddles and loose stones.

Neville let himself into the pen and coaxed Betty back into her rope halter. She was covered in a thick layer of mud. She needed to be sponged off with a bucket of warm water. A time-consuming process. And he hadn't any time to spare.

But there was no shirking his duties.

He led Betty back into the stables, Firefly at her side. Clara was seated on the mounting block. She'd removed her wet cloak, bonnet, and gloves, but she was still shivering. And he could see why. The rain had seeped through her cloak to soak into the bodice and skirts of her gray woolen dress. It was covered in dark, wet patches.

"Stay there," he said as he led Betty past her.

Clara didn't argue. Her teeth were chattering too much to speak.

He put Betty and Firefly away in their loose box, leaving them with some fresh hay to tide them over until his return. And then he went to collect Clara. "Come with me."

She stood. "Where?"

"I have rooms upstairs."

"Oh…I couldn't." She hung back. "It wouldn't be proper."

"It's all right." He put a hand on her back to coax her forward. She was trembling beneath his touch. He couldn't tell if it was because of the cold or because of him. "I'll light a fire. We can k-keep the…the door open."

Clara didn't look entirely convinced at the wisdom of such a thing. She nevertheless permitted him to escort her up the single flight of creaking wooden stairs behind the feed room. It led to a small landing in front of a closed door.

He opened it and ushered her inside.

Hugging herself with her arms, she looked about the room, examining the worn wingback chairs, old mahogany wardrobe, and metal bedstead. Her gaze lingered on the mattress with its heavy quilt and pillows. She bit her lip. "This isn't at all—"

"Here." He guided her to one of the chairs near the cold hearth. "Sit down."

Again, she did as he bid her, albeit reluctantly, perching on the very edge of the seat, as if she might spring up at any moment and bolt from the room. She was silent as he made up the fire and stoked it to a roaring flame. When he turned again to look at her, some of the color was back in her cheeks.

"Will you stay here?" he asked. "While I t-tend to Betty?"

"Are you going to bathe her?"

He shook his head. "I'll sponge her d-down. And…I n-need to wrap her leg."

"I can't wait long. I've already been gone over an hour. Mrs. Bainbridge—"

"It won't t-take long. Just…" Words eluded him. All the things he wished he could say to her. All the emotion he wanted to convey. It was tangled up in his head and his heart. There was no way to express it. Only a simple request. A husky plea. "Just…wait for me."

Her chocolate brown eyes glistened. He was reminded of the day they'd met. Of how she'd looked at him. How she'd offered him her hand.

She'd only just come into his life, and now she was leaving just as quickly. And he wasn't ready for it, lord help him. He wanted—needed—a little more time.

She nodded slowly. "Very well, I'll wait."

Chapter Seventeen

Clara was true to her word. She waited for Neville, for goodness knew how many minutes. It was long enough for the fire to dry her dress and take the shivering chill from her bones. Long enough for her teeth to cease chattering.

All the while the rain pelted the curtained window of his room, and storm clouds moved across the sun, casting dark shadows across the furnishings and floor. She rose from her chair to light a lamp. There was one located on a wooden table near the bed. A slim book bound in red morocco leather lay closed beside it.

She didn't like to pry. What Neville chose to read of an evening was none of her business. But as she removed the globe from the oil lamp and lit the wick, she couldn't keep her gaze from drifting over the gilt-stamped title on the ridged spine.

Poems

—

First Edition

—

Tennyson

—

Vol. II

Her mouth went dry. Neville was reading Tennyson? And not only Tennyson, but the very volume that contained *Sir Galahad*?

She reached to touch the book, only to draw her hand back. She hadn't read poetry in four years. Not since the scandal in Hertfordshire. No one had expressly forbidden her from doing so. Not Mama, and certainly not Simon. But both of them had implied it was a contributing factor to her shame. And she'd known it to be true. Poetry, especially the sort which rhapsodized about gallant knights and fair damsels, had only served to exacerbate her tendency toward romantic daydreams.

And now the pleasure she'd once felt in reading Tennyson or Wordsworth was forever tainted. How could she enjoy any of it when all it did was serve to remind her of her own humiliation?

She returned to her chair by the fire, an ache settling into her heart. She was resolved to think about things logically. To focus on reality, not romance. Even so, the idea that Neville was reading the poetry she'd once loved so dearly moved her deeply. It was as if he was seeking to know her. To discover who she really was.

And she wished…

Oh, but she wished things could have been different. That she had met him before, when she was younger, and life was full of possibility.

Which was a grim way of thinking of things.

Her life wasn't over. She had a plan. A vision for her future, as an educated lady. A sensible secretary to her brother, dealing with lists and ledgers, and cataloguing quantifiable facts.

And that was precisely the reason she must go to Cambridge. She couldn't permit her brother to jeopardize his standing there. Not when her own life depended so much on his. Without Simon, she had nothing to look forward to, save a dreary future as a companion.

A floorboard creaked outside the door.

Clara turned sharply at the noise. Her eyes widened.

Neville entered the room, coat in hand, looking very much like he'd fallen into a slurry. His shirtsleeves were wet, and his waistcoat and trousers were streaked with mud.

She stood in alarm. "You haven't been hurt?"

"No. This is what happens when you…when you sponge a wild p-pony who's rolled in the mud." His mouth hitched in a rueful half smile. "She's clean now."

"And you're wet through."

He glanced down at his clothing. "I'll dry."

"Nonsense. You need to change into a fresh shirt. And I need to go. It's past time I—"

"Don't go." He came further into the room, his expression losing all trace of humor. "I d-don't mind it."

"I mind it for you." She heaved a breath. "Do change into a dry shirt. I'll…I'll turn my back."

A flush crept up his neck. For a moment it looked as though he'd rebuff her offer. But he didn't say anything. He only gave a stiff nod.

Clara turned away, staring fixedly at the fire. She was aware of every sound and movement behind her. The click of the wardrobe door opening. The rustle of fabric as he removed his waistcoat and stripped his linen shirt off over his head. She closed her eyes, willing herself not to blush.

"Are you warm enough?" he asked.

"Yes, thank you." Her voice was high-pitched with nerves. She brought it back to a normal level. "I've been quite comfortable here in front of the fire."

"Has your dress dried?"

"Yes."

He came to join her at the fireplace, garbed in a clean shirt and black woolen waistcoat. His trousers were still muddy. He hadn't changed them, thank heaven. It would have been doubly embarrassing if he had. The very thought of it! As if it wasn't already awkward enough between them.

"Neville," she began.

He motioned for her to sit.

She shook her head. "I'm too restless." Arms folded, she walked to the window, putting some much-needed space between them. She was conscious of him watching her from his place in front of the fire. "Why are you reading Tennyson?"

The question escaped before she could stop it. She'd have given anything to call it back again.

His gaze flicked to his nightstand. "It's Lady Helena's book."

Clara had assumed as much. The Abbey's library was filled with books of every variety. "Yes, but...why are *you* reading it?"

He shrugged. "Curiosity."

"About Sir Galahad?"

"About you."

Warmth suffused her chest. She'd suspected his interest was in her and not in Arthurian poetry. But to hear him admit it...

"I don't like Sir Galahad," he said.

"Don't you?" She privately confessed to a faint flicker of disappointment. "He's noble and pure of heart. The noblest of all the knights."

"He's n-never been kissed," he said. "Or held a lady's hand."

She blinked. "Oh, that." She leaned back against the windowsill. The ridge of it pressed into her hips, pushing her crinoline out in front of her. "It lends to his purity, I suppose. The reason he's deemed worthy to find the grail."

"Is that what you think of…of me?"

"I don't—" She broke off. "It was just a foolish fancy. I don't know why I gave voice to it."

He slowly crossed the room to join her. She'd only seen him in his shirtsleeves once before, and then she'd been too distracted by Betty's labor to get a proper look at him. But now…

Great goodness.

Without his coat and cravat, he looked even bigger, if that was possible. All broad shoulders, and lean, masculine strength.

It was quite easy to imagine him in a suit of polished armor, atop that enormous gray horse of his. A horse that did rather resemble a charger.

He propped his shoulder against the window frame. "Because I lived at the c-convent."

"Yes. I daresay that was part of it. And because you're so very handsome, and so very kind."

His mouth quirked.

Good lord, had she just called him handsome?

She rushed to explain, her words tumbling over each other. "It's all silliness, of course. I have a tendency for such things. To romanticize gentlemen who are kind to me. Some people shouldn't read poetry or novels. It gives them all sorts of romantic ideas about life, and about people. It's not at all healthy."

He frowned at her. "You're not silly."

"You don't know me, sir. I have a long and undistinguished history of fantasizing. But I've grown up since. I've committed myself to being sensible. I'd thought I was succeeding at it until I met you." An unexpected swell of sadness clogged her throat. "It's good that I'm leaving. If I stayed through Twelfth Night, I'd likely end up making a fool of myself."

"Over me?"

She forced herself to meet his eyes. "I'm not imagining it, am I? That we're attracted to each other? Drawn to each other?"

He gazed steadily back at her. "No." His voice went gruff. "I…I admire you. Very much."

She compressed her lips to stop their trembling. She wouldn't make a spectacle of herself. No matter that no gentleman had ever admitted to admiring her before.

"Must you go?" he asked. "Can't someone else…?"

"There is no one else. My mother teaches at a girls' school in Edinburgh. Some of the students stay on over Christmas, and she remains to chaperone them. She couldn't leave even if she wanted to. It's up to me to find out what's happened to Simon and help to resolve things, if I can."

He was silent for a long while. "Will you return?" he asked at last.

"I don't expect so. Mrs. Bainbridge says there's no point in traveling all the way back to Devon for only a day or two." Clara had spoken with her again last night, and with Mr. and Mrs. Archer, too. The three of them had been excessively practical about the situation. "Which brings me to a favor I must ask of you. And you mustn't feel obligated to say yes."

He came closer, looming over her. It should have been intimidating, but it wasn't. Quite the reverse. She felt protected. As if his presence could somehow shield her from the cares of the world. "What is it?" he asked.

"I wonder if you might keep Bertie with you while I'm gone? I can't take him with me. That is, I could, but it would be very hard on him."

"Of course." He paused. "How…how will you…?"

"Mrs. Bainbridge has promised to bring him back to Surrey with her on the train. But she's ill-equipped to care for him while she's here. Bertie requires constant looking after."

"I'll look after him."

She managed a tremulous smile. "Thank you. I won't forget."

"Nor will I." He looked down at her, gazing into her eyes for a taut moment. And then he brought his hand to her face, tracing the line of her cheek and jaw with a gentleness that bordered on reverence.

Her pulse beat an erratic rhythm at her throat. She knew what was going to happen. Just as she knew that she could stop it happening if she wished it. All she need do was pull back from him or voice an objection. But she found herself incapable of doing either.

Instead, she listed against him. And when he bent his head and kissed her, her lips softened beneath his, yielding to his mouth with a sensual warmth she hadn't known herself capable of.

"Clara," he said. It was a murmured breath of enquiry. As if he was asking permission to continue

In answer, she twined her arms about his neck. Her heavy skirts bunched against his legs as she stretched up to brush her lips to his.

He responded instantly, enfolding her in a powerful embrace. Holding her so tightly that the bones in her corset gave a creak of protest. And he kissed her again. A deep, soul-stirring kiss, as passionate as it was poignant.

She felt the heat of it thrumming in her veins. It weakened her knees and limbs, forcing her to cling to him almost desperately. Like some poor shipwrecked soul clinging to a rock. The only solid and dependable thing in a stormy world.

He was saying goodbye to her.

And suddenly, she could no longer hold back the tears that stung at her eyes. She pressed her face into his neck.

His breath was heavy against her hair. He moved his hand over the curve of her spine, up and down in a slow, reassuring caress. Long seconds passed.

"I'm sorry," he said.

"I'm not."

"Clara…"

"I mean it." She drew back, her damp eyes finding his. "I only wish we had more time together."

He rested his forehead gently against hers. And the emotion imbued in that single gesture was so sweet, so tender, she felt she might drown in it. That she might lose herself entirely.

Until he spoke.

"I have nothing to offer you," he said.

Her hands slid from his neck. She stood there, frozen, as he released her from his arms and moved away from her. "I haven't asked anything of you. I wouldn't."

"You d-don't understand." He ran a hand over his hair. "I c-can't ever leave here. I'm…" His throat worked on a swallow. "There's n-no future with me."

The bare wooden floor seemed to shift beneath Clara's feet, like the deck of a ship. She reached behind her to grip the windowsill. "Yes, I see."

But she didn't see at all.

All she knew was that she'd done it once more. Despite his professions of admiration, and her abundance of caution. Despite everything she'd been guarding against these past four years. Somehow, she'd managed to make an idiot of herself again.

She turned briefly to dash a tear from her cheek. "I've been very foolish."

He didn't disagree.

Indeed, he didn't say anything. She didn't know if he was struggling for words or merely bereft of them. She couldn't bear to look at him to find out.

Was he regretful? Ashamed?

In other circumstances, she'd have endeavored to discover the answer. But not now.

Now, all she wanted was to leave his presence. To abandon the scene of her latest disgrace as swiftly as possible.

"It was a mistake to stay so long. I must get back." She moved past him to the door, her footsteps brisk and purposeful, for all that her heart was breaking.

And she waited for him to object again. To tell her, as he'd done before, that he wanted her to stay.

But he didn't say anything. He didn't offer to escort her back to the Abbey or even bid her good day.

When she walked out the door, he simply let her go.

Chapter Eighteen

Neville stared, unseeing, at the column of figures he'd entered into the ledger. They blurred before his tired eyes. He'd been hunched over the library desk for hours, trying to distract himself with work.

A fruitless endeavor.

He was unable to focus on anything.

At times like these, he was best suited to being out with the horses. But he'd already spent most of the morning in the stables, avoiding the house guests.

Avoiding *her*.

Across the room, Justin stood at the window, gazing out through the rain-streaked glass. His countenance was grim. "Miss Hartwright won't be leaving tomorrow."

Neville's head jerked up. His heart gave a bitter lurch at the very mention of her name. "Why not?"

"Because," Justin said with infuriating logic, "by this evening the cliff road will have washed out."

Tom folded his newspaper and rose from his chair to join Justin at the window. He peered out, frowning. "It looks as though it already has."

"Not yet, but soon. Given the way this storm is progressing, we'll be lucky if it's passable again by Twelfth Night."

"What do you suggest?" Tom asked.

"If she can make herself ready within an hour's time, I'll have Danvers drive her to the railway station in Abbot's Holcombe. It will be easier for her than enduring the mail coach all the way to Barnstaple."

Tom nodded. "I'll tell Alex." He strode from the room, shutting the library door behind him.

Neville returned to his work. He scratched out a figure in the ledger and entered a new one, his fingers clenched around the quill so tightly it threatened to break in his hand. He forced himself to relax. To turn his attention to something else. Anything other than the stricken way Clara had looked when he'd told her he had nothing to offer her.

And now she was leaving.

Not on Twelfth Night, and not tomorrow, but this very day. Within the hour. And there was nothing he could do about it. Not even if he wanted to. She would climb into the carriage, and Danvers would drive her straight out of his life.

Neville was paralyzed by the emotion of it.

He lay down his quill and rested his head in his hands.

"Do you know," Justin said, "I don't believe I've ever observed Boothroyd looking half so miserable balancing the estate accounts as you do."

"I'm not Boothroyd."

"No, indeed." Justin came to stand beside the desk. He flipped through the last two pages of the ledger. "He has a knack for poring over paperwork for hours at a time without suffering the smallest degree of boredom."

Neville sat back in his chair as Justin closed the ledger. "I'm not bored. I'm…distracted."

"It is rather distracting having so many people about. I've enjoyed it, of course, but I shall be glad when everyone returns to their own lives and leaves us to ours."

Neville didn't say anything. In truth, he didn't know what to say.

Somehow, over the years, his life had become knotted up with Justin's. It was a bond forged in the orphanage, born of shared misery. A tie of brotherhood and friendship. The same thing that bound Neville to Alex and Tom.

He'd long thought of them as his family. And they were that. Neville couldn't imagine a world without them in it. But that bond hadn't stopped the others from striking out on their own. From finding love and personal fulfillment.

In the past year Tom had married Jenny, the pair of them traveling the world together. Alex had wed Laura and would soon be leaving for France. And Justin and Lady Helena were expecting a child. All of them had forged separate lives.

All of them except Neville.

He supposed he existed as part of Justin's family. An appendage from the past, kept close for reasons of affection, loyalty, and lingering guilt over Neville's accident.

But Neville's life was his own, surely. He deserved happiness as much as the rest of them. He deserved—

He started at the feel of a hand coming to rest on his shoulder.

"You drifted off," Justin said.

Neville glanced at the clock. He didn't know how long he'd spent staring fixedly at the closed ledger, thinking about the orphanage, and his accident, and what it was he deserved. Minutes, probably. Perhaps longer.

"Is it happening more often?"

"No." Neville stopped himself, realizing at once that that was a lie. "Only when…when I'm still for t-too long."

"Sitting at the desk?"

"Sometimes." And at dinner, or in the drawing room with everyone talking all around him. He couldn't predict exactly when it would happen. All he knew was that it never happened when he was active. When he was engaged with the horses or some other physical activity.

"You get lost in your thoughts."

"I lose time. I…I don't realize until afterward."

Justin frowned. "I've been thinking about that. About some of the difficulty you've had with the more mundane aspects of filling Boothroyd's position."

Neville didn't respond. In his opinion, most of Boothroyd's duties were mundane. Whereas some stewards spent the bulk of their time out on the estate, Boothroyd preferred to remain indoors. He'd structured all of his responsibilities to revolve around his desk.

"I wonder," Justin said, "if it wouldn't be more efficient to separate the paperwork, letter-writing, and ledgers from the work that must be done on the estate. Monitoring repairs, collecting rents, and so forth."

"Who would…?"

"I'd have to hire someone. A secretary, perhaps." Justin squeezed Neville's shoulder before releasing it. "Don't look so glum. Boothroyd's had decades to learn his role. It's not realistic to expect you to take over his post immediately."

"Stewards are educated men." Many of them had gone to university and knew how best to make an estate profitable. It was more than simply balancing accounts and collecting rents.

"You've had an education. First the orphanage school and then the convent. More importantly, you have common sense. You may not be as well read as Tom, or as well traveled as Alex, but you have impeccable judgment. I value it immensely."

"My judgment is..." Neville pushed his fingers through his hair until it stood half on it. "It's n-not as good as you think it is."

Had it been good judgment to take Clara to his rooms above the stable? To kiss her so passionately? He'd known all the while that nothing could come of it. That there was no prospect for a future with her.

And why not?

The three words echoed in his brain—a desperate, angry question.

But he knew the answer. It was as much because of her as it was because of him. She was beautiful and intelligent, with dreams that far exceeded the rigid bounds of his circumscribed existence.

While she went off with her brother, to a fulfilling life as secretary to a natural scientist, Neville would stay here. Frozen in time. Cursed to remain in North Devon as surely as some enchanted knight in one of Clara's Arthurian legends.

In time, she would forget him.

The prospect sank his spirits.

"Come up to the drawing room with me," Justin said. "Helena's there with Jenny having tea and cake. Doubtless they can spare us a slice. We'll get things sorted with Miss Hartwright's departure, and then we'll—"

"I...I can't." Neville looked at the implements on the desk—the inkpot, quill, and quire of writing paper. An ache built in his chest.

Dash it all to hell.

He couldn't leave it this way.

Clara's feelings meant more than his pride. More, even, than his fears and insecurities. She was that important to him. He'd be damned if he let her leave here believing he didn't care. That it hadn't been the sacrifice of his life to let her go.

"There's something I have t-to do."

"For me? Let it wait."

"Not for you," Neville said. "For me."

Clara folded the last of her petticoats and placed them inside her portmanteau. Her veins hummed with anxiety. She'd thought she had another day to get her affairs in order. To pack her clothing and belongings and to settle things with Bertie's care. She glanced at the small gilt clock on the mantel. It was half past eleven. Only twenty more minutes until her departure.

"Are you certain there's nothing else you require, Miss Hartwright?" Mrs. Archer stood near the wardrobe, a cashmere shawl wrapped around her shoulders. "An extra pair of woolen stockings or another bonnet? I'd be happy to lend you whatever you need."

Outside, the rain hammered down in a relentless torrent, beating on the roof and the windows. The winter storm was fully upon them, and with it a whistling wind and an ominous gray fog that obscured the sea from view.

Clara tried not to think about how Mr. Danvers would manage to navigate the winding cliff road.

"I'm quite all right as I am." She shut and locked her portmanteau. Her carpetbag was already packed. She stacked both on the padded bench at the foot of the bed. "I'll be on the train mostly, not out in the elements."

Bertie looked up from his place by the dwindling fire. Clara's eyes found his. She swallowed against a lump in her throat.

"And you're certain Mr. Cross is going to care for your pug? You can leave him with me if you like, or with Teddy."

"I wouldn't wish to put you to any trouble." Clara's cloak, bonnet, and gloves were laid out on the bed. She slipped them on. "Besides, Mr. Cross said he'd be happy to do it. He has a way with animals."

"That he does." Mrs. Archer went to the bell pull and gave it a sharp tug. "What about your wages? Have you put them somewhere safe?"

"In my reticule." Clara tied her bonnet tight under her chin. "Except for a single pound note, which I've hidden inside the bottom of my half boot."

Mrs. Archer's mouth curved in a fleeting smile. "Very wise."

A footman arrived moments later to collect Clara's bags.

"Thank you, Robert," Mrs. Archer said.

"Shall I come back for the dog, ma'am?" he asked.

"I'll take him myself." Clara scooped up Bertie. "I must have a word with Mr. Cross."

"Of course." Mrs. Archer cast a worried glance at the window. "Though do make it a brief one. The weather appears to be worsening by the minute."

Clara promised that she would, and with Bertie in her arms, she made her way downstairs.

She hadn't seen Neville since last night at dinner. The entire evening had been a painful ordeal, and one she'd rather have avoided. After returning from the stables, she'd been quite tempted to plead a headache and keep to her room.

But that would have been cowardly.

Instead, she'd sat at the table between Teddy and Mr. Finchley, talking to each of them in turn and smiling as much as she was able. After dinner she'd partnered Mrs. Bainbridge at cards, playing until nearly midnight.

In other circumstances it would have been a very pleasant evening. But Clara's smiles had been brittle, and when she'd played her hand, her heart hadn't been in it.

The tree stood in the hall, looking as grand as it had on Christmas, with all of its tinsel and glittering ornaments. Clara inhaled its fading pine fragrance as she passed it on her way to the library.

She didn't know if Neville would be there. It was only a hunch. Lady Helena had mentioned that he'd returned from the stables, but he hadn't come to join them in the drawing room.

The library door stood half open. She entered to find Neville leaning over the desk, applying a wax seal to a letter. Her heart gave an anguished thump.

But he wasn't alone.

Mr. Archer was at one of the bookshelves, a leather-bound volume held open in his hand, showing something within its pages to Teddy. The two of them were talking softly.

Clara announced her presence with a delicate cough.

Neville turned his head to the door. When he saw her, he straightened to his full height. "Miss Hartwright."

"Mr. Cross." How civil they were to each other. How unfailingly polite. And all the while her palms were damp inside her gloves, and her stomach was tied into knots.

"You're leaving us, are you?" Teddy asked.

"I fear I must. Mr. Thornhill says—"

"Yes, yes, the cliff road." Teddy wheeled himself across the library. "I wonder that it's passable at all. It looked rather treacherous the day we arrived."

"It *is* rather treacherous." Mr. Archer withdrew another book before coming to join them. "But I expect Danvers knows what he's about."

"All the same," Teddy remarked, "take care you don't get swept out to sea."

Neville's countenance was solemn. Almost stern. He didn't appear at all amused by Teddy's dark humor.

"I shall be quite all right," Clara said. "I've only stopped in to speak to Mr. Cross about Bertie. And then I must go. Danvers is bringing round the carriage."

"We'll leave you to it, then." Mr. Archer motioned to Teddy. "Shall we?"

"If we must." Teddy flashed Clara a smile. "Safe journey."

She smiled in return. "Goodbye. I shall see you again in Surrey."

"Goodbye, Miss Hartwright," Mr. Archer said. "Take care of yourself."

"I will, sir." Clara clasped Bertie more firmly to her chest, standing in tense silence as Mr. Archer and Teddy exited the room. She felt the weight of Neville's gaze on her face—a physical sensation, as affecting as if he'd touched her cheek with his hand, just as he'd done yesterday in the moments before he'd kissed her.

She brought her eyes to meet his. A blush threatened. "I won't keep you a minute. I only wanted to reassure myself on a few counts about Bertie."

Neville remained where he was. His jaw was set, his hands clasped behind his back. She wondered how a gentleman who was so kind, so very warm, could suddenly look so cold and imposing.

"He sleeps most of the day," she said. "And he prefers a place in front of the fire. If you could see to it?"

He nodded.

"And you won't always be taking him to the stables, will you? I hate to think of him being subjected to the elements for any length of time."

"I'll look after him."

Her throat tightened with emotion. "Of course you will." Somehow she managed to smile, though she was certain it must look more like a rictus of pain. "What a ninny you must think me. Just like the day we met. All of my strictures about Bertie. As if you don't know dogs better than I."

"Clara..."

"I don't regret any of it, you know. I daresay I should, but I don't. If you—"

"There you are, Miss Hartwright." Mrs. Bainbridge's voice rang out from the doorway. "The carriage is in the drive. You mustn't keep the coachman waiting."

Clara forced composure on herself. "No, indeed." She pressed a trembling kiss to Bertie's head before passing him into Neville's arms.

As Neville took him, his hand brushed against hers. He tucked something into her fingers. It was a small, folded envelope. The very one he'd been sealing at his desk.

She looked up at him with a start.

He stared back at her, an expression in his eyes that was hard to read.

"Come, my dear," Mrs. Bainbridge said. "Time is of the essence."

Clara discreetly slipped the letter into her sleeve. Her pulse was racing. "Goodbye, Mr. Cross."

Neville stepped back from her, Bertie in his arms. "Goodbye, Miss Hartwright."

It seemed as though he might have said more. But there was no time, and with Mrs. Bainbridge looking on, they had no privacy. Clara could do nothing but take her leave.

It wasn't until later that she was finally able to open his letter. Alone at last inside the carriage, careening down the cliff road in the driving rain, she withdrew the small envelope from her sleeve, broke the seal, and began to read.

> *My dearest Clara,*
>
> *I have thought and thought of what I might say on the day of your departure, but as with most unpleasant things, that day has come far too soon. I find myself wholly unprepared to bid goodbye to you, and as lacking in eloquence with a pen and ink as I am when I speak. I'm constrained by the limits of language. No words are adequate to express the light you have brought into my life. I can only say this:*
>
> *The past weeks with you have been the brightest period of my memory. I shall treasure them always.*
>
> *If you remember me down the years, I hope it will be as a man who was honored to know you, and to be*

in your company. And who might have loved you all of your days if things had been different.

Yours faithfully,
Neville Cross

Chapter Nineteen

Cambridge, England
December 1860

Clara stood inside the gates of Magdalene College. It was snowing in Cambridge, delicate flakes that caught on her cloak and bonnet, melting away to nothing. She scarcely noticed the cold. Her entire being was too consumed with the sights before her.

She stared in wonder at the imposing stucco-faced buildings. They were set along the sides of a quadrangle. To the east was the great hall. To the north, the chapel. And along the west side, a magnificent classical structure of creamy Ketton stone with a piazza of five connected archways at its front. She recognized it instantly from the descriptions in her brother's letters.

The Pepysian Library.

Never in her life had she dreamed she'd see it in person. And now here she was, standing less than one hundred feet from its doors.

She inhaled a deep breath and thought, rather foolishly, *I am breathing the rarified air of Cambridge.* A giddy fact. So much so it nearly made her forget the purpose of her visit.

"Hartwright, did you say?" The elderly porter at the gatehouse beetled his wiry gray brows. "Ah yes. Master Hartwright." His lined face settled into an expression of disapproval. "He's gone away with Master Trent."

She recognized the name. Philip Trent was one of her brother's school friends. Simon had often mentioned him in his letters. "Do you know when he'll return?"

"You'd best speak to your brother about that."

"That's precisely why I've come," she said. "I've traveled all the way from Devon to speak to him. Are you telling me there's no way to reach my brother at all? No way to deliver a message?"

"I suppose I could have a note delivered to Master Trent's residence. Can't promise Master Hartwright's still with him. He might have gone off on his own, given the circumstances."

She went still. "What circumstances?"

"Not my place to say anything. I'll have a note sent round, but as for the rest of it, I leave Master Hartwright to explain. Are you staying hereabouts?"

"At the Bell and Swan. I'll await word from my brother there."

"As you say, miss."

Clara would have liked to question the man further, but she sensed the fruitlessness of the exercise. Better to wait for Simon to explain for himself.

Tugging her cloak more firmly about her shoulders, she exited the gate and made her way down the narrow thoroughfare to the Bell and Swan. It was a humble tavern but a clean one, and at present, fairly quiet. She saw only a few gentlemen in the taproom as she climbed the stairs to her room on the second floor.

It was comfortable enough, with a soft bed and freshly washed linens. Far superior to the room she'd stayed in last night, when she'd been obliged to break her journey in Basingstoke.

She let herself in and promptly discarded her bonnet, gloves, and cloak. Her back ached from the railway journey, and her legs were stiff from walking up one street and down another—always briskly, as if she knew exactly where she was going. A lady must never look uncertain when she was traveling alone.

The mattress beckoned. She couldn't resist kicking off her boots and lying down upon it. She willed herself to rest awhile, but no sooner had she closed her eyes than her tired mind drifted back to the contents of Neville's letter.

She'd reviewed it countless times since leaving Devon, and on each occasion she felt the same ache of emotion. The same prickling of anger.

He might have loved her if things had been different?

An infuriating statement.

She knew what he meant by it. He was referencing his limitations. As if she cared two snaps of her fingers for the fact that he couldn't speak as easily as others. What did eloquence matter? Words only had value if they were honest and true. If a person actually meant them. She'd rather have had a dozen stammered meanderings from an honest gentleman who loved her than a pretty speech from a villainous cad.

But perhaps she was oversimplifying the matter.

He'd said he could never leave Devon. That there was no future with him.

She suspected he was afraid to leave. Afraid of what the world might hold for someone who was different from other people.

And perhaps that was an end to it.

It wasn't her place to force him to do things he wasn't comfortable with. No matter that he'd said he admired her. That he might have loved her. Love shouldn't be turned into a cudgel. *If you love me, you must do this, and this.* She couldn't imagine wielding her feelings that way.

With a weary sigh, she turned her face into the pillow.

Sometime later she was awakened by the sound of a knock at her door. She sat bolt upright in the bed. Outside, the sun had lowered in the sky, bathing her room in shadows. She lifted a hand to her rumpled hair. Goodness. She must have fallen asleep.

"Yes?"

"There's a gentleman come for you, miss," the tavern-keeper's wife called out. "He's waiting in the dining room."

"Thank you!" Clara called back. "I'll be right down!"

She scrambled out of bed, swiftly combing her hair, slipping on her boots, and tugging her skirt and bodice back into order. Her hands brushed over the wrinkled fabric. There was nothing she could do about it. And Simon wasn't likely to care anyway.

Making her way down to the tavern's public dining room, she heard a chorus of deep, masculine voices rising from the tap room. A crowd of gentlemen must have arrived while she was asleep. They sounded a trifle rowdy.

The dining room was less boisterous. Two older gentlemen sat together at one table, a small family at another. And near the back, not far from the fire blazing in the cavernous stone hearth, a young gentleman was seated alone. As she entered, he leapt to his feet.

"Miss Hartwright?" He crossed the room to greet her. "I'm Oliver Trent. A friend of Simon's."

She looked around for her brother but didn't see him. "He's not with you?"

"Alas, no. He was called away yesterday and doesn't return until tomorrow." Mr. Trent tugged at his cravat. He was a slim fellow, with a shock of chestnut hair. "Will you sit down?" He motioned to a small table. "I can order tea, or coffee if you—"

"No, thank you." She sank into a chair. "I'd prefer you simply tell me the worst of it. I've come a very long way."

He sat down across from her. "How much do you know?"

"Only that my mother believes Simon is in danger of being rusticated." Her words were met with silence. "Is it true?"

"I believe we've managed to prevent that, at least. I've convinced him to offer a written apology, both to the school and to the gentleman involved. All that remains is to speak with the local authorities."

Clara's breath stopped in her chest. "The authorities?"

"A mere formality. That, and twenty guineas in compensation. But we've taken up a collection, and—" He broke off with a look of concern. "I beg your pardon, ma'am. Are you quite all right?"

Twenty guineas?

She paled at the very thought of it. Families had been brought to ruin by less.

"Compensation for what?" she asked.

"Lord knows. It's a figure the fellow's solicitor has come up with. But there's nothing to worry about. We've taken up a collection, and—"

"A solicitor is involved?" If a twenty-guinea debt didn't ruin them, a lengthy lawsuit certainly would. Either way, things were far worse than Clara had imagined. "Do you know, Mr. Trent, I believe I shall have that cup of tea, after all."

Mr. Trent immediately waved a hand to one of the tavern maids and ordered a pot of tea, along with a plate of bread and butter. It was brought almost at once.

Clara poured for both of them, rather amazed at the steadiness of her hands. "You had best start at the beginning."

Mr. Trent stirred sugar into his cup with an agitated clink of his teaspoon. "You'll forgive me, Miss Hartwright. I never thought I'd be the one doing the explaining. I confess I'm that put out by it."

"As am I, sir. But here we are."

"Quite." He lay down his spoon. "The truth is, I don't know the whole of the story myself. Simon has been extraordinarily tight-lipped about the business. And none of us were there that night. So we only have his word on the matter. And that of a half dozen or so witnesses who appeared on the scene in the aftermath. You see... your brother was involved in a brawl."

Her teacup froze halfway to her mouth. A brawl? Simon? It was impossible. She slowly lowered her cup. "I don't believe it."

"It's the truth, ma'am. It happened a month ago, at the railway station. That is to say, it began at the railway station and then made its way into the street. The altercation was, er, rather violent."

She stared at Mr. Trent, at a complete loss for words. Her brother didn't have a violent bone in his body. He was a scholar. A lover of books, and nature. He was no brawler.

"It was late in the evening," Mr. Trent went on. "Which was a blessing. Fewer witnesses, you know. But the authorities were on the scene in a trice. And it looked to them as though Simon was the aggressor."

"He can't have been."

"Oh, but he was. He admitted to it." Mr. Trent helped himself to a slice of buttered bread. "As much as I can understand it, he saw this fellow at the station, and the two of them exchanged harsh words. They'd both been drinking, and"—he shrugged—"one thing led to another."

"Are you claiming that my brother is some variety of violent drunkard?"

Mr. Trent gave her a bemused look. "A drunkard? Lord no. Simon can hold his ale better than any of us."

"Then why—"

"It wasn't the drink that caused the dustup. It was whatever the blackguard said to him."

"My brother wouldn't just go about assaulting strangers willy-nilly, sir. It doesn't matter what they said to him. He has more countenance than that, and a great deal more self-control. Whatever he's being accused of—"

"But this fellow wasn't a stranger, Miss Hartwright. Simon knew him. Or used to know him. He was Simon's old tutor from Hertfordshire. A gentleman by the name of Bryce-Chetwynde. Perhaps you remember him?"

The remaining blood drained from Clara's face. If not for the strength of her corset holding her upright in her chair, she might have crumpled straight to the tavern floor.

Andrew Bryce-Chetwynde.

It was a name she hadn't heard spoken in four long years. One she'd hoped never to hear again.

She pressed a hand to her midriff, willing herself to breathe. "Yes," she said at last in a voice quite unlike her own. "I remember him."

Chapter Twenty

North Devon, England
December 1860

Neville ran a brush and currycomb over Adventurer's dappled neck and shoulder, loosening the hair from his thick winter coat. Rain pattered gently on the roof of the stables. The storm had passed sooner than expected, leaving the cliff road swimming in rainwater and knee-deep in mud—but passable. Only that morning, Danvers had pronounced it so.

And now, Neville could leave.

The possibility of it had been preying on his mind since the day Clara departed for Cambridge.

It was a ridiculous idea.

What need had Clara of him? She was intelligent and competent. Capable of taking care of herself. Who was he to interfere? Not her brother or any other sort of relation. He was only her friend.

Only. As if it were nothing very important.

"Friendship is a precious thing," she'd said.

Infinitely precious. He hadn't realized quite how much her friendship had meant until she'd gone.

"The turning isn't as swampy as I feared." Justin's deep voice sounded from the entrance to the stables. He entered with Danvers at his side. The two of them had been out inspecting the road. "You don't think the wheels will get stuck?"

"I reckon we could add more crushed stone," Danvers said. "It would bind it up nice."

Justin nodded once. "See to it."

Danvers disappeared down the aisle, shouting for two of the grooms.

Justin lingered to address Neville. "The dogs aren't with you?"

"They're in the kitchen b-by the fire." The Cook, Mrs. Whitlock, had given them each a bone. Earlier, when Neville had left, Bertie had looked up from his, but he hadn't followed. Some dogs did better in a pack, and the little pug was one of them. He was beginning to take his cues from Paul and Jonesy.

"Good thing," Justin said. "It's vile out here."

"Less than it was."

"True. Miss Hartwright was wise to leave when she did. Lord knows what state the road might have been in if the storm hadn't passed."

Neville focused on brushing Adventurer. *Tried* to focus. "She'll...have arrived by n-now."

"I expect she has. And I'm sure she's fine. Which is just what I've been telling Teddy. Ladies are remarkably efficient these days."

Neville's gaze shot to Justin's. "What has Teddy to do with it?"

"I suppose he fancies her. The two of them did spend time together, drawing and painting, and such. And they'll have more time together still when Teddy and Mrs. Bainbridge return to Surrey."

Jealousy ignited in Neville's veins. A smoldering bitterness, as potent as liquid poison.

Foolish.

Teddy was just a lad. Hardly a rival. Clara had scarcely mentioned him at all. And yet…

She'd seemed to enjoy his company. Who wouldn't? He was mentally quick and agile. Always ready with a sharp retort or a wryly humorous remark. More than that, he *looked* intelligent. There was something in his eyes. In his expression. Something Neville knew he didn't possess.

And now—when Teddy returned to Surrey—he'd have Clara all to himself. She'd be there to look at. To talk to. With her gentle ways, and her sweet orange-blossom scent.

"He d-didn't want her to go?"

"He hasn't said so. But he's worried about her being alone in Cambridge." Justin's mouth curved in a brief, wry smile. "I blame Helena and Jenny. They mentioned how rowdy Giles and his friends used to get at university. Made them sound like a right pack of savages."

Neville's hand stilled on the brush. His heart beat hard. Lady Helena, of all people, would comprehend what went on at university. She was the only one of their ranks to have had family who attended. Her brother and father, and every other aristocratic male relative going back for hundreds of years. "What…what did they…"

"Drinking, pranks, and the like. You know how it is with young men." Justin didn't appear at all concerned. "I saw those ponies of yours this morning. They're looking well."

Neville marshaled his thoughts. It was near impossible to do so when an image of Clara alone in Cambridge amid a pack of roving, inebriated males kept creeping into his mind. "Betty still favors her leg. But she's…improving."

"And the foal?"

"He'd like to run."

Justin's expression was thoughtful. "Tom mentioned you were contemplating returning them to Dartmoor."

Neville resumed brushing. "I'm thinking about it."

"You realize, of course, that that's no guarantee someone wouldn't catch them again, and take them back to the horse sales."

"I know that." It was the very reason Neville hadn't made a decision yet.

None of the options for Betty's future were good ones. He began to fear he'd have little choice but to break her to harness. Such a thing wasn't unheard of. Miners often used the Dartmoor ponies for cart work. They were a strong and surefooted breed.

But Neville was reluctant to force such a life on Betty. She belonged with others of her kind, running free on the moors. Not hauling coal or pulling a child's cart.

"I haven't m-made a decision yet. I'm…" Neville shook his head. "It's t-too soon."

"And what about this one?" Justin came up behind Adventurer, laying a reassuring hand on his rump. "How's he getting on?"

"He's restive."

"Aren't we all?" Justin stepped back, allowing Neville room to continue brushing. "You should give him a good gallop on the beach. It always serves to blow the cobwebs off of Hiran."

"I've b-been galloping him. He wants…" Neville's hand tightened on the currycomb as he worked it over Adventurer's side. "He wants more."

"More than a gallop?"

"Just…more. A change of scene."

"Understandable, with a name like Adventurer."

Neville hadn't bestowed the name upon him. It had been his racing moniker. A name that suited him well—and that didn't suit Neville at all. "And ironic, c-considering he's mine."

Justin's expression sobered. "You've had adventures enough for a lifetime."

"My accident wasn't an adventure."

"I didn't mean the accident. I meant that—while I comprehend why you might occasionally pine for greener pastures—the Abbey is the safest place for you. Here, you're surrounded by people who care about you. Who have your best interests at heart."

"What do you…" Neville struggled to verbalize his thoughts. It was always more difficult when he was upset about something. "What d-do you think would happen if…if I left?"

"I don't know," Justin said. "And that's the hell of it. I wouldn't be there to know. You'd be out of the reach of my protection."

"You d-don't have to protect me."

"I don't *have* to do anything. I want to do it. When we were boys…" Justin grimaced. "It rankles that Alex was the one to save you. That I couldn't do it myself."

"What difference does it make?"

"It makes all the difference in the world. I was the reason you were up on the cliffs that day. It was because of me and my infernal obsession with the Abbey. What had any of you to do with it?"

Neville remembered well enough why they'd used to climb down the cliffs at Abbot's Holcombe. All those trips in the little rowboat down the coast to Greyfriar's Abbey. All that mischief-making and digging for buried treasure.

Sir Oswald Bannister had been a source of sick fascination to them. An archvillain, as sinister as a rogue in a Penny Dreadful. Justin had been both angry and intrigued to learn such a man was his father. Alex had only suspected the truth of his own parentage, but that had been enough to spark his obsession. As for Tom, he'd always been more interested in the treasure than in Sir Oswald himself. While Neville…

Neville had simply been loyal.

"You were my friend," he said. "*Our* friend."

Justin snorted. "Some friend. Putting you all in danger."

"I…I n-never blamed you for the accident. I was never… n-never angry with you. Not for that."

Silence stretched between them.

"But you *were* angry with me." Justin's eyes searched his. "Why?"

Neville was amazed he had to ask. The answer seemed evident. "You left m-me behind."

"Neville…"

"I c-could have…"

But the words wouldn't materialize. What he wanted to say—to express—after all these years. That he could have weathered any storm if his friends had been there. That without them, he might as well have perished in that fall.

His fingers clenched on the brush. He wasn't upset with Justin. He *wasn't*. It was the past. Decades ago. He told himself it didn't matter.

And then the words came. Dozens of them, rushing out, all at once, in a broken, disjointed tumble of pent-up emotion.

"The orphanage…the accident… B-but you…you left m-me there. Do you know what…what it was like? To b-be entirely alone? I had n-no one of my own. No one to…to c-care if I lived or d-died."

Justin's face was ashen. "I cared."

"You weren't there."

"I know that. At the time I thought it was best. To break my apprenticeship, and to join Her Majesty's Army. To find some way to make money for us all. But I was just a lad myself. A boy, like you and Tom and Alex." He briefly looked away. "I didn't leave until I knew you were safe."

Neville didn't respond.

"You were safe, weren't you?"

"Yes." He was that. Safe inside the walls of the convent. Just as he was safe here at the Abbey.

"The money I sent back—"

"It helped me. I was…grateful."

"Grateful." Justin repeated the word with disgust. "We both know it wasn't enough for any sort of life for you."

Neville's fingers slowly loosened on the brush. Some of the emotion dissipated. He regarded Justin from over Adventurer's withers. "I had a life."

"In a convent? Little better than a servant in their stable?"

"It was better than the orphanage. I…I didn't mind it. Not once I…adjusted. I liked b-being with the horses. Outdoors. I n-never wanted anything else."

"You didn't know anything else."

Neville didn't argue the point. It was the truth. He had no experience of the world.

But he wasn't a recluse.

He regularly went into the village, stopping in at the King's Arms, the telegraph office, or the new bookshop. When strictly necessary, he could even deal with strangers.

He'd dealt with that horse trader who had been abusing Betty.

The memory of it brought a certain satisfaction to him.

"I'm genuinely sorry," Justin said. "For everything."

"I'm not angry."

"I know that." Justin ran his hand over Adventurer's back. "You're only like this horse of yours."

Neville gave him a questioning look.

Justin smiled slightly. Wearily. "You want more."

It was a blunt statement. A true one as well. The truth was often simple. Neville let it sink into his soul He *did* want more. He wanted a life of his own choosing.

He wanted *her.*

"Perhaps," Justin said, "you might like to spend a few weeks in London with Tom and Jenny?"

Neville dropped the brush and currycomb into a wooden grooming box nearby. "Why London?"

"If you're getting the urge to see the world, it seems the likeliest place to start." Justin paused. "I take it you aren't interested?"

Neville shook his head. He didn't have the urge to see the world. He wasn't an explorer, and he didn't crave the excitement of London, or the teeming industry of Manchester or Liverpool. If he ever left the Abbey, it wouldn't be for a place. It would be because he was required elsewhere. By a needful creature.

Or by a woman.

His woman.

But Clara didn't need him. That much he'd already established. He was of no use to her in Cambridge. No use to her anywhere.

A part of him rose up in protest at the thought.

He was of no use?

It was a dashed lie. A lie he would no longer permit himself to believe. No matter his own insecurities over the years, he'd always had value. He was useful to those around him, to people and animals alike.

And he could be useful to *her*, too.

But not here. Not by being safe.

In order to help Clara—to *win* Clara—he would have to face his fears. To summon his courage, and strike out on his own. Like one of those Arthurian knights she spoke of, embarking on a quest.

"Not in London," he said abruptly.

Justin's mouth tilted up at one corner. "You have somewhere else in mind?"

Neville met Justin's eyes over the back of his horse. "As a m-matter of fact…I do."

Chapter Twenty-One

Cambridge, England
December 1860

Andrew Bryce-Chetwynde.

The name reverberated in Clara's head. With it came every memory—every emotion—of that summer four years ago. It was all she could do to focus on Mr. Trent's face, and to attend to the remainder of his unfortunate tale.

She doubted he realized just how unfortunate it was.

Indeed, Simon hadn't appeared to have confessed anything to Mr. Trent aside from the barest minimum.

"I understand he and his tutor parted years ago on not very good terms," Mr. Trent said. "Apparently, Simon was holding a grudge against the fellow. I couldn't comprehend why. Your brother was extraordinarily tight-lipped about the matter."

"Is...is Mr. Bryce-Chetwynde still here? In Cambridge?"

"No, ma'am. He'd only come up for the week to meet with one of his old masters. After Simon thrashed him, he returned to Hertfordshire."

Clara's shoulders sagged.

Thank God for it.

She had no wish to ever see the man again. Four years later, the image of him was still burned on her brain. Slim and dreamy, with an artfully knotted necktie, curling dark hair, and the eyes of a romantic poet.

"You grace us with your presence, Miss Hartwright," he'd said the first afternoon she'd joined him at the table for her brother's lessons.

And he'd smiled at her. A secret smile that had seemed reserved for her alone.

Within a month, he was sharing his poetry with her. Not only the works of Wordsworth, Coleridge, and Tennyson, but poems he'd written himself.

"You inspire me, Miss Hartwright," he said one afternoon as he walked her home from the village schoolhouse. "Something about your face, and the lilt in your voice. The way you sound both prim and provocative at once."

She reddened to the roots of her hair. "I surely don't."

"You do, ma'am. I shall write a sonnet about it. You see if I don't."

It was thusly all summer. He overwhelmed her young heart with poetry and flirtation. Everything airy, and pretty, and...vague.

And then one day he kissed her.

She blurted out the good news to her mother that very same evening as the two of them sat in the small parlor of their cottage. "He wants to marry me."

Mama looked up from her mending. "Who does?"

"Mr. Bryce-Chetwynde."

"Bah."

"It's true, Mama. He kissed me today."

Her mother's eyes narrowed behind the lenses of her spectacles. "He what?"

"He kissed me," Clara said again, smiling giddily. "In the field behind the cottage. He says we will soon be husband and wife."

At least, that was what she *thought* he'd said.

She was so certain of it—of his love, and of his words—that she allowed her mother to march her straight into the squire's drawing room. Clara had stood there in her best Sunday dress, in the presence of the squire and Mr. Bryce-Chetwynde, as Mama demanded that Mr. Bryce-Chetwynde acknowledge the secret betrothal he had with her daughter. Clara had been confident he would.

More fool her.

That confidence had cost her everything. Her pride, her job, and her reputation.

It had cost Mama and Simon, too.

Clara recalled how badly her hands had shaken as she'd held the newspaper a week later, desperately scanning the employment advertisements. That there was a listing for a lady's companion was nothing short of a miracle. Clara responded to it at once, and within a fortnight, was on a train to York—as far away from Hertfordshire as she could manage.

She'd thought never to see Andrew Bryce-Chetwynde again. Never to hear his name.

And yet it would have been a lie to say she hadn't thought of him in the years that followed. Indeed, she'd spent that first six months in York going over and over every interaction the two of them had had, trying to light on the instance she'd first misconstrued things. The moment she'd diverged onto a course that had very nearly ruined her, and her mother and brother along with her.

She'd never discovered it.

Which just went to show that her own judgment was faulty. That she'd spent too much time with her head in a book, daydreaming about epic poems and legends.

She'd resolved then and there to be done with such foolishness. If her imagination was so powerful it could make her see things that weren't there, she couldn't afford to keep feeding it. Better to starve it of its sustenance. Of poetry, novels, and plays. To force it to function, instead, on a diet of provable scientific facts. Everything sensible and orderly, fitting into neat rows and columns.

Coins clinked onto the table as Mr. Trent settled the bill for their tea. "Do you have relatives hereabouts?"

"Why do you ask?"

"You'll need somewhere to stay. I'd offer you a room myself, but..." He stuck a finger into his cravat, tugging the rumpled linen as he cleared his throat. "The lads and I have rented a hunting lodge for the holiday. It's no place for an unmarried lady."

"You've no need to trouble yourself. I'm already established here. I see no reason I shouldn't remain for the night."

"At the Bell and Swan?"

She cast a pointed look around. "It appears respectable enough."

"Yes, but wouldn't you rather return to wherever it is you came from? It's still early. I could easily find you a cab. And Simon would—"

"My brother can discuss matters with me directly when he returns. I gather he's one of the lads with whom you've rented your hunting lodge?"

"He is."

A fresh flicker of anger sparked in Clara's breast at the imagined expense of such a thing. "Then you may tell him where I am, and that I shall remain here until he sees fit to call on me."

"Simon won't like it," Mr. Trent said before taking his leave. "He'll rake me over the coals for not putting you directly back onto the train."

"I should like to see you try, sir."

The next morning Clara emerged from her room to find that the establishment had grown significantly more crowded. She hadn't any idea why. Some of the students returning to Cambridge after their holidays, she supposed. Indeed, most of the guests at the inn appeared to be single young gentleman. She'd never felt so conspicuous. As she sat down to take her breakfast in the public dining room, it seemed as though every eye was upon her.

She finished her cup of tea and ate the last bite of her toast, hardly tasting either of them. Mr. Trent had said that Simon would be back in Cambridge first thing in the morning. And it was already half nine.

As she exited the dining room in search of the tavern keeper's wife, the murmur of masculine voices followed, setting her already frayed nerves a-jangle. What she needed was a brisk walk and some fresh air to clear her head. She refused to meet her brother in a state of abject emotion.

She found the tavern keeper's wife in the taproom, wiping down the high, polished wood counter with a dirty cloth.

Clara caught her gaze as she approached. "I beg your pardon, ma'am. I'm expecting my brother this morning. If he arrives while I'm out, will you tell him I've gone for a short walk and will be back by ten o'clock?"

"Aye, miss. Will you be needing anything else? I can fetch you a hot coal to warm your hands."

"No, thank you." Clara didn't possess a handwarmer. Gloves would have to suffice. She fetched them from her room, along with her cloak and bonnet, and made her way out onto the street.

It had snowed during the night, blanketing Cambridge in a light dusting of sparkling white, as pristine as powdered sugar. She walked briskly through it, eyes straight ahead, in the direction of Magdalene College.

There were other people about. Working folk going about their day. A woman at a storefront bid her good morning, and Clara replied in turn. But she wasn't interested in shopping, or even in admiring the view of the university. It was exercise she required.

Glancing to the right and left of her, she crossed the road. She'd gone no more than a few steps when a gentleman walking equally briskly in the opposite direction nearly collided with her.

He caught at her arm, bringing them both to a stumbling halt. "Clara!"

She looked up at the young fellow with a start. He was tall and thin, with floppy blond hair that fell over his forehead, and the same limpid brown eyes as her own. "Simon!" A breath of relief gusted out of her. "Goodness' sake. What are you doing here?"

"I'm on my way to see you. Trent said you were staying at the Bell and Swan."

"I am. I was waiting for you, but when you didn't arrive by breakfast—"

"You went for a walk to clear your head?" His mouth curved in a tight smile. Taking her arm more firmly, he turned her back the way she'd come. "You don't want to be walking here. Not unescorted."

"I go everywhere unescorted. It's perfectly unexceptionable for a lady in my position."

"As if you were a servant." He made a low sound of disapproval. "I must tell you, Clara, this isn't at all the thing. You should have waited to hear from me. And yes, I know Mama ordered you to come. She threatened me with as much in her last letter. As if I were tied to her apron strings! I mean to say, how do you imagine it looks for my sister to be asking after me at my college of all places?"

"I have the notion that, had I continued waiting to hear from you, I'd be waiting until judgment day. Which doesn't even begin to address the matter of my lessons."

"You've still been receiving them, haven't you?"

"I wouldn't call those lessons. The past six months of them have been half-hearted at best. And the one I lately received—"

"Must we discuss our business in the street?" Simon steered her down one narrow lane, and then another.

"The Bell and Swan is *that* way," she protested.

"We're not going to the Bell and Swan. There's a meeting of the Antiquary Society there today. You never met a rowdier bunch." He stopped outside a small coffeehouse with a glazed sash window. "It will be quieter here. We can talk, and then I'm putting you on the train."

Before she could object, he opened the door and urged her inside. The coffeehouse was empty save for two elderly gentlemen by the fire, drinking from steaming cups as they engaged in a game of chess.

Simon led her to one of the small green baize-covered tables. It was situated in the far corner on the opposite side of a decorative screen. "I know the owner. Sit down. I shall be right back."

Clara removed her bonnet and cloak and hung them on a nearby coatrack, her eyes following Simon all the while. In his fashionable plaid trousers and double-breasted waistcoat, he looked almost a stranger. He was taller than the brother she remembered, and his face had lost its boyish softness and grown more angular with age.

She wondered what differences he observed in her. Did she look shabby to him? A faded, country creature, worn down by years of servitude? Void of the glow of her youth?

A depressing thought.

Sitting down at the table, she slowly stripped off her gloves. Simon joined her a moment later. He was accompanied by a serving boy who brought them two steaming mugs of coffee.

"Would you prefer tea?" Simon asked as he sat down.

The serving boy looked at Clara expectantly.

"Coffee is sufficient," she said. The boy bowed and withdrew. She turned her attention to her brother. There was no reason to beat about the bush. "Is it true? Did you really engage in a bout of fisticuffs with Mr. Bryce-Chetwynde?"

Simon winced. "Trent told you, did he?"

"Not in any great detail. He doesn't know the why of it. Only that it happened, and that you were, apparently, the aggressor."

"I wouldn't say that. It was Bryce-Chetwynde who started it."

"How? What could he possibly have said to you?"

Simon bent his head to his coffee. "It doesn't matter."

"I beg your pardon. It matters very much." Her voice dropped to an angry undertone. "If you're rusticated for it, and if you end up having to pay twenty guineas in damages—"

"It will have been worth it to have taken the smug look off of his face. My only regret is that I've had to apologize to the blackguard. He doesn't deserve it. Not after what he did to you."

And just like that, the world seemed to stop spinning.

Clara gaped at her brother. "What *he* did to *me*?"

Simon's expression hardened. "When I encountered him at the railway station, your name was mentioned. And you know what I've always thought. What I've always believed."

Of course she knew. It was the same thing her mother had believed. That Clara had spun a few commonplace civilities from Mr. Bryce-Chetwynde into a romance. That she'd dreamed it all up. An unfortunate result of her novel-reading and love of poetry.

"Bryce-Chetwynde and I might have parted without my being any the wiser," Simon went on, "but he was in his cups, and he had the gall—the unmitigated nerve—to say he was sorry for it. That things had got out of hand that summer. All because he was bored, and to pass the time, to amuse himself, he'd made you his flirt."

She stared at her brother, speechless.

He raised his mug to his lips and took a drink. "So, naturally, I knocked him down."

Clara had difficulty absorbing Simon's words. "Is that what he said? That it... That he'd made me his flirt?"

"And that he'd kissed you in the meadow behind the cottage that day. All the things you told us that we didn't believe." Simon lowered his cup. His face filled with brotherly regret. "I'm sorry for that. In hindsight, I can see he was a villain. My only excuse is, at the time, I idolized the man."

A chill, as bitter as the winter snow outside, settled into Clara's veins. "So did I."

"You'll be pleased to hear that I blacked his eye and knocked out several of his teeth."

"Why on earth would I be pleased to hear *that*? I get no satisfaction from your having beaten him."

"I do. It was the most satisfying thing I've done in ages. And something I should have done four years ago." Simon paused, his gaze turning wary. "I say, Clara, you can't blame Mama and me for believing him over you. How were we to know—"

"Because I told you so." And she'd continued to tell them so, insisting on her version of the truth, until...

Until she'd stopped believing it herself.

"Yes," Simon said, "but he denied it. Most vociferously. And you were always horning in on my lessons. Making any excuse to spend more time with him."

Her battered spirit railed at the accusation. "That isn't true. I wanted to learn, just as much as you did. It had nothing to do with what I did or didn't feel for your tutor."

"No one wants to study who doesn't have to."

"*I* did," she retorted in a burst of whispered vehemence. "And I still do. Why else do you suppose I've been so keen on receiving your lessons?"

"Yes, I know that. Which is why I agreed to send them, even though it's taken up heaven knows how much of my time organizing my notes and writing them out—"

"Did you even write the last lesson? The entire packet was a word-for-word duplicate of one you'd sent six months before."

He grimaced. "Was it that obvious? I'd hoped you wouldn't notice."

"Who—?"

"One of the lads. I paid him thruppence to copy an old lesson and send it on to you. I was away for a week on field trip and hadn't the time to come up with anything myself."

She'd suspected as much. The admission nevertheless brought her up short. "You could have simply written a few notes on what you were studying at the moment. The way you did in the beginning. It's all I ever wanted. Not regurgitated scientific rules and maxims. The last six months of lessons have been no lessons at all."

Simon's lips thinned. "University isn't what you think it is, Clara. We don't stand around with laurel wreaths on our heads, waxing on about the classics. This isn't ancient Greece. A real naturalist must go out into the world. Into nature. He must observe creatures in their natural habitat."

"Is that what you were doing when you ran up bills for a pair of engraved cufflinks, and a set of horseshoes for a horse you don't even own?"

He had the grace to turn a dull red. "I won't apologize for socializing with my friends. It's part of the university experience. Surely you don't expect me to remain in my rooms with the curtains drawn, studying by the light of a single candle?"

"I expect you to show some measure of respect for the sacrifice Mama and I have made to keep you here. Can you imagine my surprise to receive a stack of tradesman's bills for such fripperies, when I've been obliged these four years to wear thrice-darned stockings and gowns that are years out of season?"

His color deepened, whether with embarrassment or anger, Clara couldn't tell. "If you must know, the cufflinks were for a ball, at which I met Viscount Wrexham, who is keen to finance an expedition. And the farrier bill was for a hunter I rented who threw a shoe when I was riding to the hounds. All activities which have a bearing on my future as a naturalist. I gain more notice socializing than in sequestering myself like a monk."

Her mind latched onto one phrase. "An expedition? To where?"

"Nothing has been finalized yet. And it needn't concern you, in any event."

"Of course it concerns me. I'm to be your secretary."

Simon's gaze slid guiltily to his coffee mug. He made no reply.

A growing sense of numbness built in Clara's chest. It slowed her heart and breath, making her feel as if she were gradually being turned to a block of ice. "Aren't I?"

"As to that..."

"You promised me, Simon. You said I'd have a role in your work. That you'd make a home for me when you came down from University."

"And I will." He met her eyes, his color high. "When I settle, I mean to make you my housekeeper."

Something inside of Clara shriveled and died. "Your housekeeper?"

He leaned forward in his chair. "You must have known it wouldn't lead anywhere. The notes and drawings I sent you—they were just a bit of fun. A way to amuse you. It was a kindness, for I knew your life as a companion would be very dull indeed."

The chill in her blood was positively glacial now, making her shiver from the inside out. She clamped her teeth to stop them chattering.

"Come now," he said. "You're intelligent. Smart enough to have taught the young ones at the village school. But my course of study is something outside of your experience. The knowledge is far too complex for a woman."

"'Those who admire and love knowledge for its own sake ought to wish to see its elements made accessible to all.'"

"What?"

"Herschel said that."

He scrunched his brows. "I don't think so. I didn't write that in any of my letters."

"No, you didn't. I read it myself, in his *Preliminary Discourse*." She curved her hands around her mug in a futile attempt to warm them, and stop their trembling. "Do you think I've merely been studying your letters? That I haven't a mind or a thought of my own?" She paused before quoting another passage: "'Knowledge can neither be adequately cultivated nor adequately enjoyed by a few.'"

"Oh, Clara..." Simon shook his head. "He didn't mean women. Education in women is only useful insofar as it makes them better wives and mothers. What wife and mother needs a thorough understanding of beetle classification? You're better off, truly. In time you shall see I'm right."

Her throat constricted. "You've wasted four years of my life."

"That's rather hard. What else might you have been doing these four years? After the scandal in Hertfordshire —"

"Which you now acknowledge wasn't of my making. If you and Mama had only believed me—"

"It's rather too late to split hairs on the matter. The damage has been done. We've all got to move on from it, as best we can. I'm only sorry you had to come all this way. I daresay I should have written to you and Mama about what happened with Bryce-Chetwynde, but there seemed no point in reopening old wounds. Better to let things lie." He glanced at her coffee. "If you're not going to drink that, we may as well go."

Her hands dropped from her mug, as cold as they'd been when first she put them there.

"We'll collect your bags from the Bell and Swan and then I'll put you in a cab." He stood. "You can catch the midday train back to—"

"I don't require your assistance."

Simon heaved a sigh. As if he were the put-upon elder brother instead of the much-sacrificed-for younger. "Don't make things worse, Clara."

"I mean it." She rose from her chair and gathered her cloak and bonnet. She slipped them on. "I'd rather fend for myself."

"But you *are* going home, aren't you?"

She tugged on her gloves. "Where is home, Simon?"

Another sigh. "Clara..."

"I'll collect my things and return to my employer's cottage in Surrey. You're right. There's no reason for me to remain." She snapped open the drawstring top of her reticule and withdrew the stack of tradesman's bills. "You may take responsibility for these." She thrust them into Simon's hand. "I won't deplete my savings on your account. Not so I might one day aspire to be your housekeeper."

He crumpled the bills into the pocket of his overcoat. "Mama won't be pleased."

Clara didn't respond. She simply turned and walked out of the coffeehouse. She was relieved when Simon didn't follow. The last thing she wanted was a witness to her loss of composure.

At the moment, she was numb. Quite frozen to the heart. But a storm was brewing within her. Four years' worth of tears and anger sealed behind a dam that was about to break. She could only pray that, when it did, she'd be alone in her room at the tavern and not on the street for the world to see. For, once those emotions were unleashed, she had no earthly idea how she'd ever dam them back up again.

Chapter Twenty-Two

North Devon, England
December 1860

Neville leaned back in his corner of the carriage, bracing himself as the wheels rolled along the rain-slick coastal road that led to the railway station in Abbot's Holcombe.

Justin was similarly braced in the green-velvet-and leather-upholstered seat across from him. "Almost there."

Tom consulted his pocket watch. "Only half an hour until the train departs."

"He won't make it," Alex said.

"Nonsense. Trains are always delayed for some reason or another. Jenny and I have been known to wait hours on a platform."

"In India, perhaps." The carriage skidded, and Alex lurched sharply in his seat next to Neville. He steadied himself with a hand on the carriage wall. "But this is England."

"This is North Devon," Justin said. "I know these roads. He's not going to be late."

Neville didn't say anything. He was too anxious.

He was also resolved.

His bags were packed and tied to the roof. He had money in his purse and the direction of not one but three hotels in Cambridge to which he might seek a room on his arrival.

And he had his friends.

They'd insisted on accompanying him to the station. To see him off. Even Justin, who rarely left Lady Helena's side these days.

Neville was deeply touched by their show of support.

"Nervous?" Alex asked.

"Yes," Neville admitted.

"You'll feel better once you're on the train," Tom said. "I know I did when first I left London with Jenny. As soon as I sat down, I knew I'd done the right thing."

"It's n-not the…the rightness of it," Neville said. "It's… all the rest of it."

He didn't expect his friends to understand. They never seemed to mind his halting speech and occasional inattention. He doubted whether they even noticed it any longer. It was so much a part of him.

Only Alex had betrayed any response. When he'd arrived in Devon on the train last month—when Neville had spoken to him and embraced him for the first time in two decades—there had been sadness in Alex's eyes. Sadness, and something like regret.

He was sorry for Neville. Sorry for himself, too. And for all of them. For all they'd gone through as children.

Neville was sorry, too.

But one couldn't build a life on regret.

"Don't worry about the people," Alex said. "You'll intimidate most of them. You won't have to say a word."

"Silence is a powerful weapon," Justin said.

"Especially," Tom added, "when paired with a steely gaze, and fists the size of dinner plates."

Neville's mouth quirked. He'd never engaged in fisticuffs with anyone in his life. No one had yet challenged him. And if they did...

Well.

He supposed he could manage to fight, if it was Clara he was fighting for.

The carriage slowed as it approached the station.

Justin gave Neville a bracing look. "I admire you. I was too much a coward to go after Helena. In the end, it was she who had to come after me."

"Jenny came for me, too," Tom said. "Not but that I wouldn't have returned to her given another day or two to work up my courage."

"What about you?" Justin asked Alex. "I suppose you did something daring?"

"To win Laura?" Alex's gray eyes flickered with humor. "That was fate. Pure and simple."

Tom laughed. "In other words—"

"In other words," Alex said, "she was obliged to marry me or face social ruin."

"It's as I suspected." Justin smiled warmly at Neville. "You've always been the best of us."

"You still are," Tom said.

"Quite," Alex agreed.

The carriage rolled to a halt. Outside the window, the railway station came into view. The train waited on the tracks, a gleaming black behemoth belching clouds of smoke and steam. Passengers were disembarking onto the platform, and others were beginning to board. All manner of people. Fine ladies, well-heeled gentlemen, and children bundled up in their winter coats.

Neville's stomach clenched.

"We can wait with you," Justin said.

"No." Neville shook his head. This was something he had to do on his own. It was frightening, yes. Enough to make him feel rather ill. But this was his battle, not theirs.

The carriage shook as his trunk was removed from the roof. Danvers's voice echoed, shouting to a porter to retrieve it. "First class passenger here!"

Neville looked first at Justin, and then at Tom, and Alex. He vaguely registered that his hands were shaking.

"Safe journey," Tom said. "And good luck."

"Good luck," Alex echoed.

Justin gave Neville a solemn nod. It conveyed more that words ever could. *You're strong enough. Capable enough. You have nothing to fear.*

Danvers opened the door. A gust of cold air blew into the carriage. "Train's leaving," he said. "Best hurry if you want to make it, guv."

Neville climbed out. He only turned back once to raise a hand to his friends in a brief farewell. It wasn't goodbye. But he was on his own now.

The layout of the railway station was somewhat familiar from when they'd all gone to fetch Alex last month. Neville easily found his way to the booking office. There, he purchased his ticket.

"Anything else, sir?" the clerk asked.

Neville shook his head. He didn't intend to talk any more than necessary. Nods and head shakes weren't ideal, but they were far better than losing his words. And he *would* lose them. The stress of the situation practically guaranteed it.

Crossing the platform, he made his way to the first-class railway carriage. It was a wood-paneled compartment with carpeted floors and upholstered seats. He sat down in one near the window.

Another gentleman boarded shortly thereafter, taking the window seat opposite. A well-to-do businessman by the look of him. He was carrying an attaché case not dissimilar to the one Tom carried.

He gave Neville a measuring look. "Afternoon, sir."

"Afternoon."

"Going to London?"

"To…to Cambridge."

It seemed as though the gentleman wanted to continue the conversation, but before he could ask anything more, another gentleman boarded. He was an elderly fellow, with a middle-aged lady on his arm who might have been either his wife or his daughter.

"Beg pardon," he said to Neville. "Mind if we change seats? The wife and I prefer sitting together."

"Of c-course." Neville stood, moving to an empty seat on the other side of the carriage.

It wasn't a window seat.

Neville's jaw tightened. There would be nothing to distract him now. Nothing to keep his attention and prevent him from drifting off in his head.

He cursed himself for not remembering to bring a book. He *had* done, but the two volumes Lady Helena had given him were out of reach, packed away inside of his trunk.

"Obliged to you, sir," the lady said.

Neville inclined his head in acknowledgment. Folding his arms, he leaned back in his seat.

The gentleman beside him drew out a newspaper and opened it. He glanced at Neville. "Had a nephew who attended Cambridge."

Neville didn't reply. There was no need. Unprompted, the fellow launched into a lengthy monologue on university education—the expense and practical use of it. From there he progressed to the subject of his health.

Across from them, the elderly gentleman had fallen asleep with his mouth open. His wife had produced a bag of knitting and was busily winding a skein of yarn. She made soft sounds of sympathy as the fellow elaborated on his many and varied ailments.

Some sixty miles later, the fellow disembarked. Another thirty miles, and the elderly man and his wife did as well. They were replaced by a pair of aged, and rather fashionable spinsters, carrying a cat in a hamper.

The two ladies made no attempt to engage him, seeming content to talk to each other in hushed tones, punctuated by loud addresses to their cat. "Hush, Jemmy!" and "Don't fuss so!"

At last able to avail himself of the window seat, Neville spent the remainder of the day's journey staring out the window. The rain-soaked scenery rolled by. He hardly noticed it. He saw only Clara. Heard her, too. The velvet soft intonation of her words resonating in his heart and his head.

I don't regret any of it, you know.

And that kiss in his room above the stables! He could still feel her arms twined about his neck. Her lips on his, so warmly. So sweetly.

"I only wish we had more time together," she'd said.

He knew now that no amount of time would be enough. Not hours. Not days. It would have to be more than that. It would have to be forever.

Would she want that, too?

He was roused from his thoughts at Basingstoke. On arriving at the station, the two ladies rose to disembark. They struggled with their hamper. "You there, sir," the one in black taffeta said. "I say, do you mind lending your assistance with our Jemima?"

"Oh, yes," the one in green velvet chimed in. She cracked open the lid of the hamper. "As you can see—"

"Don't open the basket, sister!"

It was too late. The cat's striped head popped out, along with her white front paws. She gave a tremendous leap.

Neville lunged forward and caught her midair.

"Merciful heavens!" Black Taffeta exclaimed.

"Jemima!" Green Velvet cried.

"I have her." Neville stood, holding the squirming feline tight against his coat. "Open the…the…"

"The hamper? Yes, yes. Open it, sister."

Neville deposited the cat safely back inside. The ladies closed the lid and latched it. He picked up the hamper under his arm. "Is your c-carriage…?" *Nearby*, he wanted to say, but the word wouldn't come.

Fortunately, his meaning was clear enough.

The two women beamed up at him. "Our coachman awaits us near the cabstand," Black Taffeta said as they followed him out onto the platform.

"Wait until we tell him how you rescued Jemima!" Green Velvet drew out a handkerchief and dabbed at her eyes. "Why, if not for you, she might have been flattened on the track!"

Neville saw them to their waiting carriage. When they were settled inside, he passed them the hamper, and then, amid a profusion of thanks, he tipped his hat and took his leave.

Returning to the platform, he found a bookseller's stall and purchased a penny novel before boarding the train that would take him the rest of the way.

It was only as he sat down that he registered the decided tension in his muscles. He was out of his element. Out of his depth. He breathed deeply, steeling himself as the next group of passengers joined him in his compartment.

A family this time. Two elegant parents, and their equally elegant young daughter. The father stared at him with cold, unwelcoming eyes. As if he'd expected his family to have the compartment to themselves.

Neville returned the gentleman's stare with a cold look of his own. One he'd seen Justin use on countless occasions. The implacable gaze of a ruthless cavalry captain.

Across from him, the gentleman hastily averted his gaze, turning his attention back to his small family.

Neville opened his book and began to read, even as his pulse pounded.

Tomorrow he would arrive in Cambridge. He would find Clara. And if he had to brave the fires of hell to get to her, so be it.

Chapter Twenty-Three

Cambridge, England
December 1860

Neville removed his hat before entering the Bell and Swan, shaking the snow from its brim. The jarvey at the railway station had recommended the tavern as the likeliest place a visitor to Cambridge might stay. However, when it came to finding Clara here, Neville was beginning to have his doubts. The place was chock full of guests, the majority of whom appeared to be gentlemen. Their voices drifted out from the dining room into the front of the tavern, some of them laughing and others shouting in spirited argument.

A drab older woman in homespun appeared at the counter to greet him. Behind her, a flight of rickety wooden stairs led to the floors above. "Hope you're not looking for lodging, sir. We're full up."

He dropped his leather portmanteau onto the floor beside him. He had hoped to get a room. He'd been traveling straight through the night. A whisper of urgency had encouraged him on, growing louder the nearer he drew to Cambridge. He had the distinct sense that Clara was in trouble. That she needed him.

It was likely nothing but his own overtaxed nerves. He'd been under a fair bit of strain since leaving the Abbey. His muscles had tensed every time he encountered a new person—a porter, a coachman, or a stranger seeking to make conversation.

Several times he'd lost his words. And once during the journey he'd drifted off in his head while staring out the window. It had been awkward and disconcerting. But he'd managed to get through it. To keep going.

"You can try the Red Lion, across town," the woman said. "I won't say it's as fine a place as me and my husband keep, but it will do you for a bed."

"I..." He tried to formulate his thoughts. The noise at the back of the tavern was distracting. "I'm looking for someone."

"One of the Antiquarians? They're all in the dining room. The meeting's well under way by the sound of it. Are you a member of the society?"

"No. I'm looking for a...a lady."

Understanding registered in her weathered face. "Ah! You must be the young miss's brother. She says I'm to tell you that she'll be back roundabout ten o'clock. Gone for a walk, she has."

Behind him, the bell on the door jingled as it was opened and shut again. A brief gust of icy wind filled the entryway.

"And there she is," the tavern keeper's wife said. "Right on schedule." She raised her voice. "Your brother's just arrived, Miss Hartwright."

Neville slowly turned around, his heart in his throat.

Clara stood in the doorway, having just removed her bonnet. Her face was white as marble, her brown eyes glistening. She looked more beautiful than he remembered. Beautiful, and brittle as glass. As if at any moment she might shatter into a million pieces.

Something had happened. He could sense it. Her small form was practically vibrating with tension.

He took an instinctive step toward her.

She didn't wait for him to approach. Didn't address him or ask what it was he was doing in Cambridge. Indeed, she didn't say anything. She merely looked at him, in stunned silence.

And then, all at once, her face crumpled, and with a choked sob, she threw herself straight into his arms.

Neville enfolded her in a protective embrace. She was trembling violently, her body racked with tears. He held her close as she wept, wrapping her in his arms, and inside the warmth of his greatcoat. "It's all right," he murmured against her hair. "I'm here. You're safe now." He raised his head to address the tavern keeper's wife. "Where is her room?"

"Upstairs. Last door to the right." She gave Clara a look of motherly concern. "The poor mite. Is she unwell?"

"Just…overwrought." Neville picked Clara up easily, one arm at her back, and the other sliding beneath her knees. She clung to his neck, her face pressed into his cravat. "Will you send up a…a p-pot of tea?"

"Right away, sir. And I'll have the boy bring up your case."

He nodded once before striding across the hall and bounding up the creaking stairs to Clara's room. In other circumstances, accompanying her there would have been enough to ruin her. For all he knew, it still might. But the tavern keeper's wife seemed to think he was her brother. A fiction he prayed would hold long enough for Clara to compose herself, and for the both of them to leave.

He found her room key inside of the cloth reticule that dangled from her wrist. Shoving it into the lock, he unbolted the door and pushed it open with his shoulder. Once inside her room, he kicked the door shut behind them.

"It's all right," he murmured again. He sat her carefully on the bed and made short work of removing her cloak and gloves. Crouching in front of her, he took her hands and warmed them briskly between his own. They were like twin blocks of ice. "You'll feel b-better soon. After you've had some tea."

Her head hung on her neck, her shoulders shaking with every sobbing breath. "I've made a spectacle of myself."

"No one saw. Only that woman."

"I c-can't stop weeping. I knew…once I started…"

Releasing her hands, he withdrew a large linen handkerchief from his pocket and used it to dry her face. It was a futile exercise. The tears continued to come, at an alarming rate. In the end, all he could think to do was to hold her again. He sank down beside her on the bed and drew her back into his arms.

"What happened?" he asked. "Won't you tell me?"

She didn't answer, only wept into his shoulder.

He brushed his lips to her temple. And he let her weep. All the while, a lump of helpless torment formed within his vitals. A mass that was equal parts anguish and anger. If someone had hurt her, he would—

What?

What would he do?

He wasn't an inherently violent person. But at the thought of all the things that might have happened to cause Clara's tears, he felt as though he could tear a man limb from limb with his bare hands.

Long minutes later, a knock sounded at the door. "Your tea, sir!"

Neville eased Clara from his arms and went to open it. The tavern keeper's wife entered with a tray. A stripling lad in patched trousers followed after her with Neville's portmanteau.

"I've brought a plate of biscuits, as well." She placed the tray on a chest of drawers near the washstand. Her eyes flicked to Clara and then back to Neville. There was no suspicion in her gaze. "Begging your pardon, sir, but the room's only paid through noon. If you mean to stay, that'll be another shilling and sixpence. Two shillings if you want meals."

Neville withdrew two shillings from his purse and paid the lady. He had no intention of staying with Clara overnight, but neither did he intend to have her rushed out of the place by noon. She was in no fit state.

"Very good, sir." With a bow, and one last sympathetic look at Clara, the tavern keeper's wife exited the room, the servant boy in her wake.

Neville bolted the door behind them. When he turned back to Clara, she was blotting her tears with his handkerchief. Her hair was coming loose from its pins. Several long flaxen strands had fallen forward to frame her face.

"Tea?" he asked.

She nodded mutely.

He prepared a cup for her, just as he had Christmas morning at the Abbey. Only this time, he mixed in a hefty dose of sugar. Jenny Finchley swore by heavily sugared tea. According to her, it was the best medicine one could administer in cases of shock.

Neville didn't know how effective it was in reality, but he had no reason to doubt Jenny's wisdom. He stirred in another spoonful of sugar before bringing the cup to Clara and putting it into her hands.

She took a drink, her features contorting in a brief grimace at the sweetness of it.

"A little m-more," he encouraged.

She obliged him, taking another swallow before setting it down on the small table beside the bed. Her hands were trembling.

He sank down on his haunches in front of her once more, his face nearly level with her own. "Will you t-tell me what's upset you?"

"Yes, but…I don't understand." Her voice was a tear-clogged whisper. "You said you could never leave Devon. And yet…here you are." She touched his cheek lightly with her fingers. "I think I must be dreaming."

"Of c-course I'm here." He covered her hand with his. "I left Bertie with Justin. And I…I t-took the train. I traveled straight through the night."

"But why?"

He lifted one shoulder in a faint shrug. "I thought you might need someone."

Her mouth wobbled. She bent her head. Tears started again in her eyes.

"Was I wrong?"

"No. But I didn't dare hope—" She stifled a sob. "I thought I would never see you again."

His stomach clenched with guilt. "I'm sorry, Clara. I'm so s-sorry. I…I should have—"

"It's all right. How were you to know I'd be in such a state? I didn't know myself. Indeed, I was perfectly well until yesterday evening. And then this morning, when I saw Simon—"

"You've talked to your brother?"

"At a coffeehouse across town. He… He says…" Pulling her hand from Neville's, she abruptly rose to her feet and crossed to the other side of the room. "He says when he's done at university, he'll make me his housekeeper."

Neville slowly stood. He wasn't certain he'd heard her correctly. "His…*housekeeper*?"

Folding her arms, she went to the window. The heavy curtains were closed. She nevertheless faced them, giving him her back. Her shoulders shook as if she was weeping again.

"Clara…whatever has happened…"

"What's happened is that I've spent every day of the last four years trying to turn myself into another person. Trying to become someone else. Because I have been so ashamed of who I was." She swiped at her cheek with her hand. "A dreamer. A lover of poetry and romantic stories."

He regarded her with a frown. In Devon, she'd spoken of such things as girlhood fancies, seeming to reflect on them with embarrassment and regret. "There's n-nothing shameful in that."

"Not in and of itself. But such romanticism can lead one in an unfortunate direction. It can make one fanciful. Imagining things that aren't there." She turned at last to meet his eyes. The expression on her face tore at his heart. "I told you that my brother had a tutor. Do you remember?"

Neville went still. Something in her voice put him on his guard.

"I was a teacher then, at the village school. But some afternoons, when I came home, Mr. Bryce-Chetwynde would encourage me to join in my brother's lessons. He'd talk with me about books and poetry. It seemed we had a great deal in common."

Mr. Bryce-Chetwynde?

Neville swallowed hard. She'd mentioned her brother having a tutor, but she'd never before spoken the man's name.

"I was young. Unaccustomed to such attentions. When he complimented me or touched my hand, I imagined he was fond of me. And one day"—she brushed impatiently at the tears on her cheeks—"he met me in the meadow behind our cottage as I walked home from school. He brought me a bouquet of wildflowers and…he kissed me."

Neville stared at her, unable to think. Unable to breathe.

Clara's face was pale. "I told my mother we were engaged. Because I was certain we must have been. To kiss someone—to give them flowers, and to recite poetry to them—was tantamount to a proposal in my mind. And there was something else. Something he'd said. Something I'd *thought* he'd said." She pressed a hand to her corseted midriff, as if the recollection made her physically ill. "My mother brought me to see the squire, to confront him about his son's intentions. He called in Mr. Bryce-Chetwynde, and…he denied me. He said he'd only been kind."

"He c-called you a liar?"

"No. And that's the rub of it. He admitted to everything—everything except the kiss. He painted a picture of me as a little mouse of a girl desperate for affection, who had taken his civility—his kindness—and spun it into a romance. And you know—" Her voice broke. "I thought I must have done. For when I next saw him, he looked at me so coldly. As if I didn't exist at all. As if I were a nonperson. And I knew I'd got it all wrong. That they were right. I'd made it up. Imagined it. Because I'd wanted so badly for it to be true. For him to have cared for me."

Neville's chest tightened. Somewhere, in the back of his consciousness, his overloaded brain conjured the memory of Clara perched atop a boulder on the beach, her hands cradling his face, as the storm and sea raged all about them.

"You did mean me, didn't you?" she'd asked. "That I'm the one you wish to kiss? I wasn't imagining it, was I?"

He knew now why it was she'd doubted his intentions.

"The scandal was too much to overcome," she said. "I lost my position at the school, and my brother lost his tutor and the patronage of the squire. I took a job as a companion to a lady in York, and my mother found employment at a girls' academy in Scotland. We agreed to combine our incomes to help pay for Simon to be sent away to school. And then, when he went to university, we did the same. It was the least I could do to make up for all of my silliness. For making our family a spectacle and damaging Simon's prospects."

Neville closed the distance between them, coming to stand with her in front of the window. His searched her tearstained face. "But you didn't make it up," he said. "Did you?"

Clara wiped her cheeks with her hands, inwardly cursing her lack of self-control. She'd known when she left Simon at the coffee shop that she was due for an all-consuming bout of tears. What she hadn't reckoned on was running smack into Neville Cross.

The sight of him standing at the front desk of the tavern had fairly taken her breath away. He'd been garbed in a heavy greatcoat, his shoulders appearing at least a mile wide. He'd looked solid and strong and rather thrillingly disheveled—his blond hair windblown and his jaw darkened with a day's growth of golden stubble.

He'd traveled straight through the night to get to her. Not even stopping to sleep or to shave. All because he'd thought she might need someone.

But she hadn't known that at the time. All she'd known was that she wanted nothing more than the formidable safety of his arms.

He'd been more than willing to give it to her.

Great goodness. He'd left Devon. The thing he was most afraid to do. And he'd done it. For *her*.

But she couldn't reflect on any of that now. The thought of how brave he'd been—the courage it must have taken—only served to make her more emotional.

"No. I didn't make it up." She gave a choked laugh. "Not but that I didn't convince myself that I had."

He looked incredulous. "You believed him…over yourself? Over your own knowledge of…of what happened?"

"Everyone else did," Clara said.

They'd more than believed him. They'd vilified her. She'd been called a fantasist. An outright liar.

"I never said anything about marrying her," Mr. Bryce-Chetwynde had declared to his father.

"You did," Clara had insisted. "'When next we kiss, it will be as man and wife.' You said that to me in the meadow."

"I said nothing of the sort, Miss Hartwright."

"But you did, I know it."

And he *had* said it—or some variation thereof. *When next we kiss, we will be man and wife.* Or: *When next we kiss it will be the kiss of man and wife.* Clara could no longer be certain of the exact phrasing.

"It was right after you kissed me," she'd said. "I can't have mistaken it."

"You've mistaken a great many things, madam. A kiss? A promise of marriage?" His tone had dripped with disdain. "We were speaking of romantic poetry, not of reality. Certainly not of any romance between the two of us. Really, Father. This is too absurd."

"Romantic poetry!" the squire had scoffed.

"Miss Hartwright has a love of poetry," Mr. Bryce-Chetwynde had said, "and is rather prone to painting her own life in such terms. I regret I encouraged the habit."

Clara hated to recall it.

"It made me doubt my own judgment. I began to accept that I'd embellished my encounters with Mr. Bryce-Chetwynde beyond all recognition. It was the only rational explanation. And so I believed it." She paused. "Until today."

Slowly, she related it all to Neville. Her meeting with Simon at the coffeehouse. What he'd said about his altercation with Mr. Bryce-Chetwynde, and what Mr. Bryce-Chetwynde had admitted to.

In light of Simon's revelations, she now understood that there had been no reason to doubt herself. She might have been foolish—a romantically minded young girl caught up in all the attention—but she hadn't been imagining things all those years ago. The flirtatious words. The teasing and innuendo. Encroaching familiarities that had never seemed wholly appropriate.

He hadn't valued or respected her. To him, she was just a poor country miss. A young lady, to be sure, but one with no protection. Had his intentions been honorable, he'd have told her straight out that he found her beautiful. That she was intelligent. Worthwhile.

But Mr. Bryce-Chetwynde had done none of those things. He'd overwhelmed her young heart with poetry and flirtation. He'd had her dancing on a string, and had been in the process of reeling her in when Clara had blurted out the good news to her mother.

What she'd believed to be good news.

Had Mama not intervened, Clara knew now that she'd have ended up losing more than her reputation. More than her pride. She'd have lost her virtue.

Neville listened in silence, his expression growing stonier by the second. When she finished, he had only one question: "Where is he now?"

"Probably gone back to Magdalene. Or else he's returned to the hunting lodge with Mr. Trent."

"Not Simon," Neville said. "The other one."

Clara blinked. "Mr. Bryce-Chetwynde?"

"Is he still in Cambridge?"

"Not that I'm aware. Simon says he's gone back to Hertfordshire. Why do you ask?"

"Because I m-mean to throttle him."

Her mouth fell open. "*You?*"

He looked mildly offended. "Do you think I couldn't?"

"I daresay you could, and with one hand tied behind your back, besides. But I'd really rather you didn't."

"Do you still…?"

Care for him?

The very idea made her vaguely ill.

"No. Goodness, no." Her brows knit. "I don't know that I ever really did."

"Then why—"

"Because he's hired a solicitor and has already forced my brother to pay twenty guineas in damages for the thrashing he gave him."

"I have a solicitor, too. A better one."

"Mr. Finchley wouldn't thank you for making him travel all the way to Cambridge to defend you on an assault charge. Not at this time of year." She set a hand on the front of his waistcoat. "But I am grateful for the sentiment. Truly. It means more to me that you can possibly know."

He covered her hand with his, holding it flat against his chest. She could feel his heart beating, strong and sure, beneath her palm. "What will you do?"

"About Mr. Bryce-Chetwynde? Nothing. There's nothing that *can* be done. It's all in the past." She exhaled an unsteady breath. "I only regret that my studies must come to nothing. I don't know what I'm going to do with myself now. I've had no other dream these four years except to be Simon's secretary."

"Did he never mean it?"

"I think he must have in the beginning. He made such an effort to send me everything he was learning. But he's been under the influence of his schoolmates and the masters for years now. I suppose it was only a matter of time before he adopted the usual male opinions on women and education." Her mouth tugged into a frown. "I know it's childish to say, but it's not fair. It's simply not. I've studied so hard."

He looked down at her. "I've sometimes wondered…"

"What?"

"Do you even like classifying insects and…and plants?"

Her throat closed up. She bent her head, very much afraid she was going to start weeping again. "Not the beetles or crawling things, but the flowers and butterflies, and learning about nature. I love it so much. Being out of doors, with the animals. The way we helped Betty to deliver her foal. I felt useful. As if I was important. Could make a difference."

He gathered her into his arms. She went into them gratefully, closing her eyes as he held her close. After a time, during which she was mortified to dampen his waistcoat with a few more of her tears, she felt his lips brush against her hair.

A delicate shiver went through her.

"It d-doesn't have to…to be over," he said.

"No." She couldn't keep the trace of bitterness from her voice. "I suppose I could find another dream."

"Have you any others?"

"Other than being someone's secretary? I might ask you the same."

"I've been thinking about it."

She drew back to look at him. "Have you come to any conclusions?"

"I'm no good at ledgers. I'd like a…a horse farm. The one I t-told you about."

A smile touched her lips, remembering the evening they'd sat together on the settee in the drawing room. "With paddocks, and a barn, and rolling fields of clover?"

He nodded. "Somewhere near to m-my friends."

"And you'd live there? All alone?"

"Not alone," he said. "With someone like you."

Her mouth trembled. She didn't know quite how to respond.

"I said that wrong," he amended before she could speak. "I d-didn't mean someone like you."

Her heart sank. "No?" She affected a bright tone. "What did you—"

"I meant you," he said. "Just...you. Clara Hartwright. No one else would do."

She set her forehead against his chest. "Oh, Neville."

"I'm n-not asking anything from you." He stopped again. "That's n-not true either. I do have something to...to ask you." His fingers came beneath her chin, gently tipping her face up, compelling her to meet his eyes. "Will you go somewhere with me?"

Anywhere, she wanted to say. *To the ends of the earth.*

But she hadn't abandoned all of her good sense. Not yet, anyway.

"Where?" she asked. "Back to Devon?"

"Yes. To the Abbey. But first, I...I want you to c-come with me to Tavistock. To see Mrs. Atkyns."

She couldn't conceal her surprise. "You're going to talk to her about the ponies? But I thought you'd decided to have Mr. Finchley do it in your stead?"

"It has to be me. They're my responsibility." He looked steadily at her. "Will you c-come?"

Her heart swelled at the gruff request. She realized then that he needed her, just as she'd needed him. Someone to be there. To lean on during the difficult moments. He'd been that person for her almost from the day they'd met. She could be that person for him now. An unfailing support. A true friend.

Her spirits lifted a little. "Yes," she said. "I will."

Chapter Twenty-Four

They left Cambridge almost immediately and within an hour and a half were settled in a wood-paneled first-class railway carriage on the train back to Devon. Clara didn't like to ask how Neville had afforded the fare. Her single attempt at reimbursing him for her ticket had been met with a very stern glare. Gentlemen could be prickly when it came to matters of money.

She smoothed her skirts as the train left the station, chugging down the tracks in a shriek of grinding metal and a cloud of steam. Her small curtained window looked out on austere buildings of Ketton stone and brown fields dusted in winter snow. Her last glimpse of Cambridge. It was bittersweet.

"I brought something for you," Neville said.

She turned her head from the window.

He sat beside her, unbearably handsome in his hat, coat, and neatly tied black cravat. He'd shaved and changed before they'd left, availing himself of the washstand in her room while she busied herself at the front desk, arranging for a hansom cab to take them to the station.

"Have you?" she asked politely. They weren't alone in the carriage. Two gentlemen travelers were established in the upholstered seats across from them, one reading a newspaper, and the other already dozing. Clara was determined to do nothing that would draw their attention.

Neville reached into an inner pocket of his greatcoat and withdrew a slim leather-bound book. He offered it to her. "I thought you m-might like something to…to read."

She took it from him, her gaze drifting over the familiar gold-stamped spine.

Poems

—

First Edition

—

Tennyson

—

Vol. II

Her eyes lifted back to his in question.

"I've been reading it," he said.

"Sir Galahad?"

"All of the poems."

She cradled the book reverently in her hands. "Have you found any you like?"

"One," he said. "I've…I've marked it."

"With notes? I trust Lady Helena won't mind."

His mouth quirked. "She gave them to me."

Clara blinked. "Both volumes?"

He nodded. "The other is in my case. But this one…it's my favorite."

A small thrill of anticipation went through her as she opened the book, turning to the first page with one gloved finger. It had been years since she'd read anything by Tennyson. Years since she'd read any poetry at all.

Did she dare?

"Read," Neville encouraged her. "We have a long journey ahead."

Clara didn't require his permission, but having it gave her courage to begin.

And that's exactly where she started—at the beginning.

The first entry in the volume was "The Epic," set on Christmas Eve. It was followed by "Morte d'Arthur," and then "The Gardener's Daughter." She read them slowly, with long-suppressed pleasure, savoring every word.

She hadn't forgotten them, but she'd forgotten how they made her feel, as if her heart was overflowing and her spirit had taken flight. Some lines made her smile, and others made tears prick at her eyes. Each was moving—powerfully moving—and yet she saw no sign of Neville having marked any of them.

The journey to Tavistock was a long one, broken by stops at obscure railway stations and long delays, which the passengers took advantage of by disembarking to stretch their legs on the platform.

At every opportunity, Clara continued reading. She feared she wasn't much of a companion to Neville. But though she made little conversation, he didn't appear to mind. She was warmly aware of him beside her. It was a rare gentleman who would so readily indulge a lady's love for reading, especially if that reading involved poetry or novels. It made her care for him all the more.

And it made her doubly curious to discover which of the poems had resonated with him.

It wasn't until they were approaching the breaking point of their journey that she found it. Not five miles out from Basingstoke, she began reading "Ulysses," Tennyson's poem about the great hero, finally returned home from his adventures. It was a monologue, given by Ulysses himself, and while not her favorite poem, was certainly one of deep meaning.

Neville must have thought so, as well, for he had marked the final lines of the poem, underlining them in heavy black ink. The words blurred in front of her eyes as she read them.

Tho' much is taken, much abides; and tho'
We are not now that strength which in old days
Moved earth and heaven, that which we are, we are;
One equal temper of heroic hearts,
Made weak by time and fate, but strong in will
To strive, to seek, to find, and not to yield.

Chapter Twenty-Five

Tavistock, England
January 1861

Neville held an umbrella for Clara as they descended from the platform at Tavistock Railway Station. It was a newer structure, built less than a year ago, and fairly modern in every respect—which did nothing to ameliorate the typical problems of the season. It was muddy and wet, and growing wetter by the second.

A jarvey at the cabstand greeted them with a cheerful smile. "Sir, madam." He doffed his hat. "Welcome to sunny Devon."

Clara smiled. She'd been in fairly good spirits since they'd broken their journey at Basingstoke. The potential scandal of the two of them traveling together hadn't yet seemed to register with her. And if it had, she hadn't yet given voice to her worries.

Neville prayed they'd been careful enough. He suspected they had. At the inn, he'd engaged a serving girl to act as Clara's temporary lady's maid, staying with her in her room overnight. And for their meals, they'd dined in the public dining room, everything proper and aboveboard.

Not that anyone had seemed to notice them one way or the other. It was one of the rare benefits to being nobody very important.

"The Atkynses' farm?" he asked.

"Hadley House? Aye," the jarvey said. "I can take you there. Though Reverend Atkyns ain't with us no more." He opened the door of his hackney. "Come down for the sale, have you? You're a mite early."

Neville helped Clara into the cab. It was a four-wheeled vehicle pulled by a team of sturdy bays. "We're n-not here for the sale."

The jarvey eyed them with interest but asked no more questions. He waited until Neville climbed in, and then shut the door behind him. The cab shook as the jarvey leapt onto the box and gave the horses the office to start.

Neville leaned back in his seat across from Clara.

She gazed out the window, giving him an enviable view of her profile. The intelligent arch of her brow, the fine curve of her cheekbone, and the plump bow of her lips. She was as lovely in outward form as she was in spirit. And yet...

He had the queerest feeling that he was the only one who was privileged to see just how beautiful she was. As if it were a secret, locked up tight, to which only he held the key.

"Are we very near to Dartmoor?" she asked.

"On the edge of it. Less than a mile." He'd consulted the map before leaving Devon.

She looked at him, her face aglow. "I wonder if we'll see any ponies?"

He smiled. "We might."

They didn't. Not in the wild. But as the cab rolled through the gates of Hadley House Farm and past its stone outbuildings and pristine paddocks with white-washed wooden fences, Neville saw first one Dartmoor pony, and then another, and another.

Clara sat up tall in her seat. "Good heavens! There must be a half dozen of them!"

Neville stared at the passing scenery in silence. He didn't know what to think, let alone what to say. It was only recently that he'd dared put his dreams into words. A horse farm, he'd told Clara. With a house, and stables, and miles of pastures.

He couldn't have envisioned a more perfect manifestation of that dream if he'd tried. And Hadley House Farm *was* perfect, all the way down to the neat stone manor house that stood at the end of the drive.

The jarvey brought the cab to a halt in front of it.

Neville let himself out and then turned to help Clara down from the cab. While she straightened her skirts and brushed off her sleeves, he gave the jarvey an extra shilling to wait for them.

"Do you suppose we'll be here long?" Clara tucked her hand in Neville's arm as she accompanied him up the steps to the door.

"I don't know." It was the truth. His reply to Mrs. Atkyns's letter had only gone out a few days ago. She hadn't yet responded. For all he knew, she wasn't in residence at the moment.

But someone was.

The door was opened before Neville and Clara had finished ascending the steps. A heavyset woman with a careworn face emerged. She was garbed in a servant's dress—a plain black gown with a white cap and apron. "Can I help you, sir?"

Neville's mind briefly went blank. It took him several seconds to rally. "We've c-come to see Mrs. Atkyns."

The woman looked from Neville to Clara and back again. "And who might you be?"

"Neville Cross. And this is... Miss Hartwright."

Clara gave his arm a reassuring squeeze.

"Cross?" The woman peered up at him. "Him who wrote to the missus?" She brightened. "Lord bless me. Do come in, sir. The missus said you might be calling." She held the door open to admit them, and then waited with them in the modest entry hall while they removed their outdoor things.

"Is Mrs. Atkyns at liberty?" Clara asked as she handed the woman her bonnet and gloves.

"She is, right enough, miss." The woman directed them to a parlor off the hall. "I'll tell her you're here."

The room was furnished with heavy mahogany tables covered in bric-a-brac, and an overstuffed velvet-tufted sofa and matching chairs, the backs of which were draped with antimacassars.

Clara sat down, folding her hands in her lap. "It isn't at all what I expected."

Neville remained standing beside her chair. "Nor I."

In her letter, Mrs. Atkyns had alluded to the fact that her late husband had overextended himself. It was the very reason for the upcoming estate sale. And why Neville had anticipated that the house and farm would likely be in a state of disrepair.

Instead, the fences were strong and solid, the drive was well graveled, and the roof didn't appear to need replacing. The interior—what he'd seen of it thus far—seemed in equally good trim.

He wanted to ask Clara what she thought of the place, but before he could formulate the words, the parlor door opened, and a small white-haired lady entered the room. She wore a mourning gown of heavy black crepe.

"Mr. Cross?" She extended her hand to him. It was covered in a black lace mitt. "What a pleasure it is to meet you."

"Mrs. Atkyns." He briefly clasped her hand. "May I present my…m-my friend, Miss Hartwright."

"Miss Hartwright." Mrs. Atkyns offered her hand to Clara. "You are very welcome."

Clara shook her hand. "Thank you, ma'am."

"Do sit down." Mrs. Atkyns gestured to the sofa before taking a seat herself in one of the wingback chairs. "My housekeeper, Mrs. Perry, is beside herself. She knows of our correspondence, of course, and your interest in the farm and the Dartmoor ponies. But we weren't expecting you quite so soon. Your latest letter arrived only yesterday. I intended to write my reply this very afternoon."

Neville sat down beside Clara on the sofa. "I apologize for the…the inconvenience."

"No inconvenience at all. I'm delighted to meet you. Indeed, I cannot express what a relief it is to know that there is someone else with an interest in the ponies. After my dear husband passed, I feared all his work would be undone. You can imagine my relief when I received your letter."

Clara gave Neville a bewildered look.

He was no less confused than she was. "I'd thought… I'd hoped you…you might t-take the mare and foal I rescued. That they could come here."

"And live in safety near to the moors? A splendid notion. Mr. Atkyns often kept the young or injured ones thus, until they were well enough for release. We have many who still reside in the paddocks and shelters. And many more in the main barn, awaiting the annual sale on the moor."

"You sell them?" A hint of disapproval crept into Clara's voice. "But I thought—"

"And breed them, too. Mr. Atkyns was resolved to replenish their numbers. Because of him, there are more ponies on the moor, and more ponies in use hereabouts, as well. It's the only way to save them." Mrs. Atkyns smiled. "Were my husband still alive, he would undoubtedly invite you to bring your two ponies here. You could have released them onto the moor yourself one day. Or kept them here, if they had become too tame."

The door creaked open again, and the housekeeper entered with the tea tray. As Mrs. Atkyns poured, she chattered on about her husband's work, and about the many virtues of Hadley House—the superior drainage, the quality of the meadow hay, and the proximity to Dartmoor.

"I declare, I will be sad to leave this place, but as I told Mrs. Perry, with the right people, the farm will continue on just as if Mr. Atkyns was still alive. And God willing, the next residents will keep on Mrs. Perry and the other servants. They'll find it more efficient than hiring new staff."

"I beg your pardon, ma'am." Neville feared he hadn't heard her correctly. "Are you saying that…that you're selling the farm?"

"Not selling, sir. But I am, regrettably, unable to renew the lease on the property. It's far too much to manage at my age, and conserving the Dartmoor ponies was my husband's passion, not mine." Mrs. Atkyns sipped her tea. "No. I'm to retire to Bath, where I shall share premises with my sister. It will give me an opportunity to finish the book I'm writing on the flora and fauna of the West Country."

Neville stared at her as understanding sank in. A faint sense of excitement stirred within his breast. "You're looking for someone to…to t-take over the lease."

"Quite," Mrs. Atkyns said. "It isn't a bad bargain. Indeed, my solicitor assures me that, after the estate sale next week, the farm will be in a position to once again turn a small profit." She offered them each a slice of fruitcake from the tea tray. "I pray that the new residents—whoever they may be—will be able to assist you in your endeavors. Alas, I cannot. Unless…" Her eyes sparkled. "You wouldn't be interested in the farm yourselves?"

Clara set down her teacup. "Oh no. We're merely trying to find a safe place for our Dartmoor ponies." She paused. "For Mr. Cross's ponies, I mean."

"Are you certain? I shall be happy to give the both of you a tour of the house after tea. And our groundskeeper, Mr. Rigby, can take you out to view the rest of the property. As for the financial aspect, I must leave that to my solicitor, but you won't find him a difficult man. He's as anxious to settle things as I am."

"We're obliged to you," Clara said. "But truly, we're not—"

"No. We aren't." Neville met Clara's eyes. "But a tour c-can do no harm, surely."

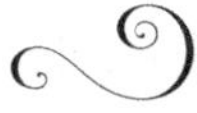

Clara walked over the property with Neville and Mr. Rigby, examining the stables, the orchard, and the paddocks near to the moor. It was a farm in every respect. Practical and well-ordered. And yet each pastoral prospect was lovelier than the last. Horses munching hay and grass, sheep huddled together like fluffy clouds, and dormant flower and vegetable gardens, kissed by sweet winter breezes redolent of rain and fresh earth.

It was acres of peace and natural beauty. A paradise for some lucky farmer and his family.

Someone who could afford it.

She wondered what it would look like in the spring and summer. What it would smell like when the flowers had come into bloom, and the butterflies gathered to drink.

"Mind the mud," Neville said, guiding her around a deep puddle.

She cast a rueful glance at the hem of her woolen dress. It was a little late to worry about the elements. Their tour was nearly at an end. The rest of the property was only accessible by horseback.

"About ten acres of clover," Mr. Rigby said, surveying the fields in the distance. "The best in the district. They'll lease it separate if they have to, but I advise the new tenants to keep it on. With less stock, it's sufficient to its purpose. And they'll have less stock if the sale goes aright. The listing is for 300 healthy Dartmoor ewes, along with the odd ram, cow, and steer."

Clara's gaze drifted over the bleak Dartmoor landscape. There was a haunting beauty to it. As if it were the setting for some grand romantic adventure. "Mr. Atkyns raised sheep as well?"

"He were a vicar, ma'am," Mr. Rigby said. "He didn't know aught about farming and livestock. Got in a mite over his head. But he knew those wild ponies, sure enough. They was his life's work." He turned his head, squinting in the direction of the farmhouse. "Best get back. Mrs. Atkyns will be wanting to hear your thoughts on the place."

"We know the way," Neville said.

"As you please, sir." Mr. Rigby inclined his head to them. "Careful how you go, ma'am."

Clara tucked her hand in Neville's arm as they walked back to the house, retracing their steps along the muddy path that led through the orchard—the trees bare of their leaves—and down past one of the paddocks that abutted the moor.

It was no longer raining, nor even drizzling. But it was cold and quiet. Rather eerily so. A white mist had rolled in, as delicate as gossamer, settling over the moorland and brushing at the edges of the outbuildings. Like something from a fairy story. A subtle enchantment.

"What do you think of…of the farm?" Neville asked at last.

"It's idyllic. And it would be perfect for Betty and Firefly. Close to Dartmoor yet safe enough for her to recover her health."

"But?"

"There seems little point in admiring the place when Mrs. Atkyns is on the verge of leaving it."

Neville stopped at the fence to face her. There was no one else about. No human beings, anyway. Only a few shaggy Dartmoor ponies far off in the paddock, standing in the mist, munching on what was left of the grass. "That's… It's exactly the point."

"How so? Do you believe the new tenants will have as much care for the wild ponies? I daresay they might, but there's no guarantee. And even if they do, they'd be strangers. How could we trust them with Betty and the baby?" She stopped herself, feeling her cheeks warm. "I meant you, of course. Not we. I have no say in the matter."

"You do."

"You're very kind, but Betty isn't my pony. It was you who rescued her. You who have developed a bond with her and Firefly. I'm merely an admirer of what you've done." She leaned against the paddock fence. "Who is caring for her in your absence?"

"Danvers, and…and Justin."

She inwardly winced. "They all know you came for me."

"Of course."

"What they must have thought…"

Neville's mouth hitched in a wry smile. "They weren't surprised. Tom and Alex suspected. And Justin… He understood."

A blush crept up her throat and into her face. "Was Mrs. Bainbridge as understanding?"

"Does her opinion m-matter?"

"Well…yes. She's my employer. And she…" Her words trailed away as Neville reached to brush a stray lock of hair from her temple. He tucked it behind her ear with gentle fingers.

"Clara…"

Her heart beat hard. "Yes?"

"You…you never said what your other dreams are. What else you want b-besides being a…a secretary."

"Oh. That." It took her a moment to get her bearings. "I'm afraid my dreams aren't very realistic."

"Tell me."

"I'd be embarrassed. It's silly to want things you have no way of getting. A goal should be practical."

"I d-didn't ask about your goals."

"My dreams, then." She fell quiet a moment. Her face heated with a self-conscious blush. "I suppose—if everything were perfect, and there were no concerns about money or propriety—I'd want this. This moment. Here with you, on this farm. With the ponies, and the stone manor house, and the gardens. I'd want to be here with you in the spring to see the flowers bloom. To see Betty and Firefly run in the sunshine."

"Is that all?"

She huffed a short laugh. "As if it's not already too much!"

"What else?" he prompted.

"Very well. As long as I'm dreaming, I'd like books to go along with it. Research books on flowering plants, butterflies, and bees. And fiction, too. Books of poetry and prose. A whole library of them. I've a great deal of reading to catch up on. Indeed, I believe I shall have to spend the next year with my nose firmly in a volume of poetry in order to make up for lost time."

"If you m-marry me, you may read as…as m-much poetry as you like."

She stared up at him, her smile fading. "I *beg* your pardon?"

A flush of color darkened his cheekbones, but there was no hesitation in his manner—or in his words. He spoke them in a deep, unwavering voice, as if they were bold and clear in his mind. An incontrovertible fact. "I love you, Clara. More than anything."

Her vision blurred, even as a glow of pure happiness spread through her heart, and soul, and limbs. She swallowed hard.

"You don't have to love me back," he said. "But if you'll be m-my wife, I promise, I'll—"

"I don't have to love you back?" She was incredulous. "Do you think I don't love you? That I haven't been in love with you since we parted in the Abbey stables?"

He loomed over her, his pale blue gaze burning with a peculiar intensity. "Clara—"

"What possessed you to write to me as you did? To say that if things had been different you might have loved me the rest of my life? I don't need things to be different. And I certainly don't need *you* to be different. I love you exactly as you are."

His hands closed about her shoulders.

"And yes," she added. "I will marry you."

A spasm of deep emotion crossed over his face. "Do you mean that?"

"With all my heart." She might have said more, but in the very next instant, his head lowered to hers, and he captured her mouth in a slow and thoroughly devastating kiss.

Heat sparked in her veins, flooding her body with knee-weakening warmth. There was nothing she could do but circle her arms around his neck, stand up on the toes of her muddied half boots, and kiss him back. Softly, sweetly. A deep, clinging kiss that left them both breathless.

He made a sound low in his throat. Rather like a growl.

She smiled against his mouth. "If we haven't yet caused a scandal, I suspect we're about to."

He nuzzled her cheek. "No one can see us."

"That we know of." She slowly drew back from him. "It's a wonder Mrs. Atkyns hasn't asked what I'm doing here."

"If she does, we can t-tell her we're engaged." He took her left hand in his. "I must buy you a…a ring. Something bright and beautiful, just as you are."

She blushed rosily. "A plain wedding band will suffice."

"You deserve the best."

"It's lovely of you to say so, but truly, I don't require anything expensive." She twined her fingers through his. "You shall see, I can live as cheaply as you do, and will be quite content to do so, in the rooms above the stable, or wherever you choose for us to settle. I'm accustomed to being frugal."

His brows lowered. He searched her face. "What about here?"

She gave him a questioning look.

He turned her attention to the paddock. The ponies were still standing, grazing in the mist. In the distance, the clouds had parted, and a faint rainbow shimmered in the sky.

Clara inhaled a breath of wonder. "Do you know, with all the rain in Devon, I'd have expected to have seen one sooner."

"Haven't you?"

She shook her head. "This is the first. And it's fitting, isn't it? To see such a thing in this magical place, and on such a day as this."

"You find the farm magical?"

"With the moors, and the mist, it seems an enchanted landscape. I do believe it could be the setting for an epic romance."

"Perhaps it will be."

She turned to look at him, her pulse quickening.

He looked steadily back at her. "But only if you want it. Only if…if you approve."

"Of course I approve. It's the most beautiful place I've ever seen. But…" She could think of no delicate way to put it. "The expense is too great. We couldn't possibly afford it."

"No," he said. "Not to buy. But to lease, yes. Easily."

Easily?

"But how?" she asked.

Amusement flickered in his gaze. "Do you think I've b-been a slave to Justin? Or a slave to the sisters at…at the c-convent? They paid me, Clara. And Justin has invested it all for me."

Her mouth went dry. All at once, she recalled the elegant dinner clothes he'd worn at the Abbey, cut to his figure as if by an expert tailor. The first-class railway tickets he'd purchased for their journey from Cambridge. And his fine horse, Adventurer. A gentleman's horse, to be sure, and an expensive one, at that.

She moistened her lips. "You have investments."

"In the railway, m-mainly. Enough to lease this place, if… if it's what you want."

"Oh." Tears started in her eyes. She had a vague thought that she was rapidly becoming a watering pot. Indeed, she'd wept more in these three days than she had in the past three years combined. "I'm sorry."

Neville's expression darkened with concern. "We d-don't have to live here. We can—"

"It's not that. It's just all too much. Your coming to Cambridge, and your proposal. And the very idea that we could live here together. You and I, and the ponies, and Bertie." She gazed up at him, her heart full to bursting. "I never dared dream in all my life that I would get a happy ending of my very own."

Understanding registered in his face. With it came a look of such love, such tender affection. He drew her back into his arms. "My dear love…" His words were slow but sure. "This is only the beginning."

Epilogue

Tavistock, England
June 1861

Neville found his wife in her butterfly garden, her head bent over a sketch pad. She was garbed in a loose-fitting skirt and fitted caraco jacket, a flat-brimmed straw hat pinned to her flaxen hair. Bertie dozed at her feet, snoring as only an aged pug could snore. "The post came."

Clara looked up. A smile brightened her face. After several months of marriage, that smile still had the power to stop Neville's heart. "Did we receive anything interesting?"

"A letter for you from…from Jenny." He sank down beside her on the wrought-iron garden bench. "Here you are."

Setting aside her sketch pad, Clara took the letter. She paused before opening it to tilt her face up for his kiss.

He bent his head, his lips meeting hers halfway. He loved her to distraction. It took all of his strength of will not to gather her in his arms.

She broke the wax seal on the envelope. Her chocolate-brown eyes skimmed its contents. "She and Tom are staying at the Abbey for a fortnight before they leave for Spain."

"Oh?" Neville stretched his legs out in front of him. His trousers were all over mud.

He'd been out with the ponies most of the morning. Betty and Firefly were enjoying their newfound freedom in the pasture near the moor. Almost too much. It made the pair of them difficult to catch.

Clara read on. "Justin and Helena are well, and so is little Honoria. Oh! Jenny says she's grown bigger. Thank heavens for that. She was so small to begin with. I did worry for her."

Lady Helena had given birth to a slightly underweight baby girl in January. Honoria Alice Thornhill had her mother's delicacy, and her father's black hair and gray eyes.

Justin had wept when first he'd held her. An event that had left Tom and Neville speechless and had Alex clearing his throat repeatedly, as if he were in danger of weeping, too.

"Blast the lot of you," Justin had said, as he'd cradled his daughter. "We'll see how you behave when your first child is born."

"Jenny hints at an impending announcement from Laura." Clara glanced up at him. "Do you suppose she's expecting?"

"I don't know." Neville wouldn't be surprised. Alex was mad over his wife. It was only a matter of time before the two of them started welcoming children. Though how babies would fit in with the Archers' thriving perfume business in Grasse, Neville had no idea. "Perhaps it's m-merely a new variety of...of lavender water."

"Perhaps so." Clara resumed reading. "Mr. and Mrs. Boothroyd are in fine fettle. It sounds as though they're putting off a move to Barnstaple for the present."

Mr. Boothroyd had wed Mrs. Bainbridge not long after Neville and Clara had married. "It's cheaper than hiring another companion," Neville had overheard Teddy joke to Alex.

The truth was, Mr. Boothroyd and Mrs. Bainbridge were quite fond of each other. They were also rather fond of Justin and Helena's new baby.

"Boothroyd won't leave the Abbey," Neville said. "Not n-now he's seen Honoria."

"No. I didn't expect he would. That baby has worked a spell on everyone in residence." Clara turned to the next page of Jenny's letter. "She has news of Teddy. He's thriving in France, apparently. Alex has found an art teacher for him." Her eyes drifted down the page. Color bloomed in her cheeks. "The rest is about us."

His brows lifted. "What about us?"

Clara folded the letter and returned it to its envelope. "Only that she hopes we've found contentment here."

"Are you content?" he asked.

She certainly seemed so. Just as content as he was in their new marriage. The friendship of it. The growing intimacy. He'd never imagined it could be so sweet. So perfect.

"More than content," she said.

He took her hand in his, bare skin against bare skin, warmed by the summer sunshine. "What more is there?"

"There's happiness." Clara rested her head on his shoulder. "There's this. Every day. With you. For the rest of our lives. The stuff of dreams."

Neville turned his face into her hair. The scent of orange blossoms tickled his nose. "Then I pray I shall n-never wake up."

Author's Note

The character of Mr. Atkyns was inspired by Edward Atkyns Bray, a vicar living in Tavistock who died in 1857. Bray was a great proponent of the Dartmoor pony and actively worked to replenish its dwindling numbers. According to his wife, Anna, who wrote extensively on the flora and fauna of Devonshire after her husband's death, Mr. Bray "reared great numbers of these horses, which were disposed of at an annual sale held on the moor. Since the death of that gentleman the breed is become almost extinct."

Clara's experience "shadow-attending" Cambridge was also inspired by Victorian fact. Ambitious girls of that period, often schooled at home along with their brothers, could find it very hard when said brothers departed for college and left them behind. This very situation comes up in Charlotte M. Yonge's 1856 novel *The Daisy Chain*.

Ethel is schooled at home with her brother, Norman. When he goes to Oxford, she tries to keep up with him. The situation leads Ethel's elder sister, Margaret, to utter a few Victorian home truths:

> *"No," said Margaret; "but don't think me very unkind if I say, suppose you left off trying to keep up with Norman."*
>
> *"Oh, Margaret! Margaret!" and her eyes filled with tears. "We have hardly missed doing the same every day since the first Latin grammar was put into his hands!"*
>
> *"I know it would be very hard," said Margaret; but Ethel continued, in a piteous tone, a little sentimental, "From hie haec hoc up to Alcaics and beta Thukididou we have gone on together, and I can't bear to give it up. I'm sure I can—"*
>
> *"Stop, Ethel, I really doubt whether you can. Do you know that Norman was telling papa the other day that it was very odd Dr. Hoxton gave them such easy lessons."*
>
> *Ethel looked very much mortified.*
>
> *"You see," said Margaret kindly, "we all know that men have more power than women, and I suppose the time has come for Norman to pass beyond you. He would not be cleverer than any one, if he could not do more than a girl at home."*
>
> *"He has so much more time for it," said Ethel.*
>
> *"That's the very thing. Now consider, Ethel. His work, after he goes to Oxford, will be doing his very utmost—and you know what an utmost that is. If you could keep up with him at all, you must give your whole time and thoughts to it, and when you had done so—if*

> *you could get all the honours in the University—what would it come to? You can't take a first-class."*
>
> *"I don't want one," said Ethel; "I only can't bear not to do as Norman does, and I like Greek so much."*
>
> *"And for that would you give up being a useful, steady daughter and sister at home? The sort of woman that dear mamma wished to make you, and a comfort to papa."*
>
> *Ethel was silent, and large tears were gathering.*
>
> *"You own that that is the first thing?"*
>
> *"Yes," said Ethel faintly.*

It was a miserable position for a bright young lady to find herself in. Fortunately, in 1869, less than a decade after the year in which *The Winter Companion* is set, Girton College at Cambridge opened its doors to female students.

And now, a word or two on Neville's head injury…

When I first began my Parish Orphans of Devon series, I envisioned Neville's fall from the cliffs as being a pivotal event in the lives of all of the orphans. His accident was inspired by an accident of my own—a cervical spine injury after a serious car accident that changed the course of my life. Many of Neville's feelings about his condition are a mirror of my own feelings after my injury and loss of mobility.

But Neville's condition isn't entirely autobiographical. In addition to my research on traumatic brain injuries, I was also inspired by someone I know of who suffered a TBI many years ago, and kept a blog of her experience throughout her recovery and rehabilitation. She was never able to resume her former life, but with patience and support, she created a new kind of life and found great happiness in it.

Disabled people aren't a monolith. Not everyone with an injury similar to Neville's feels the same way as he did, or the same way I felt about my own injury. To that end, when writing this story, I may have inadvertently used words or expressed feelings/views about disabilities that some find offensive. For this, I humbly apologize.

Acknowledgments

This book owes a great deal to my beta readers and critique partners, Flora, Sarah, and Alyssa. Extra special thanks to Sarah for helping me come up with lesson ideas for Simon to send to Clara from Cambridge. And to Jacqueline Banerjee who was a wonderful resource when I was first researching "shadow attendance" at Cambridge via post. Jackie also directed me to Yonge's *Daisy Chain*, for which I'm eternally grateful.

Special thanks also go to my editor, Deb Nemeth, who always makes my writing better; to Rachel McMillan for reading an early draft of this story; to my cover designer, James Egan; to Colleen Sheehan for formatting; and—as always—to my parents, whose assistance made it possible for me to meet my deadline in spite of numerous personal catastrophes.

Lastly, I'd like to thank you, my readers, for sticking with this series to the end. You may wonder if it truly *is* the end. For Justin, Tom, Alex, and Neville, the answer is yes. However, I do have ideas for a few novellas to resolve some loose ends with Teddy and others, as well as possible future books featuring the children of the four orphans. Stay tuned!

About the Author

USA Today bestselling author Mimi Matthews writes both historical nonfiction and proper historical romances set in Victorian England. Her articles on nineteenth century history have been published on various academic and history sites, including the *Victorian Web* and the *Journal of Victorian Culture*, and are also syndicated at *BUST Magazine*. In her other life, Mimi is an attorney. She resides in California with her family, which includes an Andalusian dressage horse, two Shelties, and two Siamese cats.

To learn more, please visit
www.MimiMatthews.com

OTHER TITLES BY
Mimi Matthews

NONFICTION

The Pug Who Bit Napoleon
Animal Tales of the 18th and 19th Centuries

A Victorian Lady's Guide to Fashion and Beauty

FICTION

The Lost Letter
A Victorian Romance

The Viscount and the Vicar's Daughter
A Victorian Romance

A Holiday By Gaslight
A Victorian Christmas Novella

The Work of Art
A Regency Romance

The Matrimonial Advertisement
Parish Orphans of Devon, Book 1

A Modest Independence
Parish Orphans of Devon, Book 2

A Convenient Fiction
Parish Orphans of Devon, Book 3

Gentleman Jim
A Regency Romance